HI

They dried themselves vigorously. Aware that Elke was still delaying in putting her bikini back on, Tinisha realised what had been going on from the moment they swam in unison. They were playing the game, stalking each other like predatory animals. Though each of them was ready for sex, they were both still able to back out at the last moment and claim misinterpretation.

Elke eased the bikini bottom up over her hips with an unnecessary wiggle, up over the narrow fuzz of her gleaming blonde pubic hair. She grinned. 'Your mouth is open, Tinisha.'

HIGH ART

TANYA DOLAN

First published in 2000 by
Sapphire
an imprint of Virgin Publishing Ltd
Thames Wharf Studios,
Rainville Road, London W6 9HA

ISBN 0 352 33513 0

Cover artwork by Michele Serchuk

Typeset by SetSystems Ltd, Saffron Walden, Essex
Printed and bound in Great Britain by Mackays of Chatham PLC

ONE

Tinisha Weaver moved the easel. The shade closer to the wall of the bungalow was cool and refreshing. Far below in the bay an early afternoon sun was molten on the blue sea and the sails of some small craft were quiet. There was a kind of inverted violence in the darting, buzzing jet skis that sprayed high wakes of white crystals. The muted cries and laughter of the bathers closer to the shore carried to her clearly. Though remote, the sounds were company for her. Distance had her feel that she was joining in without becoming involved. Enjoyment without commitment – the way she lived her life. It was strange how a scorching, arid summer day such as this could be lonelier than a gloomy, wet afternoon in November.

Tinisha adjusted the easel and found the exact blend of light and shadow she was searching for. Her patio was an artist's dream with which no studio could compare. That was why, like a seaside trader, she worked hard in the summer months and took it easy in the winter. She mixed some carmine red with a tiny amount of white on her palette. Taking a sample of the paint on the tip of a brush, she tested the shade with that on the portrait in front of her.

The face of the girl was striking. In the way that a natural storyteller embellishes a tale, Tinisha used benign exaggeration to bring her portraits intensely alive. The mouth was the focal point here. Soft and moist, the lower lip was imbued with an expertly

1

blended-in sensuality. From some angles, in certain lights, an optical illusion would have the mouth pout. A pout was Tinisha's hallmark. She never permitted her models to smile. A smiling mouth neutered eroticism. With the freshly mixed paint, she brushed even more magic on to the canvas. The wet, glistening lips were now begging to be kissed in the compelling manner that made her portraits disturb sensitive people.

Tinisha's secret endowed all of her work with this effect. She subtly introduced a metallic element into her paints. Many artists were critical, describing her work as garish. But it was results that counted, and she sold her work for high prices, while quite a few of her critics were forever on the breadline.

Although it had begun as Kerry, the portrait had distanced itself from her as it had evolved. Both Kerry and the girl in the portrait had long black hair, and both had the same glint of sexual challenge in their brown eyes. But there was a mystique to the face on the canvas, a depth, a fire and an understanding that was beyond the senses.

Maybe there was still a slight resemblance to Kerry there, but the face seemed to have come from Tinisha's unconscious mind. Some force within her was directing the portrait. The sureness of the strokes was in no way willed by her. Too real to be a fantasy: she preferred to think it was the face of a lover she met regularly in her dreams. The portrait evoked a combination of contrasting feelings in her. It was at the same time erotically tantalising and numbingly frustrating to think that in the world of dreams she had caressed the lustrous silkiness of the glossy black hair, looked deeply into those knowing eyes and had tasted the nectar of that lovely mouth, yet had no memory of it.

This method of creation was new to Tinisha. Perhaps the adage that claimed life began at forty was true. She was facing that landmark birthday in just three days time. Maybe it would mark some crucial turning point in her artistic style.

A sparrow, noisily chasing an intruder through nearby trees, interrupted her thinking. The birds screamed their grievances at each other. Close to her, a squirrel came out of a hollow tree-trunk brought down in a winter storm. The little creature made some jerky signal that meant nothing to her, then went home again. A bee flew an erratic course over the stretch of golden marigolds that laid a solid film of perfume on the hot air.

At one side of the cottage the woods began. No holidaymakers ever ventured in that direction. To them it was the beginning of a wilderness where civilisation was in full retreat. Afraid of being alone, the herd instinct took them the other way, along the path bordered by fragrant bluebells, that led down to the crowded beach.

Tinisha had backed away a few steps to study the girl that should be – but wasn't – Kerry, when movement on the road below caught her eye. A car was turning hesitantly into the drive of the holiday cottage down the hill from her. Saturday was changeover day. Tinisha paused to idly watch strangers play out a familiar scene. The rear doors of the car exploded open. Two children, a boy aged about seven and a girl who was younger, jumped out to run round in widening circles of excitement. The parents alighted more slowly, uncertain in unfamiliar surroundings, unnerved by open countryside after the claustrophobia of a city, unbalanced by the absence of the stresses of their everyday lives. An elderly woman climbed stiffly from the car, taking a few tottering little steps before recovering.

The 'ideal' nuclear family: parents, son and daughter – and a widowed granny as a built-in baby-sitter. It suggested that the couple had come to some kind of miraculous arrangement with God. But nothing in life was perfect.

The hatchback of the car was lifted and bulging suitcases dragged out. In a week or perhaps two, though it would seem less than a day to Tinisha, she would be watching the same people do the same exercise, but in reverse order. In their anxiety to return to the known, the holiday, anticipated for many months, would fade for them within hours of getting home.

He was a big guy, wearing one of those vests that showed off a spread of shoulders and muscular arms at their best. His and the woman's movements had a unison that belongs only to those who are regularly intimate and gain the maximum thrill from each other's bodies, thought Tinisha. If not twin souls, then they were certainly twin fucks.

Tinisha was glad that she had saved the woman until last for scrutiny. Blonde and petite, her hair was curly in a way that proclaimed it was natural. She wore a white skirt that was tight enough to impart an hypnotic attraction to the swell of a truly great arse. The skirt was short, too, putting the muscular thighs of shapely white legs on display.

Experience lent Tinisha X-ray vision. When freed of the bra inside of the white vest-top, the blonde's breasts would be small but firm, made to fit wonderfully into a caressing hand. The nipples would be golden brown and elongated, ready to spring to rigid attention like miniature penises at the first brush of a lover's lips. The pubic hair would be neither heavy nor V-shaped. It would have a margin of white skin at each side as it rose up from between the thighs to finish in a fuzzy arc on a nicely rounded tummy. Well-used but not outworn, the cunt itself would be unobtrusive. But it would take little coaxing from fingers, a tongue, or the sucking of a hungry mouth to make those swollen lips distend squelchingly.

Tinisha mentally knelt in front of the woman. As the blonde unzipped the side of her skirt and let it drop, Tinisha pressed her mouth and nose against the black bikini briefs. Inhaling deeply, she breathed in the aroma of the woman, an aroma accentuated by having been sitting in the car on the long journey. Eagerly, the white woman pushed down her briefs and stepped out of them. Opening her legs, she thrust her hips forwards so that Tinisha could use the thumb of each hand to gently open her up, then lick and sip inside. Then Tinisha moved her head in further between the thighs. Her nose and mouth travelled slowly up a sweating arse-cheek valley, savouring an exotic mixture produced by the heat of that summer day.

Her raunchy imaginings came reluctantly to an end when the newcomers disappeared into the cottage. Tinisha tried to return to her painting. But the distraction of the blonde, who from a distance looked to be startlingly pretty, had been too much. Trying to concentrate on her work was hopeless. Tinisha guessed that she was really wet down there. But that was one of those things you could never be sure about unless you put your hand down for a feel. That was always a mistake that led to frigging yourself to a solitary orgasm. It was better to have someone else move a searching hand up between your thighs, to eventually compliment you on the fact that you were 'really ready for it'.

The hatchback had been left open, and the blonde came out of the cottage to do a hip-swaying walk to the car. She leaned into the vehicle, reaching unsuccessfully for something. Straightening up, the blonde hitched her white skirt up above her thighs. A flash of black panties confirmed the accuracy of Tinisha's sixth sense. Then the blonde lifted one leg to climb up into the car.

This had to be a subliminal act of exhibitionism. Prolonged high temperatures had a profound effect on the human race. It promoted both riots and sexual excesses.

Whatever, it was a sight too arousing for Tinisha to bear. An urgent need had taken over her mind and body. Further painting was definitely a no-no. She dropped the paintbrush upright into a vase of soapy water. Sliding the glass palette into a pan of water, she made a promise to clean the items later. The one drawback of her *al fresco* studio was the lack of a nearby sink and running water.

Hurrying into the bungalow, Tinisha picked up the telephone. Her breathing was heavy as she dialled.

It was Marje Tredogan who lifted the receiver at the other end. Her West Country drawl was unmistakable.

'Hello, Mrs Tredogan, this is Miss Weaver. Is Kerry there?'

'I'm afraid not, Miss Weaver,' Marje answered servilely.

Tinisha took a deep breath. She was pushing it a bit on a Saturday afternoon, but the Tredogans knew on which side their bread was buttered. Marje earned a pittance cleaning the house of the local doctor, and Jack, her fisherman husband, spent more time in The Three Mariners than he did in his dilapidated boat.

As Tinisha's housekeeper, their daughter, Kerry, was the financial mainstay of the family. The girl was paid double the average rate for seasonal work, and she was employed throughout the whole year. Running all this through her mind, Tinisha felt she was justified in calling in a favour.

She lied to the girl's mother. 'It's just that I've been given a lovely whiting for my tea. You know how useless I am at cooking, let alone having any idea how to clean the blasted thing. I was hoping that Kerry would be able to pop up. I'll pay her extra, of course.'

Tinisha didn't reveal that it was Jack Tredogan who had brought the fish up to her bungalow. Reeking of alcohol, half-hard and playful, Tredogan, as always, had hoped to get his leg over. He hadn't a hope. As always, Tinisha had given him the bum's rush.

'Oh, dear, that's terrible!' Marje exclaimed, as if Tinisha had just announced a death in the family. 'Perhaps I could do it for you.'

Tinisha gave a silent, inward, exasperated sigh. She didn't want a housewife pushing fifty, no matter how well-fleshed Marjory Tredogan might be. She was desperately in need of Kerry, that sweet-tasting, passionate girl with silky skin and the firm, athletic, thrusting body of a Wimbledon finalist.

'It is kind of you to offer, Mrs Tredogan, but I wouldn't dream of putting you to that trouble. I'll have to forget the idea.'

'That would be a shame, letting a fish go to waste,' Marje protested. 'I don't think Kerry's gone far. She's just gone for a walk with Simon.'

Simple-fucking-Simon, Kerry's occasional boyfriend. Simon Gregory was a big soft prick, in more ways than one, Tinisha was prepared to wager. Kerry swore to her that she hadn't had sex with Simon. By all accounts, the furthest they'd got was when he had taken her left breast out one night. He had put it away again quickly, as if fearing moonlight would melt it.

'She could be anywhere,' Tinisha said despondently. 'I'm sorry to have troubled you, Mrs Tredogan.'

'No,' the Cornish woman shouted into the mouthpiece. 'Look, Miss Weaver, our Kerry owes you a lot. I'll send young Reg out to find her, and get her to come straight up to you.'

'Are you sure?'

'It's the least we can do for you, Miss Weaver.'

A joyful Tinisha said her thank you and goodbye. Putting the receiver down, she rushed to the kitchen, where she expertly topped, tailed, and de-boned the large fish. She didn't want the lovely Kerry to waste one minute on household chores.

'Everyone says Tinisha is the loveliest woman they've ever seen.'

It was true. Kerry Tredogan had often heard total strangers catching a glimpse of Tinisha Weaver comment on her beauty. This was indeed a compliment for a black woman in this frequently racist, white-dominated area of the West Country. It annoyed her that Simon argued differently. In fact, whenever she mentioned her employer, he became sulky. Kerry assumed that he was jealous, and she had to admit that for once he had good reason to be. But it was very different now. Since coming home from college this summer, Simon had suggested, in his diffident way, that it was time they took their relationship seriously. She had agreed. While she wanted to keep her job, Simon now had to take priority over Tinisha. A difficult time lay ahead up at the bungalow, but she was confident that once Tinisha had got the message, then she would want what was best for Kerry. Simon had given a broad hint, in front of his parents, that they could well be shopping for an engagement ring at Christmas.

By this time next year she could be Mrs Kerry Gregory. Simon's parents would want a lavish wedding. A numbing thought hit Kerry: would she be able to wear white? Then she chided herself. Of course she could. The things that Tinisha had done to her, which always put Kerry in a state of ecstasy, didn't count. A woman couldn't take the virginity of another woman. Her sudden worry over a wedding dress was ridiculous.

Happy once more, Kerry knew how lucky she was. If it was possible for a small village to have a most eligible bachelor, then he was Simon. Apart from his wonderful good looks and kind, considerate nature, his was the most respected family in the area. The Gregorys owned a semi-mansion, riding stables and a golf course, as well as having interests in most of the summer businesses in the village. The Tredogans owned nothing but a leaky fishing boat, although her father, Kerry admitted to herself grimly, probably deserved to hold shares in one public house, The Three Mariners.

'I don't know why she has to come into every conversation we have,' Simon complained as he helped Kerry over a low stone wall.

'She doesn't, Si,' Kerry said defensively. 'It's just that living here in the village doesn't give me much to talk about, whereas you have college, Bristol and your friends.'

'I suppose,' he grudgingly conceded, as they sat down in the long grass.

From here they could hear the concerted sounds of enjoyment

coming up from a beach that they couldn't see. Only rugged cliffs and the bright blue of a far-distant sea were visible to them. Kerry was aroused to notice that Simon was covertly studying her breasts.

She had no need of a bra, and friction against the material of the sea-green overshirt she wore had combined with the heat to make her nipples try to force their way out. They were swelling and stiffening even more under Simon's sly scrutiny. The effect he was having on her fully supported her decision to devote herself to him from now on. When he tentatively reached out to gently clasp her breast outside of the shirt, Kerry made no objection.

Had it been dark, she would have encouraged him to go further – probably much further. Guided by something that she didn't think was experience, Simon moved his hand so that the erect nipple was in his palm. A twisting, titillating movement of his hand sent delightful shivering sensations down her spine.

Glancing around her, checking the fields in the near and middle-distance as well as the far away hills, satisfied there was not a soul in sight, Kerry looked archly at Simon. Slowly, teasingly, she started to undo the top button of her shirt.

She avoided the arm Simon attempted to put around her shoulders, and pulled her head back from his hoped-for kiss. This was her big moment, and she was going to make the most of it. Gladdened by the excitement in his eyes, she undid the second, then the third button, but held the shirt closed. Then, licking her tongue tantalisingly over her lips, she put her right hand inside of the shirt and scooped out her left breast.

It was tanned a deep bronze right down to where her swimming costume had covered it just above the nipple. That nipple, some-how luminously pink in the bright sunlight, was as proud to be on show as she was to display it.

'Oh, Kerry!' Simon groaned, having to put a hand to his crotch to ease the pain of a trapped, erecting prick.

Craning his neck, he brought his open mouth towards her. Still holding the breast, Kerry, her own throbbing arousal heightened by the response her bare breast was getting from Simon, leaned forwards to guide the nipple to his lips.

'Hey, Kerry!'

The shout came from behind. An alarmed Kerry unthinkingly

twisted the upper half of her body round. Her small brother, Reggie, was looking over the wall that Simon and herself had recently climbed.

'Mum says that Miss Weaver wants –' the boy began, then broke off, his eyes widening. 'What – what are you doing, Kerry? Your shirt's all undone.'

Coming to her senses, Kerry quickly closed her shirt. Buttoning it, terribly embarrassed, Kerry tried to think of something to say. She had to find some good excuse, as Reggie would go straight back to their mother to report what he had seen. But nothing would come to her.

It was the erudite Simon Gregory who saved the day. 'A wasp went down Kerry's neck,' he told the boy.

'Did it sting you, Sis?'

'No,' a still disoriented Kerry gulped in a voice that didn't sound like hers.

Seemingly satisfied by the explanation, Reggie pulled himself up to sit on top of the wall.

'Why did Mum send you out after me, Reggie?' Kerry prompted the lad.

'Miss Weaver wants you up at the bungalow,' the boy replied. 'Wants you to cook her tea, or something like that.'

'This is too much, Kerry. Don't go,' Simon said.

'I have to, Si.'

'I don't see why.'

Avoiding his eyes, Kerry looked across to the cliffs. A small white cloud, the first seen in the sky for weeks, daringly waited for an advancing sun to reach it. The unexpected little cloud fascinated Kerry in the way that you can't really remember what rain is like when there has been weeks of unbroken sunshine. She had this knack of losing herself in trivial observations when feeling vulnerable. It always worked at home when an argument, usually over too little money or too much drink, erupted between her parents. It failed now as she sensed Simon's impatience.

'I work for her,' she said firmly.

'Be that as it may,' he retorted. 'You might work for her, but she doesn't own you. It's six o'clock on a Saturday evening, Kerry!'

'You don't understand,' Kerry said lamely.

'That's one thing you're right about,' was Simon's rejoinder.

Kerry was tortured by the knowledge that she could never explain it to him. Throughout their lives together they would be haunted by the ghost of her secret love-making with Tinisha Weaver. Yet here was the ideal opportunity. This was the chance to call a halt, to make sure that the past didn't live on to spoil the future. She would go up to the bungalow, and do whatever chore it was that Tinisha wanted doing. But Kerry was determined that there would be nothing else, not even a touching of hands. She would explain to Tinisha that the only relationship she wanted, from this moment on, was with Simon.

'I'm going to go up there,' she said, watching the hurt twisting at Simon's face, 'but this is the last time. I'm going to get things straight with Miss Weaver. I promise you.'

Angrily turning his back on her, Simon strode up to the wall. He leaped over it so wildly that her brother fell off the wall while trying to avoid getting knocked off.

Tears blurring her eyes as she watched him go, Kerry told herself that all would be well. Once she had made everything plain to Tinisha, then she could easily win Simon back by showing him that he came first, even before her work.

A superb idea came to her. She would take Reggie along with her, using the boy as a fail-safe clause when drafting out an invisible new contract of behaviour with Tinisha.

At first, she could see only Kerry approaching along the cliff path. The girl's walk was always graceful, but here it was a dance. Standing in the picture window of her bungalow, Tinisha Weaver's expectant sigh changed to a muttered curse. The girl's young brother was at her side. What was going on? Kerry knew perfectly well why she had been summoned to the bungalow, so why was she bringing the boy with her? Could it be that Marjory Tredogan had become suspicious, and had sent her son along as a 'chaperone'? That wasn't likely. The fisherman's impoverished wife wouldn't be able to think past the extra money that Kerry would bring home. Perhaps Simon, a cross between a jackal and fuck-all, wasn't so simple after all. Maybe he had learned something at college other than the nonsense on the curriculum. There probably wasn't one straight man in the world not turned on by the thought of two women making love. But a proviso for the majority would be that neither of the participants was his wife or girlfriend. And Simon Gregory was a prude of the first order.

Watching and waiting, Tinisha felt a kind of despairing, almost lunatic rapture. Only the approaching girl could put out her raging genital fire that burned hotter with every passing second. Kerry had the sinuous movements and the ferocious passions of a tigress. The girl was a wild animal, but Tinisha, her trainer, had absolute control of her.

Not only did the boy accompany Kerry, but also she was wearing cargo shorts. Tinisha preferred her to wear a skirt. Not that it really mattered. The shorts could only affect voyeuristic foreplay; Tinisha knew they would mean nothing once lovely Kerry was naked. What to do about Reggie Tredogan was the major problem.

By the time a strangely subdued Kerry and her brother had reached the door of the bungalow, a lust-rampant Tinisha had the answer. Naked under the thin brown robe that matched the colour of her skin: shiny *café au lait* − a tone that was envied and vainly striven for by white-skinned holidaymakers down on the beach. Tinisha tightened the sash in deference to the boy before opening the door.

'Hello, Reggie, what a surprise,' she cooed. 'I'm glad you came with your sister, as I need a man for a tough job.'

Flattered and embarrassed, the boy enquired. 'What is it, Miss Weaver?'

'The rockery at the back needs weeding. It shouldn't take you much more than half an hour, and there'll be a crisp five-pound note for you when you've finished. What do you say?'

'Oh, yes, please, miss,' the boy half-shouted his acceptance.

Passing him a pair of gardening gloves, Tinisha shut the door, thankfully leaving him outside. Kerry, an unhappy expression on her pretty face, was leaning with her back against the kitchen wall. Moving close to her, Tinisha breathed into the girl's mouth. This was a technique that never failed, and it pleased her to see sexual arousal glaze Kerry's brown eyes.

As the girl's lips parted, Tinisha closed her eyes and moved her face closer, murmuring, 'Kiss me, darling, kiss me.'

11

As her lips came against Kerry's left ear, Tinisha opened startled eyes. To deny Tinisha her mouth, the girl had turned her head. Tinisha kissed her neck and sucked on the delicious-tasting skin, resisting the temptation to give a love-bite – a hickey being dangerously indelible evidence – then tried for the mouth again.

Kerry twisted her head away once more.

'What's troubling you, Kerry?' a frustrated and bewildered Tinisha asked.

'Nothing,' the normally vivacious Kerry answered like a sullen teenager.

'Then kiss me.'

Shaking her head vehemently, the girl spoke in a rush. 'No, Tinisha, no. This has to finish. I don't want to do the things that we do any more. Simon and me are going to get engaged. I love Simon, Tinisha. I don't want anything to spoil it for us. Please understand how much it means to me to be marrying Simon.'

Leaning back, but keeping their pelvises pressed together, Tinisha smiled tenderly. The deceit that leads to a betrayal. She placed a hand on each of the naïve Kerry's shoulders. 'Of course I understand, my love. If you really know that is what you want, then – though I shall miss our gorgeous times together – you have my blessing.'

'Thank you.' Kerry's relief escaped in a drawn-out sigh. She ducked away from the look in Tinisha's eyes, and added gratefully 'I still want to work for you, Tinisha. You are a really sweet person.'

The greedy and the lovestruck are easy to win round. Tinisha could feel the heat of Kerry through her shirt. She caught the erotic scent of the girl. There was a silence between them, except for the beating of their hearts. Outside the bees were unnecessarily loud in their search for hot-scented pollen. Tinisha lightly held the girl's shoulders, then dropped her hands to her own sides. 'Well, I guess that's it. You'd better do what I pretended to want you for, Kerry – cook my tea.'

'Yes.' Kerry nodded fervently.

'There is one favour you could do me,' Tinisha said, with a false show of hesitation that deserved an Oscar.

'Anything,' Kerry responded brightly, but was unable to disguise her apprehension.

'I'd like . . .' Tinisha began, placing the tip of a forefinger on the girl's heavy bottom lip, pulling it down a little. She thrilled at the sight of spit bubbles glistening like jewels between the lip and white bottom teeth.

'Not a kiss!' Kerry was panicking; her voice had gone up an octave, and her words were slurred because Tinisha's finger still held her lip captive.

'No kiss, I promise,' Tinisha pledged with a sly smile. 'That would be too risky for us both. I just want a taste to remember you by.'

Some of the tension left Kerry.

Moving so that their breasts were touching, Tinisha kept her finger in place and put her tongue in between Kerry's lower lip and bottom teeth to scoop up saliva.

A spasm jerked through Kerry so violently that the back of her head cracked against the wall. If this caused her any pain, then she didn't show it. Suddenly she was crying and moaning, her hands fluttering all over Tinisha, pushing and pulling at the same time. Gripping tightly, her short nails dug deep into Tinisha through the thin material of the robe.

Then she was holding Tinisha's head with both hands, fingers entwining in her mass of curling black hair. The way her mouth opened and shaped up for a kiss accentuated Kerry's cheekbones. To Tinisha she had never looked so beautiful. Kerry blossomed to her fullest. Tinisha's tongue probed and the girl drank deeply. Quivering continually as Kerry gulped hungrily, Tinisha felt the girl's fingers tighten in her hair. Kerry seemed to flower more and more and Tinisha responded by moving a hand up under the girl's overshirt, passing over bare flesh to find and cup a large but firm breast. Taking the erect nipple between a thumb and forefinger, manipulating it, she was rewarded by the increase in the heat of Kerry's kiss.

Then the kiss broke, leaving the girl panting and gasping. Keeping hold of the breast, Tinisha, herself breathless, said, 'That's told me how much you love me, Kerry.'

A sob shook Kerry before she groaned in despair, 'Oh, Tinisha, I'm so mixed up, so confused.'

Fearing that the girl was about to cry, Tinisha, still fondling the breast with her right hand, used her left to tug gently on Kerry's long black hair. Pulling the girl's head back, she claimed her mouth in a demanding passionate kiss. Arousal had increased the sweetness on Kerry's lips. Her tongue was a hot, throbbing explorer. Still caressing the girl's breast, Tinisha pressed closer.

They were melting together in the kiss, thrusting at each other with their hips, when an alarmed Kerry pulled away.

'What's the matter?' a puzzled Tinisha enquired.

'I'm sure I saw someone looking in through the glass in the door,' Kerry croaked fearfully. 'I think it was Reggie.'

'No, he'll be in the rockery out the back,' Tinisha objected. 'I expect it was your imagination. Come on, you'll be more at ease in the bedroom.'

'No, no! Oh, no! I mustn't!' Kerry was protesting, while at the same time not showing any resistance as Tinisha took her by the hand and led her into the bedroom.

Pulling down the blinds, Tinisha locked her door and walked over to Kerry. The girl was frowning, and there were marks on her lower lip where she had bitten into it. Tenderly, Tinisha kissed Kerry's lower lip, and Kerry fell into her arms, her kisses demanding. She was breathing deeply, and her whole body was warm to Tinisha's hands no matter where they touched.

With a strangled groan, Kerry pushed Tinisha away. Her action was so violent that Tinisha had to take three involuntary backwards steps to recover her balance. 'No, and I definitely mean no,' Kerry said, with a hint of tears in her eyes and a catch of tears in her voice.

'Why deny yourself something that you really want, Kerry?' Tinisha enquired mildly.

'This isn't what I want,' the girl protested. 'I want Simon and a proper life.'

'I don't think that is what you want right now, Kerry.'

Standing back from the girl, Tinisha languidly undid the sash of her robe. The robe opened just a gap, teasingly hinting at everything but not really showing anything; she left it that way for a little while.

The anguish left Kerry's face. Replacing it was the semi-orgasmic expression that always took her over from her first moments of arousal to her bared-teeth climax. Tinisha, a witch when it came to sexual power, was confident that she had Kerry under her spell.

Grasping the robe with both hands, Tinisha dramatically opened it wide. Kerry had seen Tinisha's body many times before, but her desire increased with each sighting. With her eyelids half-closed, Kerry sagged at the knees. For a moment it seemed she was about to kneel in adoration of Tinisha's body. Then she stood with her back against the wall. As Tinisha gave a little shrug that sent the robe sliding off her shoulders, Kerry's face became a mask of lust. A sensuous pout was frozen on her full lips. She was staring fixedly at Tinisha, the only sign of life being the bright reflections in the dark pupils of her eyes.

Completely naked, Tinisha spoke huskily. 'Look at this.' Putting a hand down to her crotch, she stroked and gently pulled at her curling pubic hair. Delving into it, she parted her pubes and slid two fingers into her cunt, turning them to widen the gap, a thrusting and twisting movement that created a wet and syrupy sound. Her fingers began to glisten moistly, and her voice was deeper, even huskier, as she asked, 'Doesn't this make you want to touch me?'

Kerry was sobbing in a way that had nothing to do with crying. Undoing her shirt and taking it off, she cupped both her breasts, titillating the nipples as her eyes remained fixed on Tinisha's busy hand. Pulling the cord of her shorts undone, she let them fall. She was wearing brown panties, and the sight of them caused Tinisha to catch her breath noisily. With her hand on her own stomach, Kerry slid it down inside her panties and began fucking herself with her own finger.

Tinisha walked over to Kerry, took her wrist and gently pulled her hand upwards. The panties were saturated and Tinisha could clearly see the outline of Kerry's inner lips through the tight fabric. With a hand against the girl's hot stomach, Tinisha hooked a finger in the waistband and pulled the panties down. The tight V of

Kerry's curly hair was very damp. Tinisha could see that the girl's clitoris was swollen and stiff from the brief spell of masturbation.

Tinisha's nimble finger slid gently over the slippery and wet crinkled lips of the girl's vulva, avoiding the pleasure-button at first in an arousing, tantalising way that had Kerry's hips working of their own accord. As a groaning Kerry reached to stroke the back of Tinisha's head before tangling her fingers in Tinisha's long hair to pull her head down for a sucking kiss, Tinisha let her stew in her own juice for a moment.

It was a heavy kiss, with Kerry's velvet lips working a special magic. Responding with a groan Tinisha rubbed Kerry's clit round and round in tiny circles. Kerry cried out without breaking the kiss, which had a highly erotic effect on Tinisha.

Ending the kiss, Tinisha slid down on to her knees. Her mouth travelled down over Kerry's flat and fragrant smooth stomach; Tinisha then used her lips and tongue to part the girl's pubic hair and nudge open the lips of her cunt. Then she had the clit. A low, shuddering moan escaped from Kerry as Tinisha manipulated the silken bead in perfect time to the insistent thrusting of Kerry's pelvis. It was also in perfect time to the beating of Kerry's heart and the throb of blood in her aching flesh.

It was too much for the girl to bear. Through a mind-haze of pleasure as she licked and sucked, Tinisha heard Kerry's cry. 'Please, Tinisha. Let's get on to the bed – Tinisha, please!'

Standing up, Tinisha took Kerry into her arms for what she intended to be a long kiss. But they were both too aroused to extend it. There was urgency that left no time for the sex toys in the dressing table drawer, not even the as yet unused monster strap-on dildo that was somehow lent an extra eroticism by the bright yellow of its leather harness. Neither could wait any longer. Tinisha backed Kerry to the bed and pushed her on to it.

Legs wide open, knees raised, a panting Kerry held her arms open for Tinisha to get on top of her. But Tinisha had one more trick up her sleeve that would guarantee her a super orgasm.

Standing in front of Kerry, looking down at her, Tinisha said, 'Are you sure that you want me, Kerry?'

'Oh, yes,' Kerry groaned, the twisting and thrusting of her hips becoming convulsions. The wet, swollen, protruding lips of her

16

gaping cunt seeming to mime the words as she spoke them. 'Yes,' she cried. 'Fuck me, Tinisha. Do it, please do it.'

'But you said that you don't want me, you want Simon Gregory.' Tinisha had to discipline herself to remain standing and say this. Her self-control was stretched to breaking point by the sight of the lovely Kerry in such an aroused state.

'It's you I want. I'm begging you, Tinisha,' Kerry sobbed. Then her voice rose to a scream. 'Fuck me – pleeeeeeeaaaaaase!'

Then Kerry made a choking sound as Tinisha knelt on the bed between her legs and lay on top of her. Tinisha expertly wiggled her body until their hot, sopping wet cunts were welded together.

Kerry met Tinisha thrust for thrust. They kissed passionately; words that said nothing but meant everything were lost as their tongues danced together and lips crushed against lips.

It didn't last for long. Kerry's legs suddenly clutched round Tinisha's back. Tinisha's arse began to buck and shudder as she gave her all to pleasuring her lover. All at once and in unison, their voices began to rise. The muttering of endearments first became excited little squeaks and gasps. Then these noises developed into loud shrieks of totally abandoned delight as they climaxed together in a frenzy of grabbing, clawing, panting lust.

Completely spent, Tinisha rolled off to lie on the bed beside Kerry. She listened, and then she was sure. The girl was sighing softly. The sound of Kerry's satiation miraculously dredged up a reserve of sexual energy from somewhere deep inside Tinisha. Jerking convulsively on the bed, she rubbed herself to a second, mind-rattling orgasm.

TWO

Valerie Zennor was angry. No, she was seething with rage, but she didn't want to spoil the first day of the holiday for her family. All of them had been so thrilled on arrival. The cottage and its setting were idyllic, better than they had dared hope. Valerie had expected the two children to be fretful to start with. That was normal with kids. But Jerome and Roxanne had been as good as gold, and Grace, Guy's mother, had been her usual useful self.

Though it would be out of character for her – and Valerie thought that in all modesty – she was possibly being selfish. Perhaps she was partly responsible for her reaction to the disappointment her husband had caused her.

Last night had been the kind of an unmitigated disaster that was boosted by an anti-climax. Her work as a teacher and Guy's as a sales executive was demanding and tiring. Though they still managed to have sex regularly at home, a permanent exhaustion diminished it. They made all the right moves, but not through the right motives. Valerie had to use fantasies to grunt her way to an unsatisfactory orgasm, and she was certain that Guy could come only if he indulged in something similar.

Both of them had held high hopes for this holiday. Screwing in entirely different surroundings would be as exciting as fucking with a different partner. Neither of them wanted to change the other for someone else, but both were desperate to regain the lust they had once had for each other.

They had both gone to bed naked last night. Guy had been so proud of what she had to admit had been a magnificent hard-on, that he had paraded it up and down in front of her. The sight of the hugely erect cock, and his superbly muscled body, had driven her crazy with desire.

But everything had gone wrong from the minute they'd got into bed, finding as they did so that the springs squeaked loudly. The groan of complaint from the bed, and the thought of Grace, his mother, being in the next room, had had the instant effect of making Guy impotent. Determined not to give up, Valerie had climbed up, straddling him. Alarmed by the noise her action had created, Guy had hastily pushed her off. It wouldn't have been any use, anyway, as his prick had then been as limp as a baby's leg hanging out of the pram. His own mother had psychologically castrated Valerie's husband.

Logically, she should have been able to understand. But reason and anger don't mix. To her, the hang-ups most people have where sex and their parents are concerned were ludicrous. Old Grace had done it herself, otherwise Guy wouldn't be here. The fact that her son had two children was evidence of his experience. Even so, Valerie supposed that for his mother to hear him shagging his wife would be akin to having her catch him wanking himself as a schoolboy.

But none of this rationality could have helped her last night. Unable to sleep, Valerie had got out of bed to collect an underarm roll-on deodorant. Back in bed, the penis-shaped bottle had magically turned into the stiff cock of a black parent of one of her pupils. The handsome, bronze-coloured Joseph Wade stirred Valerie whenever she was in his presence. But as she moistened the rounded cap of the bottle by sliding it teasingly up and down her slit to lubricate it, she couldn't clearly imagine Joseph making love to her.

She found it easier to bring Sonya, his beautiful wife, into the scene. Sonya helped out a lot at the school, and Valerie had several times caught herself unconsciously but hungrily breathing in the undefinable but erotic aroma that Sonya's body exuded.

Easing the bottle into herself, she began by picturing the West Indian couple kissing and starting foreplay. Eyes half-closed, beautiful face contorted by passion, Sonya swung her head from side to side in ecstasy as her man slowly undressed her, caressing and kissing her breasts, sucking eagerly on the projecting nipples. Then they were naked, Sonya on her back and the husband between her wide-open legs, entering her.

A peculiar thing had happened then. Quickening the rhythm of her strokes with the bottle, Valerie had intended to have herself take Sonya's place. Instead, she had become the husband. Sonya's thighs had tightened around her hips as she had thrust into her. Sonya's open mouth devoured hers, their tongues dancing together as they exchanged saliva.

Panting, only able to take great, gulping breaths that Guy must have been aware of, Valerie had speeded up the movements of the bottle. Only at the last moment had she been able to push Sonya out of her mind. Then, with the powerful black man on top of her, his massive tool ravishing her, filling her, Valerie had come in a mind-bursting, explosive way.

It had been necessary to bury her face in the pillow to stifle a wild, abandoned cry of sheer pleasure. If she had let it rip, Guy would probably have died of a heart attack at the thought of his mother hearing so animal a sound. Goodness knows what her husband's reaction would have been had she told him she'd wanked herself while imagining she was fucking a woman.

On awaking in the morning, she had wanted more. Still asleep, Guy had a totem pole of an erection. But Valerie recognised that he was just piss-proud. One groan of a bedspring and his cock would collapse as it had last night. Holding one of her husband's warm, hairy thighs tightly between her legs, she had worked her hot, juicy cunt against it. Trying hard to conjure up Sonya and her husband, Valerie had failed. She had come again, eventually, but it had been a fizzle rather than a banger.

But the draining of her sexual energy had left Valerie's mind crystal clear. She was filled with remorse over her raunchy thoughts. Masturbation held no shame for her. It had become a regular practice of late, but always with a man in mind – one of Guy's friends, or a work colleague. Last night had been the first time she had imagined a woman. Valerie's biggest worry was that it hadn't really been her choice. She had wanted the dishy Joseph, but something of herself that she didn't understand had selected Sonya.

Getting up really early, she had gone outside into a world she had never experienced at that time of day. A slight breeze stirred as the first ray of sunlight had been pulled up over the horizon. There had been a few sounds in the bushes and trees around her as wild creatures started their day. Then there had been silence, as if the denizens of the woods had recognised that they must become careful. An occasional rustling disturbed a quiet that had soothed Valerie.

After a reasonable morning spent fully exploring the cottage and the near vicinity, Valerie, with the help of Grace, had cooked dinner. This had helped her considerably, when she discovered that a different kitchen didn't make cooking the chore it was at home.

They had come down to the beach for the afternoon. Now, with Guy and the kids off paddling in the sea, and Grace snoring lightly beside her, Valerie felt ashamed of herself.

She, the most loyal and faithful of wives, but suddenly and seriously sex-starved, found herself looking at every passing man. They were tanned, and their skimpy bathing costumes were little more than G-strings that drew attention to the bulging loads they were supposed to keep hidden. There was a general scent in the air: a mixture of ozone, suntan lotion, and human bodies that seemed to have an aphrodisiacal effect on her. She was influenced also by the sounds all around her. In contrast to the ceaseless thunder of traffic she was accustomed to, the delighted squeals of children, the happy laughter of adults, and the gentle, rhythmic lap of tiny waves against the shore played an anthem of freedom.

A man was passing by, his golden tan and lithe body enhanced by the tiny posing pouch that he wore. He was perhaps ten years her junior, not yet out of his teens. But there was no doubting the maturity in the look that he gave her. Valerie was not in a swimming costume, but wore the skirt she had travelled down in, having changed only her vest top. But she realised that she had her knees raised, and must be showing something, for the youth had been afflicted by a very obvious erection.

21

Turning on her side to avoid temptation, she was relieved to find no men or boys in her line of vision. There was only a woman of mixed race. Sensing Valerie's gaze on her, the woman turned her head to glance at her. She looked away again quickly, but not until the sight of narrow, long eyes that slanted upwards and outwards in a smooth oval face had shivered a thrill through Valerie's body. The woman was trying to placate her crying child. Apparently halfway through changing to go into the water, she had been interrupted by the small boy's tantrum. Wearing some kind of flowered changing garment that came only partway down her golden thighs, the woman had her back to Valerie.

She bent over to wipe her son's eyes, and the flowered garment rose up high. Valerie caught her breath as she saw the cheeks of the fawn-skinned arse open up. Just a few feet separated her from the woman and an aroused Valerie could have actually counted the coarse black hairs surrounding a small, puckered arsehole. She started to pant when she saw the woman's cunt. The black pubic hair was long and wet. Though it hung down thickly, it didn't hide the purplish, swollen lips.

Unable to stop feasting her eyes, Valerie felt a sexual surge throughout her whole body as she told herself that Sonya's cunt and arsehole probably looked just like this. What was the matter with her? She wanted a man, but here she was finding it difficult to breathe because a woman was exciting her. Valerie wanted to reach out to have a feel of the cunt that was gently oozing white fluid. She wanted to smell it, touch it, kiss it, taste it, fuck it.

This was ridiculous. She was a normal married woman. Forcing her eyes away, Valerie rolled on to her stomach. That wasn't a good idea. She found herself secreting her hand under her waistband and pushing her pelvis discreetly in on and off movements against the hot sand. Within seconds, while she took a last, lingering look at the gaping wet cunt that was still on full display, her part-orgasm of that morning completed itself.

She returned to what would have been normal if it hadn't been for the trembling going on inside her, as she heard Guy and the children return. Jerome was calling to her excitedly as he ran up.

'Mum, Dad's taking us to the Sealife Centre this evening. There are loads and loads of lovely fishes there.'

'That'll be nice,' Valerie said automatically, as both she and Grace sat up. She wondered if Guy's mother had slept through it all. It would embarrass her if the old lady had witnessed her working herself off against the sand.

The woman, her aphrodisiac body now in a brief two-piece swimming costume, had calmed her child and had him by the hand ready to go down to the sea. A fleeting glance told Valerie that she hadn't been to a beauty parlour to have her bikini line done. An inverted V of fine black hair came up to her navel. Why was Valerie noticing something like that?

She gave Valerie a smile. It was no more than a friendly gesture, but Valerie was dismayed how profoundly it thrilled her. Smiling back nervously, still bemused by what had happened to her, she heard Guy speaking.

'It should be really interesting, Val,' he was saying, referring to the projected visit to the Sealife Centre.

'There's sharks there, and all,' Jerome put in, while Roxanne, his little sister, clapped chubby hands in excitement, although she didn't really understand any of it.

Trying to think of an answer, a guilty Valerie didn't even seem to be a part of her own family any more. Close relatives were people you could be open and honest with. Aware that Guy was looking curiously at her, she found it impossible to meet his gaze.

'I think it'll be great,' the children's grandmother filled in for Valerie, as they pulled her to her feet.

'Come and see the tiny fishes in a pool just down there, Gran,' Jerome urged, pointing towards the sea.

As the old woman walked gingerly across the sand on bare feet, with a child holding her hand on both sides, Guy looked earnestly at Valerie.

'Are you still angry with me, Val?' he asked.

She shook her head. Self-disgust had replaced her earlier anger. 'No, of course not. But I've got one of those funny heads, you know; not really a headache. I might let all of you go to that place this evening. I'll stay back at the cottage, perhaps take a walk.'

'OK, although I wish you were coming with us.' Guy was disappointed. He added, 'You be careful, wandering around on your own in a place you don't know.'

'I won't go far.' She made a promise that she probably wouldn't be able to keep. The woods at the far side of the cabin attracted her. Maybe she'd take a walk there.

That might be dangerous but, right at that moment, Valerie Zennor thought it possible that she might even welcome being taken roughly, alone in the woods. That was a silly, frightening thought, but no more weird than everything that had gone on in her mind since arriving at the holiday cottage.

'But you just can't afford to lose that kind of money.'

In retrospect, Marjory Tredogan realised that she would have been more honest to use 'we' and not 'you', last Saturday evening. That was when Kerry had come home to drop the bombshell that she didn't want to work for Tinisha Weaver any more. There had been something very different about her daughter. Her eyes had seemed to be looking inwards at some infinite sadness. Aware of Kerry's obstinate streak, Marjory feared that Kerry had objected strongly – possibly even rudely – to being called to cook her employer's tea on a Saturday.

But Kerry had denied this, saying that Miss Weaver and herself were still on the best of terms. It was just a matter, Kerry had explained, of wanting a change. 'After all, Mum, I'll be married to Simon soon, and I won't need to work then.' Although Kerry considered herself to be a millennium woman, she was as old-fashioned as the girls who, up to the seventies at least, believed that the good life stretched from their wedding day on into the beyond.

'But you'll need work until then,' Marje had argued.

All she'd got from Kerry was a dismissive shrug. 'I'll find something, Mum.'

Where indeed? The two cafés in the village, the small amuse-ment arcade, and one or two of the public houses courted staff in late spring in the smarmy way that politicians sought votes at election times. But come September, the local employers didn't want to know you.

That was why she considered that her daughter was being irresponsible in leaving a regular, well-paid job. It couldn't have come at a worse time, because Jack had just fully seen the error of his ways. Her husband had sworn that he had not touched a drop of alcohol for the past ten days. He had lied about his drinking before, but this time he had been working harder and bringing more money in. With Kerry's wage, they could have at last managed to start putting some finances behind them.

In fact, this Monday morning Marje had been planning to secretly open a post office savings account. But Kerry's sudden decision had knocked that idea on the head. Right now, Marje was on an errand for which she had no liking. She was aware that Kerry was putting on her, but it wasn't in her nature not to help her daughter, whatever the circumstances.

Kerry had learned last evening that Marilyn Cosgrave, who had married the young coastguard lodging at Mrs Normington's, was pregnant and leaving her job. Marilyn was the sole employee of Terry and Geraldine Dumphy, who owned a combination garage, café and country store on Sea Road. Geraldine ran the café and store with Marilyn, while Terry took care of the garage side of the business.

As she headed for Sea Road, Marje prayed that either the story about Marilyn was wrong, or Dumphy had taken someone else on. She hadn't told Kerry that she didn't want her working for the likes of Terry Dumphy. He was a crude man who got a kick from telling women absolutely filthy jokes. For some reason, he fancied Marje, and his suggestive remarks and innuendoes were all the more worrying because Geraldine openly aided and abetted her husband. This surprised Marje, because Terry Dumphy was known to be insanely jealous regarding his voluptuous blonde wife.

Marje would have none of it. She found that sort of thing repulsive – disgusting! At last year's Christmas party in the village social centre, she had been foolish enough to be press-ganged into a game of postman's knock. Young Albie Forster, an apprentice at the village hairdresser's, had got himself all worked up kissing her, literally begging her to open her mouth as they'd kissed. Marje had kept her lips pressed firmly together, the way that she always had. After all, why did a boy of twenty want that sort of thing from a plump housewife of fifty? Kerry had often tried to convince her that, particularly because of Marje's mane of red hair, she was a very attractive woman. Marje put that down to a daughter being kind to her old mum.

Not that Kerry was being kind today in recruiting her to make an approach for a new job for her. It wasn't a sensible idea, Marje had pointed out, because if there was a vacancy, then Dumphy would need to see the applicant in person. Kerry had pleaded in her wheedling way. 'I just want you to break the ice for me, Mum. It will help that you went to school with him.'

The way it turned out, nothing could have helped. Unnecessarily squeezing past her by the counter, causing Marje to shrivel inside when she felt his hard penis 'accidentally' find its way into the crack of her bum, Terry Dumphy had explained the position.

'If you'd called on me on Saturday, Marje, then the answer would have been a definite yes,' he said while ogling her body in its summer print dress. 'But Elke Fuller is coming back home today, and she's starting for me tomorrow morning. But if that should fall through, or Elke don't stay for long, your Kerry will be the first to know.'

Thanking him, Marje felt she could tell Kerry that there was still some hope. Elke Fuller, who was four years Kerry's senior, had itchy feet. When she was born, Dr Morgan, dead and gone these past twenty years, had warned George and Ada Fuller that the baby had a double crown, and they would never be able to keep her at home. The old doc had been proved right. At sixteen, Elke had gone off to work at Butlins. Back home again three years later, she had stayed a short while before going off to join the army. Now it seemed she was back home yet again.

'Hello, Marje.' Geraldine Dumphy came out of the shop to greet Marje. 'It's not often we see you on a Monday.'

She was a big-breasted, dyed-blonde woman. She had a face that must once have been devastatingly attractive, but now had the hardness of a prostitute. There were those in the village who unkindly suggested that had been her former occupation. She had come down from London on holiday in 1979, met and married Terry, and hadn't gone back home since.

'Marje came to book her 30,000-mile service.' Dumphy grinned as he gave his garage-owner's jargon a double meaning.

'Thirty thousand!' Geraldine made a joke in her good-natured fashion. 'I reckons it's more like a hundred thousand since Scrumpy-Jack dipped her oil.'

26

Though Geraldine was a very nice person when away from her husband, Marje blushed and felt sick at being made the butt of the Dumphys' dirty humour. She walked swiftly away. She would tell Kerry that the job had gone. There was no way she'd leave a daughter of hers alone with the sex-mad Dumphys.

Dried leaves carpeted the path through the forest. Unhurried, Valerie Zennor took pleasure in the spongy feeling under her feet. It gave her body strength and resilience, unlike the hard, unrelenting pavements of London. Walking along the winding trail was invigorating. Occasionally she had to step over a tree-trunk stretched across the path. They were legacies of a winter storm of long ago. On so glorious an evening, Valerie could envisage neither that storm nor the winter it belonged to. Some of the fallen trunks blossomed with leaves.

At times, fallen branches crackled and snapped when she stepped. This made the sounds of wildlife follow her. It was as though her movements were awakening the birds so that she could lead them in song. A Walt Disney analogy caused Valerie to smile. Maybe a wicked stepmother awaited her up ahead, cackling eerily as she proffered a poisoned apple.

Valerie was happy for the first time since coming on holiday. In a snatched and whispered conversation in the garden of the cottage, Guy had promised that they would definitely have sex that night. Initially that had excited her: but now, out here in the midst of nature, it was wholly insignificant. For the first time since passing through the insanity and perils of puberty, Valerie was devoid of a constantly pressing interest in, and a need of, sex.

She wondered whether, if she was honest with herself – an exercise that she found strangely difficult right now – her dormant desires might well go through an instant resurrection if it were not Guy who would be sharing her bed that night, but Sonya Wade or the woman on the beach. Valerie detested, and was terrified by, this newly discovered side of herself. But she accepted that it was due to the drastic change of location and circumstances. Once they all returned to their own home, normality would sneak back and all would be well.

Valerie paused, undecided, on reaching a fork in the path. To her right was a brook that had been diminished by the heat. It traced down through the wood before disappearing into an underground cave under a ridge. Fascinated, Valerie followed the brook to discover that it leaped melodically out of the cave further down. Walking beside it, she topped a slight rise, and stood for a moment in the shade cast by a giant elm tree.

Up ahead her trail joined a wider path that led to a yellowstone bungalow that had a roof of red tiles. On a patio, with her back to Valerie, a woman artist stood at an easel.

Moving slowly, going nearer, Valerie wondered if an approach by her would be welcomed or rejected by the woman. The artist wore a free-fitting brown dress. Her mass of tumbling, curly hair was held back by a thick yellow band with no attempt at neatness.

She turned as Valerie got closer. Not expecting to meet someone's eyes so directly, Valerie was momentarily stunned. With one hand poised, a paintbrush held in long fingers, the female artist seemed amused by the effect she'd had on Valerie. She had the exquisite looks of a film star, but none of the pretentiousness. Her eyes were a disconcertingly deep brown. It was possible to see into them, to a certain extent, the way you can crystals. But when Valerie tried she became entranced, and realised with a shock that the black woman's eyes were looking through her. It was as if she possessed some special powers.

The woman bent over to rest her palette on a small table, and the dress fell away to expose her bare breasts. There was something highly erotic about the way the artist delayed straightening up after noticing the fascination her cleavage held for Valerie. She looked as if she might be ready to smile, but didn't. An uncomfortable Valerie stood, desperately searching for some way of breaking the silent impasse.

She had known there was someone coming. Tinisha had felt the moment of tension, had heard whispers in the woods before the blonde had walked into view. Then the brief alarm was gone, as though it had served its purpose. A few birds were flying around in the direction from which the woman was coming. Tinisha heard them singing about the blonde. They were saying there was no danger, but marked her approach for all to see. Two house martins stopped bathing in the brook and flew back to their nest. They sat together, watching.

Tinisha turned, and was stunned. The woman's hair was loosely arranged and its fairness flamed as she passed through arrows of sunlight. The measurements of the full figure inside the A-line black embroidered dress had to be perfection. She looked soft and yielding, but there was a strength and firmness, too, that Tinisha found to be equally desirable.

There was a long and awkward silence between them. Though never having met before, it somehow didn't seem possible that they were strangers. They stood bemused, like two people trying to remember the future. It took Tinisha a long time to locate her vocal cords and make them work for her.

'You don't look worried enough to be lost,' she commented lightly.

The white woman put even white teeth on display in a wide smile. 'No, I was just wandering around.' She pointed at the canvas propped on the easel. 'I saw you working, and wasn't sure what response I'd get. Artists often object to people looking over their shoulders.'

'I suppose there are as many responses as there are painters,' Tinisha said, wielding a palette knife with care to scrape on some yellow ochre. The scratching sound caused the pair of house martins to turn and look questioningly at each other.

'And what is your personal response?'

'You're welcome.' Tinisha turned her head to smile at the white woman. 'I could use some company.' She looked westwards into a sky where the bright yellow sun of the day was changing to orange. 'There's not enough light left for me to go on. I'm Tinisha, Tinisha Weaver.'

'My name's Valerie, Valerie Zennor,' the blonde responded, turning her head to indicate the holiday cottage down below. 'We –'

'I know,' Tinisha interrupted her, but not impolitely. 'I saw you arrive.'

Smiling her acceptance of this, Valerie moved closer to the easel, studying the canvas. 'She's truly beautiful. Who is she?'

'Ruby,' Tinisha replied instantly, surprising herself. The name had come into her mind via the same mysterious route as the painting. A change had come over the portrait in the past few hours. It was an indefinable change, but for some reason it made Tinisha uneasy.

'Is she just a model, or a friend?' Valerie enquired conversationally.

'She's very close,' Tinisha replied, the answer creating laughter inside her head.

It was very quiet. The woods had sung a last chorus and gone to sleep. The sun was sinking fast but was leaving a memory of gold that spread through the growing shadow of a coming night, to blend with the now dark purple mass of the sea.

'I wish I had a talent like yours,' a wistful Valerie said.

'According to the psychiatrists, we don't have talent,' Tinisha said. 'They say that male artists are premature ejaculators. That could be true of us, too. Some women ejaculate similar to the way a man does . . .' She broke off. 'Oh, dear, I've embarrassed you.'

'No, not at all.' A blush coloured Valerie's face, telling Tinisha that she had lied.

Tinisha reached out to pull a shaft of wild wheat out of its coarse scabbard, then chewed on the sweet end as she studied Valerie. Holding the white woman's chin with a thumb and forefinger, she turned her head slightly.

'Hmm, just as I thought.'

'Plug-ugly.' An embarrassed Valerie giggled.

'On the contrary, you would make a perfect model,' Tinisha assured her. 'I would be more than happy to paint you.'

Though flattered, Valerie stammered, 'Th-thanks for the compliment, but we're on a pretty tight budget. I could never afford anything like that.'

There were a few sounds around them as nocturnal creatures began to come out. A rustling was followed by a distant squeal of pain or love. The last ray of sunlight was pulled over the horizon. Tinisha could see the village far below, haloed by artificial lighting, inhabited mostly by holidaymakers she would never meet. She spoke softly to Valerie without turning to look at her. 'I wasn't asking you for money, just for a little of your time.'

'I'm sorry, I didn't understand,' Valerie apologised, resting a hand on a wooden trellis intertwined by roses. 'Ouch!' Pulling a little face, she raised her left hand to her mouth, biting on it.

'A splinter. Let me see,' Tinisha said, catching hold of Valerie's hand. Examining it, she made a diagnosis. 'No, you just pricked it on a thorn.'

There was a vibration between them, a thrilling sensation that made it impossible for Tinisha to release the hand. Valerie, plainly just as excited by the contact, said a shy little, 'Thank you.'

Raising the hand, which shone wetly where Valerie had sucked on it, Tinisha said in a motherly tone, 'I'll kiss it better.'

Kissing the palm, she then took the part made moist by Valerie into her mouth. Tinisha kept the hand in her mouth for a long time. They stood together with the night going on around them and mysterious communications going on between them.

It was Valerie, so affected that she was laughing and crying at one and the same time, who broke the contact. Gently freeing her hand, she whispered, as if there was something between them that shouldn't be disturbed, 'I have to go.'

She was away, hurrying downhill towards the cottage; she turned her head back over her shoulder when Tinisha called, 'I can do your portrait whenever you can spare the time, Valerie.'

'We'll see,' Valerie said weakly as she moved on and the new darkness closed round her, hiding her from Tinisha.

THREE

The shower Kerry took after her mother had left for work had been refreshing. The moist fragrance of the bathroom air was in her mouth. It tasted as sweet as a woman's kiss. Tinisha's divine kiss! She forced that erotic thought from her mind and stepped back from the mirror. She looked really good. Just being around a seaside resort, whether you sunbathed or not, seemed to give you a tan. The deodorant stung a little under her freshly shaved armpits. She was glad that Tinisha didn't shave.

Thinking of her employer evoked two responses in Kerry: an increase of warmth between her legs, and a coldness of dread in her heart. She was pulled in opposite directions by sexual need and the voice of duty. Having been absent from work for three days, now it was time to eat humble pie. In a discussion with her family, including a much-mellowed father, she had agreed that a return to work was a financial necessity. There was a long way to go before her marriage to Simon, when the Tredogans would be sure to benefit from the Gregory fortune. She patted her tummy outside the blue denim dress. It was as flat as ever; she hadn't gained an ounce in weight, nor an inch in size – apart from her breasts – since the age of fourteen.

Going out, she passed through platoons of aimlessly wandering trippers. What they found so interesting about the village, Kerry would never know. She was as anxious now as ever to seek the sanctuary of the hills. As she slowly and leisurely ascended, so did her misgivings over how Tinisha would greet her. As always, it was as if she climbed different soil, a different life, and a new and surprising air. When Kerry looked back, the buildings in the village below were pink and ugly and unfledged, like young birds in a nest. It was only a mile or so away, but up here it was as though creation had changed its mind abruptly. The air was lighter, and the skylarks sang their song of innocence in the sweep of distance.

Wondering whether it was actually the change of environment or the thought of Tinisha that wrought the change in her, Kerry walked on. Curved and hesitant, the narrow chalk path grew whiter as she went along it. To her right, a cluster of trees huddled together, sharing their secret. That secret was the magic of the hidden-away bungalow, the home of Tinisha Weaver.

A low dry-stone wall ran along beside the path here. Kerry felt that she could almost tell where its long-ago makers had sat down to rest. Often up here she could imagine a Roman soldier relieving himself behind a bush, or raising his helmet to wipe sweat from the red ridge across his forehead.

Simon came into her mind. She desperately wanted him, both psychologically and physically. But she admitted to herself that she was frightened of him sexually. Tinisha instantly lifted her over the fear barrier of sex when they were intimate, but Kerry was convinced that it wouldn't be anything like so easy with a man. A short while ago, she had been shocked to overhear Albie Forster and some other boys discussing what they would like to do to her mother, their voices quavering with excitement. The things they had described had both aroused and sickened Kerry.

Why couldn't she see in her mother what those boys saw? Her father must have done so at one time. Yet she had seen her mother come from the bathroom to walk past him stark naked. Her body was plump, but firm and ripe, the dark nipples on her heavy breasts saucer-like, the stiff bush of red pubic hair startling in contrast to the white skin of her stomach. But Kerry's father had not raised his head from the newspaper he'd been reading. Was that what marriage did to people? How long would it take Simon, now so greedy for her, to completely lose interest in her and her body?

33

As she neared the bungalow, she was nervous but determined. This time she would make it clear to Tinisha that she would work for her, but on her own terms. She had promised the unsuspecting Simon that. Kerry knew that she owed a clean break from the woman not only to Simon but to herself. Could she do it? Once inside the lovely artist's aura, finding herself in tune with her vibrations, Kerry always became lost in the frenzy of her own desire.

With a renewed sense of confidence, she strode the last few yards. Through the bushes she could see the bungalow. Kerry's resolve started to crumble as soon as she saw Tinisha. Leaning against the door jamb, Tinisha had the pseudo-relaxed pose of a sensual woman in touch with every inch of her body at all times. And she was wearing a scanty white bikini that gave an additional eroticism to her dark skin.

Sitting in a chair outside the back door of the cottage, the hot, sweet midday sun bathing her upturned face, Valerie sensed a shadow falling on her closed eyelids.

'Sex police. You're under arrest.'

A grinning Guy was standing there. He had showered, slipped on a robe, and was holding out his driving licence as a pretend police badge. He was a bull at service, offering love in the afternoon. Valerie caught the smell of a television-advertised sexy male perfume. It was the latest, but it sickened her.

She was instantly ashamed of the flash of annoyance she felt at her reverie being interrupted. It was wrong and selfish, but Valerie excused herself in an involuntary reaction. In a semi-trance, she had been listening to a vast silence that was broken occasionally by the slight whisperings of a breeze brushing gently over the land.

'You fool, Guy,' she chided him in pretend amusement. 'What on earth are you up to?'

'Mother's taken the kids down to the beach. We've got time, lots of time,' he said a little breathlessly, catching hold of her wrists and gently pulling her up on to her feet.

Valerie dreaded what was to come. In recent times their love-making had registered on the minus side of mediocre. It was as if they were one of those crazy couples who fuck for pseudo-scientific videos, wires attached to them and with people peering at their private parts through instruments. Paddy Keegan, their cynical bachelor friend back home, believed that three months was the duration of real attraction between any couple. Puppy love was a beautiful thing when the lovers were puppies, Paddy declared, but it was sad and ugly between old dogs. Guy and she had lasted ten years, but now it seemed they were old dogs.

Groaning inwardly, Valerie accepted that she didn't have the right to deny him her mouth as he took her into his arms and kissed her. His hard-on probed against her. It was a massive battering ram. By twisting his mouth he parted her lips, eager for more of her. One of his big, dark-furred hands was sliding up the inside of her ultra-short skirt. As he cupped the bulging crotch of her panties, she struggled to break the kiss and thrust him away from her.

'No, Guy, no,' she gasped. 'Someone might see us.'

Out here in the open countryside it wasn't a valid objection. Valerie recognised that. But the lovely woman artist hadn't been out of her mind since the chance late-night meeting with her up at the bungalow. It was as if she were here now: tall, dark, willowy, perfect and devastatingly beautiful. A smouldering, sinuous, serpentine female.

Knowing nothing of this, Guy scoffed at her worry about being observed. 'The only thing likely to see us is a fucking rabbit with a pair of binoculars.'

With her arms folded between them and her hands flat against his chest, she kept him at a distance from her. 'What if they come back, Guy?'

'It's a long walk,' he assured her. 'Come on. If you're too shy to do anything out here, let's go up to the bedroom.'

Sweeping Valerie up in his strong arms, he carried her up the stairs with ease. He laid her on the bed, undressed her, then stood up to take his own clothes off. Then they were both naked and he was on the bed with her, propped up on one elbow, looking lustfully at her.

Guy leaned down and kissed her. It was a slow, lingering kiss that tasted of aftershave. She kept her lips pressed together as his fingers played at her throat and swept slowly up to her hair.

Then something fell between them like an invisible, descending curtain. Valerie's body went rigid.

'What's the matter?' he croaked.

The pit of her belly was hot and painfully tight. Guy moved his hand between her legs. Valerie's cunt felt tender and twitchy. His touch was torture, and she reached down to grip his wrist and move his hand away from her.

'I can't, Guy, I'm sorry. I'm so sorry.'

Hating the disappointment she saw on his face, the abject rejection that clouded his eyes, Valerie tried to think of something conciliatory to say, a few comforting words. There was nothing. Tears were threatening her as he rolled over disconsolately to lie on his back, asking angrily, 'Not another of your fucking headaches?'

'Yes, no . . . n–' she stammered. 'I don't know what it is.'

Getting off the bed, he stood up. Clearly agitated, he reached for her upper arms, picking her half up off the bed. He dropped her and picked up a packet of cigarettes from the bedside table. He dropped the cigarettes and picked her up again. For a moment he stood holding her, hurting her, as he obviously tried to collect himself.

Guy had never raised a hand to her, but at that moment Valerie was frightened.

But he lowered her to the bed gently and stood up. Every muscle on his magnificent body stood out in relief. Turning side on to her, his gargantuan hard-on was incongruous in the situation, even ludicrous. No, it wasn't funny: it was lamentable. Valerie lay there, having rejected sex but just as unbearably worked-up as her husband. The problem was that she didn't want to be here. Valerie had the urge to rush pell-mell up to the bungalow on the hill, like a drug addict late for a date with her pusher.

Face red from humiliation, Guy stood with his head down, obviously wrestling with an urge to wank. Then he went out of the room.

Lying still, Valerie looked idly out of the window. A jet-black crow did a vertical landing on the branch of a tree, complaining loud and raucously as it did so. Two squirrels stopped wrestling among the leaves to listen. All living creatures had their problems.

Getting off the bed, Valerie collected her clothing from where Guy had carelessly tossed it when in the grip of passion. As she dressed herself, zombie-like, she could hear the sounds of him relieving himself in the bathroom. When he returned to the bedroom his prick was flaccid and his embarrassment agonisingly acute.

Valerie sat on the bed as Guy, unspeaking, got into his clothes. Then he sat beside her, not close enough to signal that the sex-war was over, but in a way that declared a truce.

'This holiday was supposed to fix everything,' he mumbled.

'We might find that it has when we get home,' she said, knowing that she wouldn't convince him because she hadn't convinced herself.

'I suppose the important thing is that the kids enjoy themselves,' he said, brightening.

That wasn't true, for Guy and she had as much right to enjoyment as their children. But it had been a selfless thing to say. She tentatively put an arm around his shoulders. He had a right to comfort, even though she had been the author of his distress. She had a need of him that wasn't directly selfish, as it would be the first move towards saving their marriage. Valerie had to enlist her husband's help in saving her from herself.

'I know that I'm not in a position to ask you for anything, Guy,' she began slowly, 'but do you remember me telling you about that woman artist who lives up on the hill?'

He gave a confirming but disinterested nod.

'Well, she wants to start painting my portrait tomorrow afternoon, and I wondered if you'd come up to the bungalow with me.'

Now that his body and mind was no longer in a sexual uproar, he managed one of his wry smiles as he asked, 'Why? Is she an ugly old witch that frightens you?'

'Not really,' Valerie replied, adding a lie, 'but she is a bit strange, and I do feel sort of uncomfortable with her.'

'Don't worry. I'll look after you.'

As his hand closed over the back of hers, Valerie's guilt became so overwhelming that she experienced difficulty in breathing.

Worry made the beating of Kerry's heart increase in tempo when she was close enough to see Tinisha's stern face. She realised that she was, and always had been, in awe of her employer. The woman was a fantastic but somewhat selfish lover. Tinisha took; she did not give. She was beautiful, absolutely gorgeous, but even when in the throes of passion there was something of her that remained aloof, superior. Most of the real Tinisha Weaver was concealed from the world.

Tinisha had once told her – although Kerry didn't fully understand what she meant – that she used sex to enhance her art. It was an old trick that most top opera singers employed, and famous pop stars had caught on to. They had sex in the dressing room to improve their performance, to mellow the voice. For Tinisha it heightened her vision, added an extra dimension to her work.

Tinisha stood waiting now, anger making a little furrow between her eyes. Unsmiling, forbidding, glaring, causing Kerry to slow her steps. The furrow became a deep crease. Even so, the sleek, supple body and the silky smooth skin were getting to Kerry. Her vow of lesbian celibacy was already showing itself to be as feeble and transient as any New Year's resolution. Stopping in front of an unspeaking Tinisha, head bowed, Kerry looked up fearfully at her.

There was a long, awkward silence. Then Tinisha's sudden, unexpected laugh startled Kerry.

With her brilliantly white teeth on display in a genuine smile, the artist said, 'Well, just don't stand there; give me a kiss.'

Moving forwards, Kerry thrilled as her upper legs made contact with the graceful swell of Tinisha's warm thighs. She put her hands on the bare waist, holding Tinisha and tilting her own head back for the kiss they both yearned for. It was a brief, tentative kiss. They parted to exchange small smiles to confirm that their mutual desire should continue.

Their mouths, open now, came together again, their kisses becoming more passionate. Mouths smearing wetly, their breath was coarse and hot. They pressed together, breasts against breasts. Simon and everyone else, everything else, were forgotten in Kerry's need to hold, to taste, to breathe in the heady aroma of this woman. However, Kerry wisely remembered to give just enough hint of total surrender. She knew that was very important to Tinisha.

Without separating, they moved inside of the open door, away from any unlikely prying eyes. Tinisha's back was against the doorjamb. Her skin had the texture of satin. It was so smooth that Kerry's hands seemed to glide over her back. Moving her right hand to the front, she eased one cup of the white bikini top up clear of Tinisha's left breast. Warm, firm, wonderfully soft-skinned, the breast was delivered as a prize into Kerry's hand. Enjoying the magical, mind-blowing feel of it, Kerry moved her hand a little so that the long and erect nipple was in the centre of her palm.

It didn't seem possible, but their kissing had become wetter, hotter. Their mouths were fused and ravenous. Tinisha, her top lip pulled back over her strong teeth as she responded to Kerry's manipulation of her nipple, ended the kiss and bent her head. The glossy mass of black curls was against Kerry's face as Tinisha lowered her head; Kerry breathed in its scent. It was an erotic perfume that brought an immediate, gushing response of wet stickiness between her legs. She felt Tinisha's nose and mouth hotly locate the V-neck of her dress. The black woman's lips came against her flesh; then Tinisha was licking the sweat that a long walk on a hot day had produced between Kerry's breasts.

When Tinisha came up to claim her mouth again, Kerry could taste the salt of her own perspiration on her lover's lips. Carried away, they clawed and pulled at each other, each wanting everything at the same time. They sang a low duet of moans and squeals. Kerry heard an animal-like grunt. She couldn't tell whether it was herself or Tinisha who had made the noise, and accepted that she would never know.

Then she was shocked as Tinisha put a hand on each of her shoulders to force her away. Kerry feared that Tinisha must have had one of her shattering orgasms that put her out of action for a little while. But this wasn't the case. Kerry followed the artist into the bungalow.

Tinisha turned. Her eyes were heavy-lidded in total arousal, but the expression on her face was a severe as when Kerry had walked up.

'You've let me down badly, girl, haven't you?' she complained. 'I've had the housework to do as well as my painting.'

'I'm sorry, Tinisha,' Kerry said humbly.

'You will be.' Tinisha was looking at her fiercely. 'In Victorian times, disobedient servants were thrashed within an inch of their lives. Take that dress off.'

Obeying, Kerry pulled the dress off over her head. She was wearing only a scanty pair of panties. Letting the dress slip from her fingers to the floor, she stood facing Tinisha. Kerry knew that her body, lean rather than full, had a girlish appeal that Tinisha found to be irresistibly provocative.

A fully aroused Tinisha undid her own bikini top and let it fall. Breathing heavily, her lovely face transfused with lust, she stared hungrily at Kerry's body. A shudder of total desire ran through Kerry as she saw Tinisha push down her bikini briefs. The thick black hair was moist, with the moisture so prolific close to the vertical cleft that it had taken the curl out of hair that hung down long, wet and straight. Kerry watched as her employer parted her legs to rub two fingers up and down her slit.

Then Tinisha held the two fingers rigid. Moving her cunt over the tips of her fingers, she jerked her hips over them, panting and gasping as she did so. Kerry could hear the unbearably exciting noises caused by the wetness as Tinisha's fingers went in and out of her gaping redness.

It was a stirring sight, but being a voyeur wouldn't suffice for Kerry. She needed to be a participant, to have Tinisha against her again. Her body was silently screaming for sexual fulfilment, and there was a tremor in her voice as she pleaded, 'Please, Tinisha!'

The naked Tinisha walked towards Kerry tantalisingly slowly. Deliberately, she delayed the last few moments that closed the remaining few inches between them. Then their bare breasts were touching, hard thrusting nipple against hard thrusting nipple.

Taking the nearly naked body of Kerry into her arms with a shuddering sigh, Tinisha kissed her. As they kissed, each of them made little movements from side to side so that their breasts erotically caressed each other. Stiff nipple brushed against stiff nipple. It was heavenly. As Kerry sucked on Tinisha's tongue, her arousal made her impatient. Wanting the kissing to continue, Kerry desperately needed other things to be happening as well. She used movements of her body to convey her desires to her lover.

'No!' Tinisha pushed her away again, and Kerry felt the surge of her passion slowly subside. 'You don't deserve to be pleasured. You have been a naughty girl and have to be punished.'

Tinisha walked across the room and picked up a leather belt, curling it in her hand like a whip. 'Do you agree that you should be punished, Kerry?'

'Yes,' Kerry agreed in a low voice. 'I will work every Saturday for nothing.'

'Not good enough.' Tinisha shook her head adamantly.

Not having ever seen Tinisha like this, Kerry found that her knees were knocking from fear.

'Kneel before me,' Tinisha commanded.

Dropping to her knees, with her face close to Tinisha's sopping pubic hair, Kerry saw that the outer lips of Tinisha's cunt had curled back. The odour from the engorged lips had a dizzying fragrance. Assuming what Tinisha wanted, Kerry was eager to lap at the opaque juice that was bubbling out, but she heard another order rap out.

'Down further, girl. I am your mistress; I hold the ultimate power. Go down and worship at my feet.'

Crouching on the floor, Kerry first kissed the insteps of Tinisha's bare feet. Then she was kissing and licking at the toes. It was a deliciously different sensation. This was something of Tinisha that she had never before tasted. As her tongue entered the whiteness between Tinisha's black toes, an astonished Kerry found herself rapidly building to a climax. If only she could touch herself . . .

Tinisha, the sexual expert, sensed this. Kerry felt Tinisha's fingers entangling themselves in her hair, pulling her to her feet. Her mouth was close to the wetly open, gasping lips of the black woman. Moving her head eagerly forwards, Kerry staggered back as Tinisha pushed her roughly away.

Kerry felt herself grabbed by her right wrist and pulled into the kitchen. Tinisha's arm came across her back, pushing her down. Tinisha said hoarsely, 'Lie across the table, Kerry.'

Doing as she was told, folding her arms so that her breasts fitted comfortably into them, Kerry laid her head and shoulders on the kitchen table. She raised her eyes to see Tinisha unfurl the belt. Fashioned of thick, brown leather, it was a strap of two feet long with a knotted end. The sight of it aroused both fear, and a more than equal amount of excitement in Kerry.

Kerry felt Tinisha lay the strap lightly across her bare back. It was smoothly cold, a high-powered sexual caress such as she had never before experienced. Tinisha's fingers curled inside Kerry's black lace panties, getting a grip.

'I'll teach you to obey me, you bitch.'

Viciously spitting out the words, Tinisha at the same time pulled on Kerry's panties, ripping them apart and then pulling them off her in two ragged pieces. Then Tinisha slapped the girl across the bare buttocks with the flat of her palm. The slap was repeated, then again, until it became a violent smacking.

Kerry could hear Tinisha's laboured breathing after the spanking had ended. It hurt so much that Kerry prayed Tinisha would be satisfied and not use the leather belt. Yet another part of her was immensely thrilled by being spanked, and came close to willing Tinisha to carry out her intended whipping.

'Think about what's coming to you next, Kerry,' Tinisha instructed breathlessly. 'From this moment on, you will belong to no one but me. I am your mistress, Kerry, and you must put me before all others. Do you understand?'

'Yes.'

'Louder.'

'YES!'

'Ready,' Tinisha half-sighed, and Kerry felt an alteration in the currents of air around her hot, stinging backside.

Then Kerry winced as a burning line was branded over her buttocks. Tinisha energetically lashed at her. Left and right, the strokes of the belt criss-crossed Kerry's bottom, bringing tears to her eyes, while at the same time creating a close to intolerable sexual tension in her.

Four! Five! How many more lashes must she endure? Kerry cried out. 'You are my mistress. I will always obey you, always!'

Though she must have heard, Tinisha plainly intended to deliver six strokes, and the belt lashed painfully across Kerry's bare bum one more time. Sobbing with relief more than pain, Kerry stayed bending over the table. She heard something thrown across the room. From the sound it made, she judged it to be the belt. Then both of Tinisha's cool hands were tenderly on her tortured bottom.

'Oh, you poor darling: what have I done to you?' she heard Tinisha moan, and sensed the other woman sliding down on to her knees behind Kerry.

Then Tinisha was kissing Kerry's stinging buttocks. Lips that were normally burning with a fiery passion were cool and soothing. Accompanied by little sympathetic cooing noises, Tinisha's kisses were taking away Kerry's pain.

The kissing stopped. Kerry was aware of one of Tinisha's hands on each of her buttocks, fingernails digging lightly into the still smarting flesh as she parted them. Then she could feel Tinisha's face in the newly opened flesh valley, sniffing her, smelling her. Exciting herself, Tinisha sent her probing tongue into overdrive.

Kerry felt hands on her hips, as Tinisha lifted her a little, bringing her into the rear entry position. Aware that her cunt was thrust back so that every fraction of it was accessible to Tinisha, Kerry cried out in delight as she felt her lover's mouth go avidly to work.

Sex had never been this good for Kerry. Sucking and sipping, Tinisha was taking her love-juice like a dedicated bee at a ripely nectared flower. Then Tinisha captured the clitoris. Manipulating the small silken bead with her tongue, the experienced Tinisha kept in perfect time with the beating of Kerry's heart, the throb of blood in her aching flesh, and the meteoric rise of her sexual responses.

And just when she believed nothing could be better than this, Kerry felt Tinisha's long tongue enter her. Unerringly it found the super-spot, the lusting core of Kerry's sexuality. Tinisha knew her stuff. She understood everything about this critically sensitive place. She found the exact rhythm and divinely applied the precise degree of pressure. Aware that Tinisha had made contact with the deepest part of her, possibly her very soul, Kerry experienced a rushing tide of heat and excruciating pleasure explode between her legs.

She released a piercing scream of ecstasy that echoed far off in eternity. Orgasm pumped like hot steam through her genitals, streaming up into her belly, down into her thighs. Then it spread further and further, eventually reaching the tips of her fingers and toes, where it vibrated in time with the insistent pulsing that tightened her vagina spasmodically on Tinisha's inserted tongue.

Coming up out of the blackness of unconsciousness, Kerry felt Tinisha pulling her urgently up from where she had lain on the table. Tinisha was saying, over and over again, 'Come on, darling, quickly. Please be quick, please help me. Come on.'

Regaining her senses, knowing what was wanted of her, Kerry dizzily stood up. Tinisha was propped on the edge of the table, facing her with her legs open. Her head was back, her top teeth bared, and her eyes closed. Kerry saw that the luxuriant growth of black pubic hair was so wet, it completely obscured Tinisha's slit.

With Tinisha making strangled pleading noises, Kerry bent forwards. As she avidly breathed in the arousing odour of Tinisha's cunt, and her lips made light contact with the wet, sticky pubic hair, Kerry felt Tinisha's legs go over her shoulders. The hot thighs closed against each side of Kerry's head, and she put her hands up to clasp the cheeks of Tinisha's arse. Deliberately slowly, so as to tease a frantic Tinisha and herself, she used her lips and tongue to part the pubic hair and open up heavy lips that were slippery with lubrication.

'Oh, yes, yes!'

Despite her head being trapped between Tinisha's legs, Kerry heard her lover's cry. She had no time to locate the clitoris properly, no time to start to move her tongue more rapidly, before Tinisha went into a dramatic series of orgasmic convulsions.

Gasping for breath, Kerry was trapped. At last, as Tinisha's body went limp, she was able to get away and move up to flop, exhausted, across the table next to Tinisha. Too weak to cuddle, they held both of each other's hands as they gradually recovered.

After what could have been fifteen minutes, but might well have been fifteen hours, or fifteen days, they sat up, bleary-eyed.

Concern on her face, Tinisha turned Kerry a little so as to examine the red weals on her bottom.

'I'm so sorry, Kerry,' she said contritely. 'It was only a game.'

Smiling at her, Kerry put an arm round Tinisha. 'I know it was. And it's a game I want to try again.'

With a feeling of satiation and contentment that spread up from her crotch to connect with her brain, Tinisha drove her red Volkswagen down the hill. The session with Kerry had been out of this world. With her bottom relieved, if not quite cured, by Tinisha's application of an expensive lotion, the girl was back at the bungalow preparing tea for them.

Topping a small rise, Tinisha glimpsed the village below. It was a distant clutter of yellow and grey stone buildings turned a uniform silvery white by the shimmering heat of the afternoon sun. Windows reflected like mirrors, and the aquamarine water beyond was fringed by emerald.

It was beautiful.

That was true, but Tinisha berated herself for never taking time out to appreciate the wonderful environment in which she lived. There was never an opportunity. Without reason for doing so, she was always rushing to the next session when she would be brushing paint on to canvas – or her next steamy involvement in the delights of the flesh.

They were out of milk. The devoted Kerry had been willing to walk to the village for some, but Tinisha wouldn't hear of it. Her only hope now was that Terry Dumphy still had a bottle or two in the fridge, this late in the day.

She switched on the radio, fiddling with the knobs to find some music to suit her mood. The Carpenters did fine – dated but ageless. She was on level ground now. Something, perhaps the disembodied voice of Karen Carpenter, sent a surge of adrenalin through her. The road ahead was the future, secured for her by the events of the recent past. For her to lose Kerry Tredogan would be to lose some vital part of herself.

Like a mirage, the pleasant section of the resort vanished as she turned into Sea Road. Dumphy's place was old-fashioned, like something out of a Hillbilly movie. It was a combination garage, grocery store and dingy café. The squat figure of Terry Dumphy paused in mid-step as she drove in, then walked on when she drove to the shop and not the petrol pumps.

A blonde girl was behind the counter. She was tall and slender, with shapely legs. A large mirror carrying an advertising message of yesteryear in gold lettering allowed an interested Tinisha to do a double-take. The girl had a nicely shaped bum encased in a shiny wet-look miniskirt.

'You must be new here,' Tinisha said unnecessarily, but as a small talk opening.

'Started yesterday,' the girl responded informatively.

'Local?' Tinisha began, breaking off the question to say, 'sorry, I'm prying.'

'Not at all.' The girl smiled.

She was bright, engaging, an absolute delight. And she was so damned beautiful. The blonde hair was short in military fashion, but attractively styled. Tinisha adored the tiny tilted nose, the limpid blue eyes. She loved the excitement that bubbled out of the girl and, above all, the animation.

The girl chattered on. 'My home is here, and I've just come back.'

Pointing to a two-pint plastic container of milk, Tinisha said. 'One of those, please.' As the girl reached for the milk, Tinisha continued, 'You've reversed the charges. Girls normally leave home at your age, not come back.'

'That's true.' The blonde girl giggled. 'I joined the army. Left the force before I was due out, though. It was awful. You couldn't go to bed without one or the other of the girls trying to get in under the sheets with you.'

'Ugh!' Tinisha exclaimed in bogus disgust, suspecting that the blonde's expression of distaste was as much of a sham as her own.

'Exactly. That's ninety-eight pence, please.'

Passing over a pound coin, Tinisha introduced herself. 'I'm Tinisha Weaver.'

Taking the coin, the girl then lightly took Tinisha's hand in greeting. 'Elke Fuller,' she gave her name, then understanding widened her eyes and excitement raised her voice an octave.

'You're the artist up at the bungalow.' Her voice, thought Tinisha, was almost over-admiring.

'I didn't know I was that famous.'

'You are,' Elke assured her. 'I'm really chuffed to meet someone out of the ordinary like you.' Her happy expression fled as the bell on the door clanged, and two more customers came in. 'There goes my chance of talking to you.'

'For the time being,' Tinisha corrected her. 'We'll meet again.'

'I'd like that,' Elke Fuller said fervently.

'So would I,' Tinisha replied, carefully concealing her own fervour.

FOUR

'You struck me as a man of action.' Tinisha smiled at Guy Zennor.

The white man had his back to her, looking out across the bay, but she guessed her compliment had him mentally preening himself. Men were far more vain than women, and their vanity had an offensiveness to it. Either in support of his macho image or because of an unfulfilled ambition, he had expressed a wish to do some serious climbing. Olive-complexioned, with dark eyes and thick dark hair that was perfectly styled, he was too big to play at being invisible, but had tried to be anonymous since he had arrived with Valerie. Tinisha enjoyed an inward smile as an old description ran through her head: a spare prick at a cow's wedding. That fitted Guy nicely.

Tinisha considered that she might have telepathically communicated her disappointment to him. No, it was more than disappointment. She deeply resented his presence.

They were out on the patio. It was hot. There was not even a slight breeze to rustle the trees, and the uppermost leaves had their bellies turned up to the sun in an arid prayer for rain. The linoleum in the gazebo had buckled, creating small air-filled mounds. Kerry's trainers made sucking noises on the gumlike floor as she prepared lemonade for them in the old-fashioned way. Tinisha had been addicted to the drink since holidaying on Montserrat two years ago.

There was a stretched canvas on the easel in readiness. A selection of oils was on a marble-topped table. A large palette and jars of brushes were on another. Valerie sat where Tinisha had positioned her, close to the stone balustrade that guarded the steep drop down into lush woodlands. Her blonde hair was tied back in a sleek French knot that made her appear almost regal. The thought of posing had her acutely self-conscious. She sat rigidly upright and very still.

'This is wonderful, Tinisha,' Guy exclaimed, keeping a hand up to shade his eyes as he turned his head to speak. 'I really envy you living in a lovely location like this.'

'You wouldn't say that if you saw the place in winter,' Tinisha told him, the kick she got from shocking people making her go on. 'Up here it rains harder than a cow pissing on a flat rock.'

'Don't spoil my dream,' Guy pleaded. 'You see that high cliff over there? Now that's what I call a challenge.'

'Then go for it,' Tinisha encouraged. 'Now is the time. That cliff will still be there when you're back home.'

Shaking his head regretfully, Guy explained his position. 'It's not that easy. This is a family holiday, and it would be selfish of me to go off climbing.'

'You have time to spare this afternoon,' Tinisha urged, pleased that an opportunity to get rid of Guy had presented itself.

'Your mum has the children,' Valerie put in.

On cue, Kerry came out carrying a tray of drinks. Tinisha brought the girl immediately into the conversation. 'Guy's thinking about climbing that cliff over there.'

'Which one?'

Disinterest made Kerry's question flat, but Guy didn't notice. He raised a muscular brown arm to point. 'That tall one.'

'Penryllen Point.' Kerry followed his finger. 'Oh, yes, that's a doddle. I've climbed it dozens of times.'

'You're a climber?' a surprised and impressed Guy responded.

'Not really. It's only a hobby. I don't use ropes or anything like that.'

Though listening to the conversation, Tinisha didn't speak for a moment. She was studying Valerie. She needed to analyse the colours she would use so as to decide on a background. That would come last, but Tinisha could not proceed with a painting unless she had ideas for a background running through her head from the start. Black? She had achieved some dramatic effects with black in the past. It would proclaim Valerie's fairness. No; Tinisha dismissed black as too gothic. Burnt sienna or umber. Either would do, or possibly a rich brown of her own mixing. Satisfied, she gave Kerry her support.

'Kerry's too modest,' she told Guy. 'Maybe she doesn't have all the gear. She doesn't need it, because she can climb like a monkey. You're lucky you came down when you did. This time next year, our Kerry will be an old married woman.'

Although Tinisha hadn't begun the portrait, Valerie acted like she was taking a big risk by moving to look at Kerry. 'You must be very excited, Kerry. When's the big day?'

'We're getting engaged at Christmas,' Kerry replied as she passed the lemonade around. 'Tinisha's exaggerating a bit, as always. We haven't exactly set a date for the wedding yet.'

'She'll soon fix that. Her boyfriend's family owns most of the village, and that's no exaggeration,' Tinisha said.

Bored by women's talk, Guy changed the subject by enquiring, 'How long would it take me to climb that cliff, Kerry?'

'You couldn't do it,' Kerry said; then, blushing, swiftly qualified her blunt judgement. 'I'm not being critical of you, but you would need a guide. Someone who knows the climb.'

'I think you've just been made an offer, Guy,' a smiling, pleased Tinisha said.

'Could I get to the top in an afternoon if you were there to show the way, Kerry?'

Pursing her lips thoughtfully, Kerry replied. 'You look pretty fit, so I'd say it would take an hour and a half at the outside.'

'What do you think, Val?' He turned to his wife pleadingly.

'I don't mind, but it's surely up to Kerry,' Valerie responded.

'What do you say, Kerry?' Guy asked hopefully. 'If I drove us over there, would you show me what to do?'

'Would it be dangerous?' a worried Valerie asked.

'Not with Kerry calling the shots,' Tinisha said, adding with a chuckle, 'it'll be as easy as falling off a log.'

'I'm glad that you didn't say cliff, Tinisha,' Guy said, mock gloomily. When they had all stopped laughing, he asked, 'How about it, then, Kerry?'

'Guy's really keen.' Valerie smiled wryly at her husband, moved by his boyishness.

'I don't mind, but it's up to Tinisha.' Kerry shrugged.

'You've done everything you have to do, Kerry, so off you go.' Tinisha, her heart thumping as she looked at Valerie, hoped that she sounded magnanimous.

When Guy and Kerry had left to head down the hill to the holiday cottage, there was a difficult spell of silence between Valerie and Tinisha. It gave Tinisha the opportunity to get some paint on to canvas. Her daubing justified the psychologists' premature ejaculation theory. At this stage, it meant nothing. No layman would recognise it as the foundations for a portrait. But, if she had her way, it would be the only paint she would use that afternoon.

It was Valerie who spoke first, when they heard the roar of a car's engine as Guy and Kerry pulled away down below. Unsure whether or not she should alter her pose by moving her head, she spoke without looking at Tinisha.

'Are you sure about this, Tinisha?'

'Painting your portrait?' Tinisha checked. 'You'd better believe it. I really enjoy my work, and you make a beautiful model.'

Tempted out of her characteristic shyness by the compliment, Valerie said demurely, 'If you promise not to laugh, I'll tell you something.'

'I promise, cross my heart,' Tinisha responded, disconcerting Valerie by using one finger to trace an invisible elaborate cross over her crotch instead of her heart.

'I once wanted to be an actress. I suppose every girl has that dream at some time in her life, but the fantasies were extremely vivid for me.'

Valerie took a sip of her lemonade to ease the embarrassment of her confession; Tinisha thrilled, watching the soft lips moisten as they closed over the rim of the tumbler.

Tinisha found it necessary to clear her throat before saying,

'With those marvellous cheekbones alone, you'd have made Hollywood. What happened to your dream?'

'I exchanged it for another when I met Guy Zennor,' Valerie replied ruefully. 'I wouldn't have been much good before the cameras, anyway. I'm really uptight about sitting for this portrait.'

Walking over to stand behind her, Tinisha ordered softly, 'Lower your shoulders, Valerie.'

Placing her hands on the slim shoulders, Tinisha pressed her thumbs into the back of Valerie's neck. Exerting exactly the right amount of pressure, she moved the thumbs in a gentle massage.

'Mmm . . . that's sensational,' Valerie moaned. 'You have magic fingers.'

This made Tinisha chuckle inwardly. *You don't know the fucking half of it, Valerie.* She said aloud, 'Your shoulders and neck are all knotted up.'

'You probably don't realise it, but you are working miracles, Tinisha.'

'Why don't you really relax?' Tinisha moved the shoulders of the white button-through vest Valerie was wearing, so her hands were on bare skin, squeezing and releasing, moving sensually.

'You're terrific. Do you know, I can actually feel the tension draining out of me.'

Relaxation and tiredness were blurring Valerie's words. Delighted with the effect she was having, Tinisha murmured, 'Your body deserves to feel good. It is so beautiful that it should only know pleasure.'

'But I do feel so guilty,' Valerie dreamily admitted.

'What about?'

'Well, I'm taking up your time, and my husband has taken your maid away.'

'I'm not complaining.' Tinisha smiled, then became serious as she added, 'In fact, I'm indebted to you for keeping me company today. You'll keep me away from morbid thinking.'

'Has something unexpected happened, something bad?' Concern brought Valerie out of her relaxed state.

'Oh, no,' Tinisha assured her. 'It was expected and it is perfectly natural. Today I've reached the big four-O!'

'Your birthday!' Embarrassed, Valerie gasped. She reached out and a little behind her to touch Tinisha's arm. Her fingers felt like a cool breeze. 'Oh, dear, you've made me feel worse than ever. If I'd known, I could have brought you a present.'

'Don't worry about it,' Tinisha said brightly, sliding a surreptitious hand down into the vee of Valerie's vest. The tips of her fingers made thrilling contact with the swell of an unbrassiered breast. 'A birthday kiss will suit me fine.'

She felt Valerie's whole body stiffen defensively. Tinisha felt the forgotten ache of long-ago teenage love. Always convinced that every woman, even those who have men as lovers, has a natural desire for the touch of another woman, she now dreaded that Valerie would prove an exception to the rule.

But remembering Valerie's reaction on her first visit defeated that supposition. She had known what it was all about, then. Now, she had been taken by surprise. She was disorientated by what must be, for her, a new and disconcerting situation.

Tinisha bent and put her lips lightly against the side of Valerie's face. Breathing in the woman's scent, tasting her, Tinisha felt a flush of warmth in her loins, a sensation that warned her she had passed the point of no return. Her fingers searched inside of the vest. Hiding in a surprisingly wide circumference of areola was the reluctant little rise of a nipple. Moving her mouth down to kiss Valerie's neck, Tinisha teased and coaxed the nipple with a finger.

Close to Valerie's ear, Tinisha's whisper held a tremor. 'You're neither woman nor child, but there's much of both in you, Valerie.'

Then Valerie was saying, 'Yes, yes! Oh, yes!' over and over again. She attempted to squirm away. She was struggling; her head turned sideways, back and forth. Each time she said 'yes', like the ticking of a clock. Each time she mouthed the word, her slack, wet lips puckered to further inflame Tinisha's desire.

Tinisha rejoiced as she felt the nipple responding, becoming erect. She saw Valerie's legs jerk out straight, tightening the red shorts against her white thighs, then the blonde woman opened her legs wide.

Valerie's mouth was partly open as she surrendered to Tinisha's kiss, and her long, sharp fingernails were blissfully painful as she held Tinisha close.

She'll have to cut those nails soon, thought Tinisha.

Why did disasters always occur just when everything was going right? Always when you were in a hurry, too. Marge Tredogan had showered early to give herself time to put on make-up and arrange her hair so that she looked her best. Dr Gilbert and his wife were having visitors for tea, and had asked Marje if she would prepare the food and wait on them. This was a step up from cleaning work. A golden opportunity, so to speak. If she made an impression, there were sure to be other occasions, meaning more money each time. That was important now that Jack had stopped drinking and was earning more at the fishing. The family was at last getting its act together. The way things were going, they would be able to face the Gregorys unashamed when Kerry got engaged.

She should have known that her luck would let her down. Skin tingling from the refreshing water and heavily scented, thanks to Kerry's body lotion, she had come out of the shower wearing just a robe when it had happened. Maybe she had banged the door against the wall, or perhaps she had nudged against the piece of furniture with her shoulder. Marje would never know. Whatever, the cheap flat-pack wardrobe she had assembled herself had collapsed.

It would have been a minor, inconsequential incident had not one of the heaviest pieces knocked an electrical socket from the wall on the way down. Positioned close to the floor, the oblong porcelain socket dangled on one thick wire. What panicked Marje was that two other wires, one brown and the other blue, had brassy bare ends that were kissing. Each time the ends touched there was a threatening crack, and bright yellow sparks flew about like tiny falling stars.

Although she was tempted to bend down and part the wires, something in Marje's mind cautioned that it would be dangerous to do so. She needed help, but the Tredogan drastic financial position had resulted in the telephone having been cut off yesterday. They could afford to have it reconnected now, but it would take a few days. Until then, the nearest public call box was in the next road. By the time she reached there, the house would be on fire at best, or demolished by a mighty explosion at worst. She needed immediate help.

Hearing a steady thudding noise outside, Marje hurried to the bedroom window. In next door's back yard, Adam Croad, her neighbour's eldest son, was keeping a football in the air by alternately bouncing it off each raised knee. Occasionally he would twist his head as if greeting someone, and hit the ball off his forehead. Adam wasn't a bad lad for a seventeen-year-old. Though a friend of Albie Forster, he wasn't precocious like Albie, and most certainly didn't have the Forster boy's dirty mind.

Raising the window, fighting the stiff, noisily complaining sash all the way, Marje called out to Adam, asking him to come up and help her.

He charged in the back door and rushed up the stairs. Apparently expecting to find her collapsed, or at least in some physical distress, the boy stopped inside the bedroom door, bemused.

She pointed to the miniature firework display, cautioning, 'Be careful, Adam, please.'

'I know about electrics,' he assured her. 'I'll turn it off at the mains.'

'Do you know where the switch is?'

'It'll be the same as in our house,' he called over his shoulder as he ran down the stairs.

Did she have time to dress? Definitely not. The wires were no longer sparking, and she could hear him reach the foot of the stairs. He called, 'Have you a screwdriver up there, Mrs Tredogan?'

'No.' She went to the door to shout down the stairs. 'But you'll find one in the little cupboard beside the sink.'

'Righto.'

He was back with her then, working methodically, as confidently as an experienced workman, despite him being just seventeen. He reconnected the wires, then offered the plug up to the wall. As he replaced one screw, he was looking around for the other. Marje saw it lying trapped between the edge of the carpet and the skirting board. Sitting on her heels, she used a forefinger to flick the screw from its hiding place. Passing Adam the screw, she noticed that he was looking at her slyly. Worried for a moment, Marje relaxed in the knowledge that, though she was crouching, her robe still covered her upper thighs. Then she was horrified to realise that the fullness of the dressing gown had allowed it to fall away below. Adam's eyes were now staring fixedly up between her legs. He made a pretence at aligning the socket, plainly to get a good look.

She was about to get up in a hurry, when he asked her to hold the socket tightly against the wall while he secured it with the second screw. This meant staying in the same position, sitting on her heels. Feeling that she was doing the boy – who was putting himself out to help her – an injustice with her suspicions, she reached a hand to the socket. Too eager and clumsy, she moved the socket a little. The screw flipped out and bounced on the floor to go under her robe. Adam was reaching after it when Marje thoughtlessly spread her thighs apart to look for the missing screw.

A silent scream echoed inside of her head as she realised the boy was touching her naked body. He was feeling her, caressing her; then he used a long finger to begin exploring her inside. Trying to close her robe and her legs at the same time, she only succeeded in falling over backwards. The robe, entangled under her, fell open.

The fall had parted her from him. But he had opened his trousers. His hot eyes were on her, and this time she screamed a real but muted scream as she realised that he was masturbating. Knowing that she should close her legs, cover herself, get up and chase the boy out of the house, she was unable to do any of those things. Transfixed like a rabbit held in the stare of a stoat, she lay still. All Marje Tredogan found it possible to do was shut her eyes so that she could no longer see the scene that horrified her.

After what seemed to her to be hours, she heard his footsteps running down her stairs. Then the back door slammed and she knew that she was alone: she was safe.

She had some clearing up to do, otherwise Jack would be asking questions. Sickened by the whole episode, she concentrated her thoughts on the doctor's tea party. But when she took her robe off and caught sight of her naked body in a mirror, a strange and disturbing feeling came over her.

Studying herself, she looked at what the boy had seen to become so excited. Telling herself that she should be ashamed, she realised that she had no reason to be. She didn't want Adam to do things to her, or any other man. Ridiculous though it was, she had an urge to feel and kiss the full-bodied, big-breasted, red-headed woman in the mirror. It shocked Marje that she wanted to make love to herself.

Seeing that her nipples were distended, she self-consciously raised her hands to cup both of her breasts. Taking an erect nipple between each thumb and forefinger, she caressed and tweaked. It was sexually stimulating. With her left hand still toying with her left breast, her right hand slid slowly down over her smooth belly to her cunt. She began to gently massage the soft flesh either side of her clitoris.

Marje found a darkness creeping into her mind, and then, as it is said to happen with a drowning person, her life started to flash before her eyes. But it was fragmented, selected parts of her life. In chronological order, she relived her sexual experiences. It began with her first and only summer holiday. Aged seventeen, she had rented a caravan for a week at Weymouth with Brenda, her best friend. Sharing a double bed, the two of them had cuddled together under the bedclothes. There had been little affection in Marje's life and, when she had remarked to Brenda how pleasant it was to have the warmth of someone so close, her friend had said, 'Here, feel something *really* warm!' Brenda had guided Marje's hand between her legs and had held it there firmly, until she gave a muffled cry and the subtle motion of her pelvis had ceased. Then Brenda had whispered, 'Now it's your turn,' and slipped her hands under Marje's nightgown: Marje had surrendered to sensations she had never known before. Her budding breasts had eagerly responded to her friend's caressing fingers.

That was the first time in her life that Marje had felt desired. It was also the last time in her life that Marje had felt desired.

In her teens, a few boys had lied to her before lying with her. They had simply used her body for their own selfish gratification. Marje hadn't been revolted by those encounters, but neither had she been thrilled. Even though she had loved Jack before and ever since their marriage, Marje would be stretching the truth if she claimed the physical side of their relationship had ever meant anything to her.

Yet she had never had an experience such as this. It was the first time she had ever touched herself in this way. Fifty wasted years, Marje told herself as she worked on her granite-hard clitoris, between whimpers of absolute pleasure. Somehow, it was as if she had become a mirror image, so that the second Marje moved close to enjoy the delights of the body of the first. The walls of her vagina, contracting and relaxing in a throbbingly exciting way, created a suction that was pulling her working fingers up inside of herself. Marje Tredogan was carrying on a love affair with herself, and it was absolutely wonderful. She was doing to herself what men had done to her, what the boy from next door had wanted to do to her. Remembering the look on young Adam's face, she lifted one leg to open her cunt with both hands. Looking in the mirror, she excitedly studied exactly what the boy would have seen.

The movement of her fingers speeded up. Her body jerked; sweating, moaning, muttering and grunting out filthy words that excited her even more, she rode her high waves of pleasure into an unbelievably fantastic orgasm. Needing to rest one hand on the bed for support, Marje was bewildered. She would never have believed that sex could be so good.

Letting her fingers slide out of herself, she looked at their glistening wetness, at the translucent stickiness that covered her hand. Some of it gathered at the side of her palm, forming a pear-shaped drop that dangled over the edge of her hand.

'How about a cream tea, Dr Gilbert?'

Hearing her own voice say these words, Marje thought it was screamingly funny. She started to laugh and couldn't stop. The laughter went on and on until it tripped over a sob that had got caught up in her throat. No longer were her cheeks wet with tears of laughter. Crying hysterically, she fell face down on to the bed, clinging on, her body wracked by sobbing.

Not understanding what had just happened to her, Marje was afraid. She had a foreboding that, having discovered how stupendous sex could be, her future life would be different to the past. It seemed that she had discarded some sort of protection, and she felt very, very vulnerable.

*

Tinisha teased herself by slowly undoing the buttons of Valerie's vest. The blonde's back was against the wide bay-windowed wall of the bedroom. The sunshine outside was so brilliant that closing the drapes had darkened the room very little. A golden light filled the bedroom, making everything seem surreal. Tinisha had the notion – probably a sacrilegious one, she told herself – that having sex in heaven would be similar to this.

Valerie gave a quick little nervous smile as the last button was reached and Tinisha opened the blouse wide. The exposed breasts matched exactly the mental image Tinisha had formed of them from seeing them in their thin covering of cotton and from feeling what lay beneath.

She fondled the left breast; the one nearest the heart was always the most sensitive. The soft roundness of its warm flesh caused a little tremble in Tinisha, who moved closer for a kiss.

'I've never done anything like this,' Valerie said in a quiet little voice as Tinisha's mouth neared hers. Tinisha drank in the other woman's sweet breath as Valerie spoke, before her own opened lips contacted Valerie's compliant but as yet quiescent mouth.

The other woman's shyness, the retiring manner that had her seemingly begging to be subjugated, aroused Tinisha dramatically. Trembling with desire, Tinisha nevertheless was aware of a feeling of shame. An incurable romantic, she had fallen in love with Valerie the first time she had met her. But what was she feeling right now? It could be pleasure at being able to manipulate this lovely woman, or the thrill of being able to control, to have absolute power over another person. Maybe it was a fear in Tinisha of being left alone. It could have been any one of a thousand emotions. One thing for sure was that it had nothing to do with love or devotion. Tinisha wasn't proud of herself.

But that moment of self-criticism passed and was forgotten. Deliberately making the kiss a short one, Tinisha released Valerie's breast during it, and put her hand down to undo the waistband of the red shorts. Tinisha stepped back and watched the shorts drop to Valerie's ankles.

Valerie stood, looking embarrassed, in just a tiny pair of white panties. She wasn't a natural blonde. Wisps of dark curly hair spilled over the top and around the sides of the panties. For Tinisha, it was an erotically tantalising glimpse of what lay within. She was a little irritated by Valerie's apparent need to talk.

Placing one hand concealingly over her crotch, Valerie said hesitantly. 'It doesn't seem right with a woman.'

'Of course it's right. You want it as much as I do, my sweet Valerie,' Tinisha assured the slightly quivering woman. It was only too patently true. 'Only a woman can understand the physical needs of another woman. Only a woman understands the need for gentleness.'

As she spoke, Tinisha reached for Valerie's hand. The other woman let Tinisha lead her to the bed. As she knew she would, Tinisha felt the full charge of electricity from Valerie as she ran her hands down the white woman's slim body, a move that took the tiny white panties off without Valerie realising they had gone.

'Roll over. Lie on your tummy, darling.' Tinisha's voice was tender. 'Yes, just like that.'

Valerie lay prone and Tinisha was over her, breath sobbing. She buried her face in Valerie's hair, breathing deeply. The tip of her tongue flicked in Valerie's ear. And then her other ear. And then she was licking the white skin down along the spine; her hands were opening the cheeks of Valerie's arse and her darting, flicking, rimming, reaming tongue sent a thrill like a chill shivering through Valerie's small body. Tinisha turned Valerie, her head coming up between Valerie's thighs. Lips lightly meeting Valerie's cunt-lips in a tender kiss, Tinisha then darted her tongue into the woman, causing the juices to flow readily, licking and sucking until she could hear Valerie choking for breath.

Then a sudden change came over Valerie. Moving away from Tinisha, she pulled Tinisha up so that they were lying on their sides, face to face. No longer a shy, reserved little woman, Valerie came at Tinisha like a tigress. First licking her own juices from around Tinisha's mouth, she kissed her demandingly.

An astonished Tinisha felt Valerie's soft lips writhing against hers. The tip of Valerie's tongue ran over Tinisha's teeth, licked her gums, then thickly rammed into her mouth, swabbing. Tinisha could taste the lemonade. They lay rocking, enclasped, quivering, body to body, tongues lashing.

Valerie took control. Pushed on to her back, Tinisha was

enraptured. Jesus H. Christ, what a lover Valerie was proving to be. She was kissing her so delicately, ears, lips, neck, breasts, belly and – oh, fucking hell – her cunt!

Valerie Zennor's head was hidden within the fuming recesses of Tinisha's thighs. The baton of Valerie's tongue was leading an orchestra of nose, mouth, lips and chin that played a musical masterpiece of sex on Tinisha's body. With an innate skill, Valerie, a complete amateur, did a professional job on Tinisha's vulva, sucking in the labia, her scorching tongue burning at the erect clitoris in a way that had Tinisha swooning.

Just as Tinisha was reacting to the incipient shivers of a building orgasm, Valerie, purely by accident and not design, broke off the cunnilingus engagement and came up to lie facing Tinisha.

Rolling away from her, Tinisha reached out a hand to open a drawer of the dresser beside the bed. She took out the dildo with its yellow leather harness. It was still unused; she had been saving it for a special occasion. This seemed to be that occasion.

But as Tinisha invitingly held the instrument up, Valerie gave an urgent, negative shake of her head. Tinisha understood. Both of them were too far gone to spare the time needed for her to strap on the dildo. Knowing exactly what to do, Tinisha raised herself up on the bed. Valerie opened her legs in anticipation, bending her knees so that she was in the missionary position. Kneeling between Valerie's legs, Tinisha put her hands down to open up the other woman's cunt. As Tinisha lowered herself, Valerie, ready for deep kissing, reached up for her with both hands. Exchanging tongues with the now sex-crazy Valerie, Tinisha expertly guided her cunt against Valerie's. With her clit resting directly on Valerie's own, she commenced a rhythmic thrusting.

Valerie picked up the tempo, matching Tinisha thrust for thrust. They were pube against pube, with Valerie writhing and fucking upwards, while Tinisha writhed and fucked downwards. They threshed, bathed in sweat, until Valerie cried out, 'Now! Tinisha, please, now! Now, Tinisha!' She sucked on Tinisha's tongue, and Tinisha sucked on Valerie's tongue as they came together, hitting a mutual orgasm that had a truly unbelievable intensity. It was cunt upon cunt, clit upon throbbing clit, woman to woman . . .

When it was over, Valerie clung to Tinisha. Holding her tightly, she gasped out three words. 'I love you.'

Tinisha considered replying in a similar vein. To do so would be an investment; it would buy assurance that she could have Valerie again before she went back home. But to respond in that way – despite the wonderful sex – would also be dishonest, giving Valerie a false hope.

Though she kissed Valerie softly, tenderly, lovingly, Tinisha remained silent.

FIVE

It was quiet at the top of the cliff. The long grass was still under a scorching sun. They lay side by side, he with his hands clasped behind his head. Their feet were facing the sea. Why didn't people ever stretch out parallel to, or with their heads towards, the edge? Kerry stopped herself contemplating on that. This was a habit she'd picked up from Tinisha, who tended to muse on things psychological when her mind wasn't seething with sexual thoughts – which wasn't often. Far below and to Kerry's right, the stretch of silver beach was crowded. There was a steady traffic of holiday-makers on the rickety flight of wooden steps leading down to the sand. Half a mile away was a craggy mass of rocks as indistinct as a Constable landscape in the shimmering heat.

She turned to look at Guy Zennor. He was the strong silent type. She liked that, but would welcome knowing what he was thinking right now. Talking would enable her to slow her mind down, stop it from racing round in circles that became increasingly confusing. The afternoon had been far more pleasant than she had dared hope for when they had started out. Instantly aware of Tinisha's carnal interest in Valerie, Kerry had been neither jealous nor resentful. Well, that wasn't quite true. She had been drawn to the petite, delicately beautiful Valerie Zennor, and it both excited her and caused her pangs of envy to think what Tinisha might be doing to the delicious woman with the corn-silk hair that very

63

minute. Tinisha, hot, tasty and incredibly sexy, was the only woman Kerry had been with. It would be nice to sample unfamiliar kisses, the feel of different soft flesh. Valerie had a lovely long neck.

That sort of thinking confused Kerry further, and she decided to discipline herself. Being with the superbly built, impressively athletic Guy had stirred something in her that she would have preferred to remain dormant. It had added another dimension to her longings, as well as increasing her mental torment over Simon. On coming away from the bungalow with Guy, it had soothed her to think that maybe her feelings for Tinisha would vanish if Tinisha could satisfy herself with Valerie. Without the temptation presented by the luscious Tinisha, Kerry felt that she would find it easy to go straight. That way, there would be no risks, no obstacles along the route to marrying Simon.

Not that Tinisha was her problem now. Guy had been great company, a quick learner on the climb, but at all times deferential to her knowledge and experience. A witty conversationalist, he had been a gentleman throughout. Just once he had made a risqué remark. That had been when she had clambered up on to a ledge above him and, looking up, he had jokingly expressed his regret that she was not wearing a skirt.

Had he continued along those lines, they might not well be lying apart right now. Was that what she wanted? Kerry hated the fact that she couldn't be sure. The heat was no excuse for the way that her nipples were prodding at the thin fabric veneer of her jersey top. Their straining erection was an advertisement for her sexual arousal.

She wondered what Tinisha and Valerie were doing right at that moment. What would Valerie's mouth taste like? Exotically sweet, judging by her looks. From the moment Tinisha kissed her, Valerie would have no control over herself. Kerry had kissed more than a few boys, in her schooldays and since, but nothing had prepared her for the whirling tornado of passion that Tinisha's first kiss had created in her.

They had been slow, due to Kerry's shyness. They had kissed regularly, and Tinisha had gradually coaxed Kerry into letting her fondle, kiss and suck her breasts. The day when Kerry had been led across the border of what Tinisha termed 'the undiscovered land' remained Kerry's most momentous memory. It was on an afternoon when they were both naked and Tinisha, whose desires were ever at boiling point, was even more worked up than usual.

Holding up her right hand, the long middle finger extended, she told Kerry, 'You've teased me long enough, sweetheart. I'm going to fuck you with this.'

Experiencing her usual mixture of surging sex and fear, Kerry had accepted that she must let her lover break her in. But, wary of a possible and humiliating accident, she delayed Tinisha, explaining that she had to take a pee.

This made Tinisha change her mind about the fuck. Going into the bathroom with Kerry, Tinisha had climbed into the empty bath, taking Kerry with her. Not knowing what was going to happen next, Kerry had looked down as Tinisha had stretched out below her. Then Tinisha had got Kerry to squat over her, facing her feet. Hands on Kerry's bare hips, Tinisha had pulled her back so that Kerry could feel the outer lips of her cunt just brushing Tinisha's face.

Satisfied that she had Kerry in the right position, Tinisha breathed, 'Now, let it go, my lovely.'

In no doubt as to what was wanted of her, Kerry had urinated gushingly. She hadn't known if Tinisha's mouth was open or closed, and she hadn't cared. Whatever Tinisha wanted, she would give it to her. In relieving herself, she was relieving her lover, and that was vitally important. And then she was done. The final drips were leaking out, and she heard Tinisha splutter, 'Oh! oh! oh! That was wonderful, my darling.' Then she was licking and sucking at Kerry.

From that moment onwards, Kerry had had no inhibitions whatsoever. Tinisha and she had become full lovers.

A couple wearing bathing costumes passed by. Walking hand-in-hand through the tall grass, they were in the middle distance, but close enough to snap Kerry from her reverie and bring Guy out of his semi-trance. He came up on one elbow to look at her; his eyes lingered on her breasts before he raised them to meet hers.

'I'm sorry, Kerry. You gave up your afternoon for me, and I'm poor company.' Aware that she was looking at the mighty bulging at the crotch of his tight jeans, he apologised contritely. 'I'm sorry. I remember that I was having a kind of half dream.'

'Should I feel flattered?' she asked without thinking, and then cringed on realisation that she was begging for a compliment.

'You deserve to be, Kerry. You're really lovely, but I don't like lying,' he told her shame-facedly. 'It was Valerie, my wife, in the dream.'

Tell me about her. Kerry was screaming out the plea inside of her head. Tell me what it's like to kiss her, feel her, lick her, fuck her. But she could not make those torrid requests out loud. Guy was plainly eager to get away from the subject of sex. He was pointing to a cliff to the east. It was hugely white, towering above the clifftop they were on.

'Have you ever climbed that one, Kerry?'

'Three times,' she answered. 'That's Trimenen Head. It's a pretty tough climb.'

'Do you think I could do it?'

'You proved this afternoon that you can,' Kerry said. The couple in the swimming costumes were kissing, standing with their arms round one another, body to body, mouth to mouth. It was a voyeuristic turn-on for Kerry.

'If I can get another afternoon free of the family, would you help me climb it?' Guy asked, as hesitant as a schoolboy stammeringly asking for his first ever date.

'I'd love to.'

'Thanks, Kerry.'

Leaning over her, he reached out a big hand towards her breast. Expecting him to cup it, squeeze it, Kerry was bitterly disappointed when he just teased the extended nipple with his fingertips.

The effect of the contact on Guy was electrifying. They were sprawling together in the grass, his big, muscular body partly covering hers. His dark eyes looked at her, then deeply into her, reaching her very soul. There was a cruelty to the shape of his mouth that excited her, as he lowered his head for what she anticipated would be an explosive kiss.

Wanting the kiss, needing him, Kerry moaned softly and ran her tongue over her parted lips to moisten them for him. He hardly noticed. The sudden hot spasm of desire that had taken him over had passed, draining him of his need for her. Kerry could see something else building up inside him, something very different, something slow and heavy that throbbed like a pulse. Her own surge of sexual feeling was numbed by his instant and unexpected coldness. Kerry saw his lips tighten in a straight line.

Scrambling to his feet, Guy tried to make his voice sound casual, but failed miserably. 'We'd better be getting back.'

Valerie Zennor had made a deal with herself. Still unable to believe the things she had let Tinisha do to her, the things she had done to Tinisha, she was determined that nothing like it would ever happen again. Shame at what she had done caused a vague but awkward separation between her children and herself. Though it couldn't be so, she was certain that her mother-in-law knew in detail what had gone on, and facing Guy had sent Valerie off on an agonisingly extended guilt trip.

She agreed with the wise-woman who dwelt in the back of her mind, that sex with a woman had been a one-off. She would enjoy it again, and probably again, but only in recall when she masturbated. Though she would continue to sit until her portrait was finished, she would make certain that she was never again alone with the voluptuous artist.

This afternoon was different, she told herself as she watched the red Volkswagen curving down towards the cottage. An afternoon's shopping in the nearest town would be enjoyable. Even a grope would be out of the question on a crowded high street.

The bright sun glinted off the car's paintwork, the deep shine complementing the gleaming chrome perfectly. The engine purred contentedly, like the cat Valerie had back home, as Tinisha pulled in beside her. The little nod of greeting and the white-toothed smile from behind the steering wheel was a crashing, crushing reminder for Valerie of how stunningly attractive Tinisha was. As Tinisha leaned across to open the passenger's door, her low-cut pink print dress fell away putting her large but firm coffee-coloured breasts on display.

'Are you ready for some fun, honey?' Tinisha's smile was as ambiguous as her words.

Getting into the car, Valerie found herself hungrily breathing in the black woman's perfume. Amplified by the heat inside the vehicle, it had both the lure of manufactured perfume and the raw, overwhelming compulsion of the body aroma of a highly sexed woman. Feeling her own body respond, juices beginning to ooze from her as she longed to do with this beautiful woman what they had done together before, Valerie was dizzy. She became painfully aware that this trip to town wasn't a treat – it was a mistake. A huge mistake.

Tinisha drove fast but confidently, like someone who never doubts her own reflexes. Though Valerie could see from the speedometer that they were just under the legal limit, it was fast enough to be challenging as Tinisha powered the car through a series of bends.

Her skirt was riding high on her deep-bronze thighs as she drove. Desperate to keep her eyes away from Tinisha's legs, Valerie found she lacked the willpower to do so. She wanted to kiss those thighs, run her tongue up the insides until she came to the darker, sweat-stained area, where the nectar of more perspiration would be gathering. She could remember the rousing odour of that sweat now, actually feel the slide of it on her tongue. Then her mind went further up and she was sucking at the drooping labia, taking in the opaque love-juice from the black-haired, luscious flower that was Tinisha's cunt.

'Stupid fucker!'

Tinisha's shout brought Valerie's mind back to normality. A stereotypical holidaymaker, his stomach bulging over a pair of ridiculous shorts, and his bare upper body sun-pinked and peeling, had run across the road in front of the VW. They were passing through the village, weaving among meandering trippers with blank faces and disappointed, empty eyes.

Then they were out in open country. A snaking line of sharp bends caused Tinisha to drop the car's speed to forty. Ahead was a bright yellow sports car. Cars weren't Valerie's thing, and she didn't know the make or model. But it was obviously a fast vehicle. Its only occupant was the driver, a young man whose long hair was lifted and twirled by a self-generated wind. Valerie was alarmed to see Tinisha's brow crease as she stared at the sleek body of the car in front of them. Going into the next bend, Tinisha changed down to second gear. She pushed the VW so hard into the corner that it began to drift. Panic was threatening Valerie until she recognised how Tinisha was expertly using the steering and throttle to balance out the vehicle.

They had taken the bend at a good ten miles faster than the yellow sports car. As both vehicles came out on to a short straight, Tinisha swung the wheel to overtake and rammed the gas pedal to the floor, the souped-up engine under the red bonnet responding instantly. Eyes flicking back and forth from the roadway to the rear-view mirror, the man in the sports car dropped down a gear and his twin exhausts roared angrily as he gunned the car. Speedometer needle rising, Tinisha kept her foot down. They raced side by side towards the last bend. The driver turned his head to take a quick look at them. He was young, and in the topless car his face was distorted by G-force. For a moment his face loomed in Valerie's window and his mouth opened as he shouted something. His words were swallowed up by the wind.

Tinisha waved a challenging hand at him. Clinging to her seat, a terrified Valerie watched the car clock one hundred, then five above as side by side the two cars headed for the ever-nearing, tree-lined bend. Tinisha and the other driver were playing the chicken. Neither would give way. It was a test of nerves, and she couldn't imagine someone like Tinisha surrendering.

She didn't. It was the sports car driver who braked at the last second. But they were on the corner, still almost side by side. A farm tractor loomed up right in front of them. It and Tinisha's VW were on a collision course. Cringing down in her seat waiting for the inevitable impact, expecting to hear tearing, rending metal just before she died, it astounded Valerie to see how cool Tinisha was. Biting her heavy bottom lip lightly in concentration, the black woman glanced at the opening between the yellow car and the tractor. Studying the angles, getting it right, her hands tightened on the wheel. She swung the car to the left. What seemed to Valerie to be a miracle happened. Tinisha's car shot between the sports car and the tractor, skimming both with what must have been minute fractions of an inch to spare on either side.

They had a wide road to themselves then. The driver of the sports car had dropped right back. Seeing this in the driving mirror, Tinisha roared with laughter. Valerie could see a veneer of sweat shining on the other woman's brow, but otherwise she was euphoric.

'That frightened me,' Valerie confessed. 'Terrified me.'

'Life ain't worth living if you don't live it dangerously.' Tinisha grinned. 'Driving makes me horny, Val. I could pull into the next lay-by and fuck you to destruction.'

'We're going shopping,' Valerie reminded her primly.

'Right,' Tinisha smilingly agreed, driving with one hand while she put her left on Valerie's knee and slid it upwards, palm against the inside of the thigh.

Annoyed by the liberty, Valerie pushed the hand away. The rebuff only made Tinisha laugh, and her hand returned to its task. It shocked Valerie to find that now the danger was over, the fast drive had excited her. She couldn't prevent her thighs from parting so that Tinisha could move her hand up to rest on the over-full crotch of her panties. They were tight, and Tinisha's finger was painful for a moment as it tried to find its way in the side of the crotchpiece. Without giving a thought to the move, Valerie eased her bum up off the seat so that she could pull her panties down a little to permit Tinisha's hand to find her bare, squelchy cunt. As expertly as she had driven, Tinisha parted Valerie's hair to find her wet slit.

They continued on towards what Tinisha had earlier referred to as a 'one-horse' town, with Tinisha fingering Valerie, and Valerie loving every second of it.

There was something special about Marje Tredogan. It wasn't that she was a beauty or particularly intelligent. Geraldine Dumphy was convinced that a fire that had never been fanned burned slowly and constantly inside the woman. It was like one of those dual-coloured coats you used to be able to buy, which could be worn either side out. Marje wore her sexuality inwards, and her bland side out. Normally placid, oddly detached, Marje vibrated with excitement in the Dumphy shop that afternoon. She was euphoric about having her daughter's soon-to-be fiancé as a dinner guest that evening. She asked for Geraldine's advice on what meal to cook.

'I want to put on a nice spread, but nothing out of the ordinary,' Marje said, her profusion of red hair nodding with the punctuation. Her bright blue eyes sparkled as she searched for further comment. 'Until you get to know someone's likes and dislikes, it's difficult, isn't it?'

As she agreed that it was, a familiar voice within Geraldine told her that Marje could be taken advantage of in this excited state. Watching Marje's too-full lips and long white teeth as she spoke, Geraldine lapsed into a sexual daydream. The intensity of her imagery sent a chill down her back, frightening her.

Probably all that was special about Marje was Geraldine's need to be near her. She felt no affection, no love. It was a biological thing in which she simply wanted to feed herself. Marje was no more than an instrument to fulfil a need. But Geraldine knew that she would have to pretend otherwise to succeed.

'Please believe that I'm asking this in the most respectful way, Marje,' she began diplomatically, aware how the deprived can be deeply offended by a reminder of their poverty, 'but have you something suitable to wear? To save you buying,' she went on tactfully, 'I've plenty of dresses upstairs, and you're welcome to borrow any of them.'

'You're very kind,' Marje said gratefully.

Geraldine wasn't kind – just randy. She counted herself lucky to have found Terry Dumphy as a husband. It was fortunate that her reputation hadn't accompanied her when she'd taken a holiday in Cornwall. It had been a lucrative, if often, sick-making, profession, supplying carnal recreation for London's bigwigs. Geraldine had turned ten tricks a day before seeing the light. It hadn't been a Road to Damascus kind of revelation that had got her off the game, but a Government minister. He had been big, but running to fat. Bald as an egg up top, the rest of him was as hairy as a bear. The hair was a protective coating that concealed the puncture-marks of the needle that delivered heroin into his bloodstream. His sexual predilections were repulsively way-out, so revolting that it had been the final straw that broke the back of Geraldine's life of prostitution.

Leaving Elke to look after the shop, Geraldine had Marje follow her into the living quarters that were part of the same building. It all seemed very unreal to Geraldine, but the creak of the stairs as they went up to the bedroom confirmed that it was really happening. They went into the bedroom that had a large antique oak bed as a centrepiece. A late afternoon sun struck the skylight to cast a bright but not uncomfortable reflection in the room. It was only two days since the decorators had left, and the fresh paint was a restful perfume.

'I'd say that we're about the same size, wouldn't you?' Geraldine asked as she opened her wardrobe to take out a blue sequinned dress. Her hand shook a little as she held up the dress on its hanger. Put off men at an early age, she hadn't been with a woman for twenty years. That had been here in the resort, just before she'd met Terry Dumphy. It had been a free and easy meeting on the beach. She and the woman who had the look of a librarian, even in a bikini, had playfully splashed each other while wading into the sea.

'Catch me,' she had challenged Geraldine, running off to dive into the sea.

The chase had been on, continuing underwater, where they had touched and felt each other. The groping had been tentative at first, becoming increasingly adventurous. They had ended up in the caravan the woman, Carole – that had been her name – had hired. Hardly daring to make a noise, they'd enjoyed a double-ender while Carole's elderly mother was asleep in an adjoining compartment.

That had been all of two long decades ago. There had been opportunities, of course, with the elegant Tinisha Weaver obviously available. But Geraldine hadn't wanted to jeopardise her comfortable life with a caring husband just for a lick or a grope at a cunt. But today she was desperate for it, and the risk seemed minimal.

'I don't really know, Mrs D–Dumphy ... G–Geraldine ...' Marje was stammering.

'Call me Gezz, Marje. Everyone else does,' Geraldine invited with a warm smile. 'Now, what do you think of this dress? Do you fancy it?'

'Oh, really, I couldn't.' Marje pushed her thick red hair back from a face that blushed dark red. 'What if I spilled something on it?'

'Then I'd smack your bum,' Geraldine joked, and had to control her face to hide how her own words had aroused her. 'Now, I'll put it on and you can see how it looks.'

Undoing the waistband of the blue denim skirt she wore in the shop, Geraldine let it drop to the floor and stepped out of it. Taking off her blouse to stand in bra and panties, she looked out of the corner of her eye for Marje's reaction. Terribly embarrassed, the other woman had turned away.

Her own reflection in the mirror on the wardrobe door was displaying more interest than Marje. Irritated and frustrated, Geraldine put on her dress. It hugged her figure like a second skin. She needed to call Marje to have her take a look.

'Well, What do you think?'

'It's really lovely, Mrs Dumph– It looks wonderful on you, but I think that it would look foolish on me.'

'Rubbish,' Geraldine scoffed, taking off the dress and passing it to Marje. 'Here, you try it on.'

Taking the dress, Marje anxiously glanced at the door, seeking privacy, asking 'Could I take it into . . .?'

'Try it on here, where you can check yourself out in the mirror,' Geraldine said. 'Don't worry. Terry doesn't finish in the garage until eight of an evening. He won't come charging in.'

'I wasn't thinking – ' Marje began, and Geraldine was aware of exactly what she had been thinking, and knew that she was lying.

The ever nervous Marje feared that she might be trapped into a threesome, a heat-sticky *menage á trois*.

'Try on the dress. I won't look,' Geraldine lied.

'I know you won't.' Marje responded with a lie of her own. Bending forwards as she took her dress off, Marje unwittingly brought the top of her head close to Geraldine. Her hair smelled sweet and clean. Geraldine had to conquer an urge to bury her mouth and nose in it. As she lowered the dress over her head, Marje's massive but shapely breasts threatened to escape from the lace bra. Thick clumps of deep red hair were in each of her armpits. With Marje's red head covered by the dress, Geraldine took the opportunity to have a good look at her body.

Marje was wearing old-fashioned white-cotton knickers that were slack-crotched. But a throbbing demanding sensation came to life in Geraldine as she saw that the down of dark auburn hair that surely covered Marje's mound also extended halfway up to her navel. She was heavy, but Geraldine welcomed that. Well-built women seemed juicier than slimmer ones.

Sensing Geraldine's gaze on her, Marje looked up. She was staring into Geraldine's eyes, her eyelids half-closed. A sensuous pout was frozen on her full lips. Though fairly certain that a modest exhibitionism had turned Marje on, Geraldine knew she couldn't take a chance. A premature advance, a wrong move of any kind, could mean disaster. Women are never truly angry at a man who makes passes, but most of them don't grant another woman the same licence.

With the dress on, nicely complementing the flesh it covered, Marje looked to Geraldine, silently seeking her opinion.

'You look lovely, absolutely lovely,' Geraldine said truthfully.

Reaching down, Marje touched the dress lightly with both hands as if she couldn't believe it was real until she did so. Then her expression became sad, and she whispered. 'I'm not pretty enough, am I? I wouldn't look right in this dress.'

Reaching out, Geraldine took Marje's unhappy face in her hands. 'You look absolutely beautiful.'

A flash of fear came into Marje's eyes, but Geraldine, who could out-act Helen Mirren if necessary, made it clear that this was just a gesture of fondness. The traces of sweat on Marje's top lip stirred rather than deterred Geraldine. She kissed Marje once shortly and then a lingering kiss, striving to make it seem sisterly. Keeping her eyes open, she saw tears leaking heavily from Marje's closed lids. Uncertain as to whether Marje was crying from joy at the dinner she was giving that night, due to Geraldine's generosity, or because the kiss terrified her, Geraldine released her.

The room was quiet. There was only a faint heartbeat to be heard. It was Marje's heartbeat.

Somewhere deep in the bewildered look that Marje bestowed on Geraldine was the tiniest of promises. Accepting that there would be no immediate action, Geraldine was satisfied that she had done the necessary groundwork for the future.

She sealed the unspoken deal with. 'That dress suits you better than it does me, Marje. You keep it.'

Tinisha and Valerie shared a cubicle in the boutique. It was one of those small places that charged outlandish prices for prestigious labels attached to mediocre garments. The two of them would seem to be the only customers. It surprised Tinisha to discover that Valerie, although white, eased the ache in her that came from not being among her own people.

Both of them had been on a sexual high, a plateau of total erotica since arriving in town. They had visited an open-air market, jostling in the heat among a heaving crowd when they both desperately wanted to be alone together. The air-conditioning had the temperature just right in the boutique. A sultry young assistant, nicely packaged in a tight-fitting black uniform-dress, bought a bandeau bikini with a tropical sarong for Valerie to try on. The assistant's breasts were little half-apples. They sat apart, impertinent and sharp. Tinisha wondered if they were always so pointed, or if she was a little excited by the presence of Valerie and herself. The boobs were cute; the way they looked away from each other said the girl could not have anything on underneath the form-fitting dress.

'I wouldn't kick her out of bed,' Tinisha remarked as the girl left, closing the curtain.

But an unhearing Valerie gave a shocked gasp as she turned the price tag on the garment she held. 'Good God, Tinisha! Have you seen these prices? I can't possibly afford this.'

'You don't have to. I'm paying.'

Coming into money affects people in one of two ways. They either become misers or big spenders. Tinisha was a big spender. At the age of seventeen, with both parents divorced and interested only in their remarriages, she had been alone and penniless.

Winning a scholarship to art school had been the turning point. She had survived in a scruffy, noisy bedsit, sharing a shower and toilet with scruffy, noisy fellow bedsitters. She had been the only black student in a class full of white, middle-class dilettantes. On graduation she'd slept with the head of a titled English family, getting to paint his portrait as a reward. This was a planned exercise in self-promotion. Needing success, she had put every bit of her talent and all of her imagination into the painting. The praise had been long and loud. From that point on her fame had spread. With commissions rolling in from the rich and famous, she had amassed a fortune for herself, and had never needed to sleep with another man. After investing wisely, she had moved to Cornwall and purchased her bungalow home. Now she could paint when she felt like it, and fuck when she needed to. The only time money means anything is when you haven't got it. Right now, she wouldn't even notice buying Valerie expensive clothes. What she would get in return would repay her a hundredfold.

'But I can't let you do that,' Valerie was pointlessly protesting, as she had already stripped to her panties in her eagerness to try on the beachwear.

'You can, if you let me do this,' Tinisha said, cupping one of Valerie's bare breasts and with her other hand in her blonde hair, pulling her head back for a kiss.

Kissing with her eyes open, Tinisha noticed a narrow gap between the curtain and the edge of the cubicle. The assistant, making a pretence of arranging items in a glass counter, was watching. With a surreptitious movement of her shoulder, Tinisha moved the curtain to make the gap wider. Afforded a better view, the girl's eyes widened as both Valerie and Tinisha became hotter in the kiss.

As always, it seemed to Tinisha that there were two of herself involved. While an aroused Tinisha clung to Valerie, the other, cynically amused version of her thought of the voyeuristic shop assistant while a Noel Coward composition ran through her head: *A room with a view.*

Pausing for breath, Tinisha saw that the assistant had moved closer to them. Coming round the counter, supposedly folding some lingerie, the girl stood just a few feet away. Moving her head back, Tinisha was pleased to see the shiny silver cobweb of saliva that was suspended between Valerie's mouth and her own. Breaking it with a flick of her tongue, she licked some of it in while Valerie hungrily collected the remainder with her tongue.

Satisfied that the girl assistant was still watching, Tinisha started kissing Valerie again. Sliding her hand down over Valerie's flat tummy, taking the panties down with it, she gently inserted two fingers into Valerie's vagina, sliding it up, going deep. Valerie moved on the fingers and hand so she could blossom herself to the fullest.

When Tinisha's fingers probed, Valerie drank her kiss deeply. Tinisha quivered continually as Valerie gulped hungrily, her own fingers opening and closing in Tinisha's hair. Tinisha increased the rate of her fucking. Her fingers were ceaseless plunging pistons, in and out, all the way out and all the way in. Valerie's vagina answered the pumping with slopping, plopping, suction sounds. Watching and listening, drooling and licking her tongue round her lips, the assistant had her crotch pressed against a corner of the counter, working herself.

'I'm coming,' Valerie announced, apparently out of habit. As she approached a debilitating, excruciating orgasm, she broke the kissing to bury her face in Tinisha's shoulder to prevent the scream of pleasure rising up in her. She only partly succeeded. Valerie's stifled groaning seemed terribly loud in the soundless air of the far from busy boutique.

Then with Valerie slumped exhausted, her back propped against the wall, Tinisha opened the curtain a little further to call to the assistant. 'We'll take this.'

Valerie hadn't tried on the beachwear, but Tinisha guessed it would fit her. If it didn't, what did it matter? It was only money!

The girl came partly into the cubicle, panting heavily as she looked at Valerie's delta of wet hair, her panties halfway down her white thighs and the proud breasts with their pointed brown nipples. Handing the clothing to the girl, Tinisha purposely, fleetingly and wickedly, passed the fingers she'd been using on Valerie under her nose. The girl gave a strangled sob.

A recovering Valerie was slowly dressing, and Tinisha pointedly dropped her right hand down by her side, close to the assistant. Obviously terribly worked up, the girl showed ingenuity by dropping the bikini top. When she bent to retrieve it from the floor, Tinisha made her right hand available. Sniffing at it, moving her nose and mouth this way and that over the hand, the girl then began to suck on Tinisha's fingers. She went at it slobberingly like a calf at its mother's teat, and only stopped, straightening up quickly, as she heard the footfalls of what Tinisha took to be the proprietor of the boutique.

'Parcel that up, miss, and we'll pay when my friend is ready,' Tinisha said.

'Thank you, madam.'

Left alone with Valerie as she finished dressing, Tinisha put her fingers into her own mouth. A blend of Valerie's love-juice and the shop assistant's saliva was a heady mixture. Closing her eyes, she got every ounce of sexual pleasure she could from it.

'You're terrible, Tinisha,' Valerie complained. 'You'll have us both shot.'

'Like I said before – ' Tinisha grinned at her ' – you can't enjoy life if you don't live dangerously.

'Please warn me, in future. You're stark raving! Have you anything else crazy planned for the rest of the day?'

'Well,' Tinisha drew out the word contemplatively, 'I've got myself in such a state that I've either got to eat the lovely arse of that girl wrapping up your present, or have you.'

'You're not going to have me in here,' Valerie objected.

'I don't plan to. What I want is to have you naked, all to myself and in private, on a comfortable bed.'

'Well that's out, obviously,' Valerie said as they both stepped out of the cubicle.

Tinisha shook her head. 'No, it's not. You can telephone the holiday cottage from here and tell your old man that we are staying in town tonight. Make an excuse that we're going to the summer show. Then we'll book ourselves a room at the Eagle Motel, just out of town.'

Valerie had started to tremble. The uncertain smile on her lips, the excessive brightness in her eyes were signs of fear. She said tremulously, 'I can't do that.' But Valerie knew that she would. The Zennors had been married long enough to turn away from each other. And kisses were very persuasive, when love was all but dead.

SIX

When Marje Tredogan had lit the little candles, they gave off a smoky odour for a moment and then flared up. Put on edge by the occasion, Kerry regarded the candles as a mistake. They would be all right for a couple sharing a romantic meal. Simon was here, of course, but it was really a family dinner. Kerry's father had closed the curtains and shut out the last orange rays of the sun. Candlelight prismed off the borrowed crystal decanter and glasses. A few quick beams bounced off the tablecloth. They traced their freedom around the floor and attempted to climb the walls, but the walls were too steep and they continued to fall back. The alien shadows changed the room for Kerry so that it didn't seem like her home. There was a difference to the street sounds, too. The usual roar of traffic and loud horns were oddly muted. It was quiet, just a lazy hum with softer, distant horns.

Her mother had prepared everything marvellously. They had sat down to *filet mignon*, mushrooms, fresh peas, and baked potatoes. Then there had been a little green salad with French dressing. Afterwards none of them could get enough of an exquisite coffee mousse. Pleased by it all, Kerry suspected that her mother had sought and received good advice. Geraldine Dumphy was Kerry's guess.

With her small brother grinning at them, Kerry and Simon sat close together on the settee. The flash of madness with Guy up on the clifftop was harmless and insignificant now. Simon had revealed no definite plans during talk over dinner. He had neither stated nor suggested any dates for an engagement and marriage. Marriage could be the end of everything, not the beginning, Tinisha had once said. 'I finished with boys once I didn't need them to carry my books home from school,' the cynical artist once told her, 'and maybe you should have done the same.'

Kerry never really listened to a lot of the things Tinisha said. The conversation at dinner had a slender theme of Kerry's and Simon's togetherness running through it. They were both in love, and this dinner was a good start. If it wasn't enough, then there were other approaches.

Kerry's mother passed round cheese and biscuits. She looked great in a slinky blue dress. A white rose in her hair budded and grew as Kerry watched. The unusual restriction of wearing a tie indoors had her father sitting as if paralysed from the waist up.

'I hope that we haven't been too much of a shock for you, Simon,' Jack Tredogan said. Yawning, he covered his mouth. He had put out to sea at four o'clock that morning.

'On the contrary,' Simon responded. He was tall with dark skin and slightly foreign features. French, perhaps. A touch of the Daphne du Mauriers. A skeleton in the Gregory cupboard: one of Simon's female ancestors had maybe opened her legs on a Cornish hillside for a Frenchman ashore from a four-master moored in a blue-watered creek.

Kerry chided herself. She was convinced that she had been acting like a schoolgirl all evening, and now she was thinking like one.

Her mother stood at the table and looked off into space the way she did when gathering the confidence to say something. 'You must be used to a very different kind of life, Simon, what with living away from the village for so long.'

'To be honest, I really love the simple things. Home and family, gentle, peaceful living,' Simon replied. He added gallantly, 'That was an excellent meal, Mrs Tredogan.'

'Thank you, Simon.'

Marje Tredogan blushed a little. The flickering candlelight sharpened the colour and gave her a fragile transparency. For the first time, Kerry saw that her mother was attractive. With features too irregular for beauty, a latent sexuality made her face distinctive. Tinisha should capture that somehow androgynous attractiveness on canvas.

Kerry cancelled out the thought as soon as it came to her. Tinisha Weaver was in the past. Well, that wasn't strictly true because she still longed for Tinisha's kisses and fantasised about her in bed most nights. But Simon was now the real present, the future, her very life. If Guy Zennor was still keen to climb Trimenen Head, then he would have to find someone other than Kerry to guide him. As for Tinisha, she would have her fill of Valerie Zennor throughout the woman's holiday. By the time that happened, Kerry would have perfected a strategy of defeating her desire for the woman.

She felt Simon's hand touch hers with a gentle pressure. Too shy to hold her hand in front of her parents, he simply wanted to make contact. Kerry turned her hand to hold it, much to the observant Reggie's amusement.

'Can we have the television on, please, Dad?' Reggie, bored out of his young and active mind, asked.

'What do you say, Mother?'

As her parents exchanged glances of uncertainty, Kerry wondered if they still had sex. She doubted it. Success in bed relied upon togetherness out of it. Her father had been on his best behaviour this evening and the days leading up to it. But it wasn't some kind of born-again marriage between her mother and father. It was more of a hastily arranged and very fragile pact.

Kerry couldn't adjust to this new Jack Tredogan. Her image of her father came from a few vivid recollections from her childhood. A shirt that was dirty and smelled of fish. It was torn at the elbows, revealing hairy arms as big around as both of Kerry's legs together. He said the word 'bastard' a lot, and always breathed hard when he was drunk.

'I don't think that we should –' an unsure Marje Tredogan hesitantly began to answer her son.

'It's fine with me, Mrs Tredogan,' Simon said. 'The television's never off in our house.'

'Yippee!' Reggie cried, grabbing the remote control.

Kerry was relieved. The conversation, stilted throughout the evening, had started to drag along lamely. The screen lit up, isolating them while at the same time easing the awkwardness between them.

It was a talkback programme. Three viewers, two women and a man, were in the studio complaining about a racist programme to an indignant producer.

Kerry's father gave his opinion of television by starting to whistle a popular tune. Her mother stopped him with a rebuking, 'Jack!'

The subject on the television suddenly changed. The presenter, serious-faced, was saying how the telephone lines had been jammed following a lesbian scene in a popular soap.

A replay followed. Kerry squirmed as two young girls looked lovingly at each other on the screen. They moved closer, eyelids drooping, lips parted. They kissed like sisters to start with, but then it was a no-holds barred, open-mouthed snog.

An embarrassed Marje was scrambling to retrieve the remote control from her young son. Kerry's father blew out a long breath. His lips ballooned out and then collapsed.

Reggie suddenly shouted, pointing at the two girls, 'Look, Kerry and Miss Weaver.'

'Reggie!' Marje Tredogan shouted scoldingly, but didn't have any more words. Her panicking fingers first gripped and then dropped the remote control. It hit the floor hard, spewing out its batteries, but none of them noticed.

Wanting to run, to hide, to die, Kerry heard her young brother go on to prove to his mother that he had a point. 'Kerry and Miss Weaver, kissing. Just like them two. I saw them up at the bungalow.'

Simon freed Kerry's hand, letting it fall into her lap. Standing up from the settee, he swayed a little. Reaching out to steady himself, he found nothing to support him. Giddiness curing itself, he walked out of the room and out of the house.

He went without a word. Simon Gregory neither looked at Kerry nor thanked her mother for the dinner he had previously praised.

With a silent Valerie at her side, Tinisha drove through the now semi-deserted streets of the town. They had eaten well at a restaurant. Valerie, trying to escape from her conscience, had drunk too much. She had lied to her husband on the telephone, and complained to Tinisha that she was abandoning her children.

'It's only one night, for fuck's sake.' Tinisha had put up what, to her, was a logical argument.

Valerie didn't agree.

She was in a reflective mood herself now. Driving past people who would forever be strangers. They had their worries, ambitions, dreams, and desires that she would never know about. So many men and women moved through your range of vision without them touching you or you touching them. They might pass you full of sorrow while you were bursting with joy. There was no order in meeting people: just a chaotic random factor. The ones you do meet come and go as though they were auditioning for your friendship. Even those who get to play the part of a friend are swiftly forgotten, once they move away.

Staying in town could be a mistake. Valerie's holiday placed a time-limit on her portrait, and there was still much to do. Most of it could be done without Valerie. Tinisha only needed a sitter for the basics and an occasional refresher. That way she could let her imagination interpret how the character of the model should be seen. The portrait that had started out as Kerry, before becoming the mysterious Ruby, was causing her a strange kind of concern. The skin of the woman on the canvas was darkening. Could it be that she was portraying one of her ancestors?

And where was the girl from the boutique right now? What was she doing? Most likely at home masturbating over thoughts of Valerie. Just a few minutes in their company had probably altered the course of that girl's life. Tinisha wasn't sure whether that made her feel triumph or guilt. Whatever, thinking of the girl and then taking a covert glance at Valerie's long legs snapped her out of her meditative mood. This was not a night to be wasted.

She slowed the VW and pulled across the road into a sparsely occupied car-park. The only sign of life was a spluttering, yellow neon sign, crudely designed in the shape of an eagle. Setting the handbrake and switching off the engine, she announced, 'We're here, Val.'

'I shouldn't be here, but there,' Valerie complained. The ride had sobered her a little. She was no longer slurring her words.

It was dusk. The light from the office window glowed palely. Artificial light and daylight didn't mix well. Some paints were the same. A man's round, pale face stared out at them through the open window. Tinisha gave a curt nod in greeting as they passed. His dirty mind would be in overdrive by now. Funny how the thought of two women making love turned on all straight men, while a lot of straight women were repulsed by it. Or pretended to be repulsed by it.

When they were in the rented cabin, Tinisha was surprised. It belied the seedy outside appearance of the motel. The place was richly carpeted and well furnished.

'This is nice,' Valerie said, doing a little twirl on one foot to inspect the place. 'It's a really nice place. It must have cost you quite a bit.'

'Like I said, it's only money.' Tinisha shrugged. 'I asked for the best.'

'I'd say that you got it.' Valerie nodded as she took another look around. 'I like it.'

'I'm glad, because I like you.'

'I like *you*, Tinisha. You'd make a good saleswoman . . . a good sales-person. You have a sweet mouth.'

'Why don't you come over here and taste it?' Tinisha sat on the edge of the bed. Valerie's uninhibited behaviour signalled that she was still more than a little drunk.

'I will, but I'm very thirsty.' Valerie pointed to the plastic carrier bag that was on the floor, resting against the bed. 'When are you going to open that bag, my lovely Tinisha?'

Tinisha opened the bag, taking out one of the two bottles of Bacardi it contained. Valerie turned on the radio, tuning the dial until she got pulsing, pounding music. Turning the volume low, she deftly caught the bottle Tinisha threw to her. Not waiting for the glass Tinisha was getting from the cabinet, Valerie drank from the bottle. She danced to the music. Tinisha took a tentative sip and returned it to Valerie.

Taking a long swig from the bottle, Valerie carried on dancing, telling Tinisha, 'I'm pissed. I am pissed.'

Standing, Tinisha took Valerie in her arms and danced with her. The respectable, goody-goody housewife who had arrived on holiday was drunk, sexed-up, and abandoned.

'Tinisha, I can feel you up against me, and it's sending me crazy.'

And they danced.

Tinisha kissed her, her tongue in Valerie's mouth.

When she could talk, Valerie said, 'Can I ask you something?'

And they danced.

'What?' Tinisha said.

'Have you got that great big dildo with you? The one you showed me at the bungalow?'

'No.'

'Aw!' Valerie complained. 'I could do with it right now.'

'I'll give it to you when we get back. It's never been used. You'll be the first, I promise.'

'Why me?' a bleary-eyed Valerie asked archly. 'Why don't you ram it up your little friend, Kerry?'

'We don't want to talk about Kerry.'

'I do. You do it to her, don't you? What's she like? Tell me.'

'I know what you're like, and I want some more,' Tinisha replied. She broke away, and Valerie danced alone.

Dancing, wriggling, her arms upraised, Valerie husked out her words. 'You want some more of this? Then come and get it, lover.'

She went on dancing. She was still drinking Bacardi straight from the bottle. She passed it to Tinisha. And kept dancing. Tinisha drank a long, satisfying swig and handed the bottle back to Valerie, who kept drinking. And putting the bottle down. And dancing.

Tinisha took off her clothes as Valerie danced. She folded them carefully. Naked, she walked to the closet and put her clothes neatly away.

Naked, she came back to take Valerie and dance with her. Valerie's left arm was around her. Valerie's right hand held her cunt. She felt it take the weight of the distended lips and run a finger up and down the slippery slit. 'God, you're so wet. You're all swollen and wet.'

'Take care with that hand of yours. When I get you on that bed, Val, I'm likely to kill you.'

'That's the way I'd like to die.'

Tinisha slid away from Valerie. She could feel the effects of the alcohol. Backing off, Tinisha sat on the edge of the bed again. 'Get naked,' she said.

'I'm about to do that,' Valerie answered.

'Do it,' Tinisha said urgently.

'I'll do it gracefully.'

'Do it any way you want, but do it.'

'I'm going to do a striptease,' Valerie said. 'I've always had a fantasy about being a stripper. Maybe a lapdancer.'

'Just get naked, Valerie.'

Moving sinuously to the rhythm of the music, Valerie opened her blouse. Swinging it round and round above her head, she let go. The blouse flew through the air and landed on the bed. Picking it up, Tinisha pressed it against her mouth and nose, breathing deeply.

Moving to the rhythm of the music, Valerie unzipped her skirt, let it drop, and kicked it away. She kicked out of her shoes. No stockings. No tights. A black bra and black panties around the slender, shapely body and a marvellous arse. She kept dancing, the musky odour of her encompassing Tinisha.

'Holy-fucking-Moses, you really are something,' Tinisha said.

'Wysiwyg.' Valerie gave her a white, even-teethed smile.

Computer terminology – what you see is what you get. Tinisha loved what she saw. The booze had loosened both of them up.

Valerie unhooked the bra and, dancing, tossed it to Tinisha. Tinisha tossed it away. Valerie wriggled out of the tight little panties and tossed them to Tinisha who smelled them, kissed them, bit them, and tossed them away. And now stark naked, Valerie was dancing wildly, arms upraised, breasts jouncing, stomach swaying, pubis grinding.

'Turn around!' Tinisha ordered. 'Bloody hell, let me see that arse.'

Valerie turned, rhythmically dancing, presenting her firm white, oscillating buttocks.

Unable to stand it any longer, Tinisha grabbed. She seized. She kissed Valerie from hip to hip, then back to her spine. Kissing her spine, she kissed down along the cleavage of buttocks before driving her tongue in. She felt Valerie shudder.

'You're driving me wild, Tinisha.'

She pulled Valerie to the bed, turned her face down and opened the cheeks of her bum, guiding her hand between them. She couldn't get it in. The immediate needs of a sobbing Valerie made it impossible. One minute, she was raising her arse to aid Tinisha; the next, she was trying to twist her body round for some face-to-face kissing. She was reaching behind her with both hands, feeling whatever parts of Tinisha she could get hold of. Though Valerie wanted it every bit as much as Tinisha, her threshing defeated them.

Determined not to be beaten, Tinisha took a firm grip of Valerie's slim hips. She moved a little to collect some of Valerie's lubrication to be added to her own. Then she took aim with her fingers. 'They're going in. Oh, dear God, yes,' Valerie moaned in pleasure. 'Oh, God, that's wonderful. They're up my arse, Tinisha. If you do it slowly, I'll come again and again. Ride me slow and easy. Please let me come first, darling. Let me come and then I'll do whatever you want. Oh, that's it, that's just right. Keep it going, Tinisha. Let this one, just this one, be for me.'

'Keep moving your lovely arse, Val. I'll hold it. This one is for you.' And Tinisha held her desire in, moving slowly, aware of Valerie's sphincter muscle tightening and throbbing round her fingers. Then Valerie was rubbing herself and screaming, howling. 'Oh, it's great! Oh, fuck, fuck, fuck. Oh, I'm coming! Oh, I'm creaming! I love you and your wonderful body!'

And still Tinisha rammed her fingers in.

Valerie moaned. 'Oh, darling. Lover!'

'Move up on your knees,' Tinisha panted.

'Yes, darling.'

Her fingers went in further. They went in all the way. Tinisha controlled her strokes, in and out, deep in and out. Valerie was screaming again, loud and piercingly. She moaned and screamed as she came and came. And then Tinisha rubbed herself with her other hand and hit the high spot. Head back, she shouted out her own delight. Valerie's body flattened on the bed. Tinisha remained on her, in her.

Head sideways on the pillow, Valerie whispered, 'My God, Tinisha, you're great. No one has ever done anything like that to me. At one time, when you were thrusting in, I really thought I'd go mad.'

'You've that gorgeous arse of yours to thank for that, Val.'

Moving a little, Tinisha let her fingers slide out. The feeling came close to matching the torrid sensation when it had gone in. Their hot bodies were adhering together, sweat causing a suction between their skins. Reluctantly, Tinisha rolled off and went to the sink, washed her hands and returned. Valerie was close to falling. Then she staggered to the bottle of Bacardi. Drinking from the bottle, she staggered, dancing to the music still humming from the radio.

'Tinisha, I love you to bits.'

Tinisha was lying on her back, smiling.

Sucking on the bottle, Valerie danced again. Laughing. She asked, mumbling, 'Do you want to do it in the front?'

'Aren't you satisfied, Val?'

'I loved it up the arse, but I thought you'd want your hand in my cunt, too.'

She drank from the bottle again, making Tinisha shake her head in wonderment. 'I've got to get you home in the morning. You'll have to be in good shape for your family.'

Dancing to the music, drinking from the bottle, she staggered to the bed and stood over Tinisha. 'I've got no fucking family. I've got nobody. This is the life I want to live. Fuck 'em all.'

'Oh, good Lord!' Tinisha groaned inwardly; if you remember even a fraction of this tomorrow, Valerie Zennor, you'll die of shame.

Now Valerie sat on the bed. Her body was glistening with perspiration. There was a fairly violent tremor in the hand holding the bottle. She spoke sadly, somehow absently. 'What am I doing? I'm drunk. What am I doing here, doing the things that we've done? What's happened to me, Tinisha? I honestly never suspected that I was capable of anything like this. You do believe me, don't you?'

'I believe you,' Tinisha said consolingly, aware that the drunken euphoria of earlier was about to slide into a tearful pit of drunken despair.

'Then why have I done these things? Am I really a terrible woman, a bad wife and mother?'

'No worse than anybody else.' Tinisha ruffled Valerie's hair fondly. 'Everyone has this side to them, Val. Most don't get the opportunity to exercise it.'

Putting an arm round Valerie's shoulders, she laid her back on the bed. God they were drunk. The silky feel of Valerie's soft skin got to Tinisha, and she caressed her. On her back, Valerie responded by opening her legs.

Lying on her front, her face resting lightly on Valerie's stomach, Tinisha began kissing the hair-covered skin, moving down. She heard Valerie's soft groan of pleasure. A new wave of arousal was combating her own drunkenness.

As the effects of alcohol receded, Valerie was consumed by sexual desire. She thrust her hips up from the bed, opening herself up wide for Tinisha's hotly kissing, sucking, licking mouth. With her fingers twining in Tinisha's black hair, Valerie had sobered to the extent that she was able to judge when Tinisha was coming. With perfect timing, she synchronised her own shuddering orgasm.

Then, exhausted and thoroughly spent, Valerie released a small sigh and fell asleep. As Tinisha took Valerie lovingly into her arms, she saw the ghost of a contented smile haunting her lovely face.

Marje Tredogan needed to confide in someone. There was a strain of edginess in her now. It was early morning. Sunshine had been warming empty village streets when she had left home. Not that it seemed like home, after last night. They were no longer a proper family. Marje was aware that the Tredogan climb from the gutter was over. Now it would be a fast slide back down. Jack would be back on the bottle; new debts would be added to what they already owed, and had been paying off regularly. The biggest worry of all was what would happen to Kerry.

The Dumphy café was as yet empty. She sat at a corner table, waiting for Geraldine to join her. Geraldine had become a really good friend of late. Away from her husband, with his smutty suggestiveness and filthy innuendo, Geraldine was nice. Marje wondered if the other woman had an inkling of what had been going on. You couldn't keep much secret in a small community, and a village shop was a gossip-exchange centre.

Women making love to each other! Such a thing was once never heard of. Marje was terribly confused by it. She hadn't been troubled by Geraldine kissing her yesterday afternoon. That hadn't been sex: just friendship and kindness. What it had done was to bring a pushed-away memory of Adam back sharply into focus. Not just what the boy had done but, more perturbingly, what Marje had done to herself afterwards. The world had gone seamside out, and Marje Tredogan was now caught up in the eruption of sexual perversions.

Sitting nervously waiting, Marje felt that Tinisha Weaver's wraith had followed her. The artist had been haunting her house all last night, Marje was sure of that. The woman had been standing there in the grey transparency of the moonlit bedroom. When Marje had looked sideways with her head on the pillow, Tinisha had seemed to be lying down. It had been eerie. But maybe it wasn't Tinisha after all, she admitted to herself. Maybe it was something in herself that was haunting her.

As soon as Simon had gone, Kerry had run up to her room, crying. Marje knew that it would be difficult to talk to her daughter. They had never mentioned sex to each other. Yet this was much more serious than the birds and bees stuff. Marje had looked to her husband for comfort. But after walking up and down, repeating the word 'bastard' over and over again, Jack had gone to bed. Within minutes, he had been snoring like a pig. Marje hadn't managed to sleep a wink.

It occurred to her that the lack of sexual activity in her own life was an impediment to full understanding. She could remember that business with Brenda. Admittedly exciting, it had amounted to no more than two young girls experimenting. How one female could seduce another was not beyond Marje's comprehension, but she was angry enough to go straight up to the bungalow and tackle her daughter's employer.

Marje knew that could well be a drastic mistake. She had often started things she had been unable to finish. A feeling of inferiority made her gullible, vulnerable. She was no match for anyone. Once Marje's initial anger deserted her, a strong person like Tinisha

Weaver would swiftly gain the upper hand. Though she hated to admit it to herself, Marje Tredogan was weak. The fact that the subject was sex exacerbated the problem.

Two cups and saucers slid on to the table. Geraldine sat opposite her, big, blonde and beautiful, albeit in a heavy-featured, coarse way. Most importantly, Geraldine was self-confident. She always seemed to know what needed to be done, to whom, and when. Even being in her company loaned indecisive people such as Marje at least a semblance of courage.

It was crunch time. Marje shrivelled up inside. The tea had a tang to it. It was peculiar that the rougher the café, the stronger the tea smelled. That was a silly, petty thought to have at such a time. She looked at Geraldine Dumphy, seeing her through a kind of haze. A bluish haze that gave the blonde a halo. That was encouraging. Geraldine might be Marje's guardian angel. She could certainly do with divine aid.

'You look awful, Marje.' Geraldine frowned. 'Did your dinner party go wrong, love?'

Nodding, Marje took on her unhappiness in a tough fight. She won, keeping control of herself. But a few tears escaped to run down her cheeks. She heard Geraldine say, 'Surely it can't be that bad?'

'It is, Geraldine. I just don't know what to say, how to tell you.'

Reaching out to cover one of Marje's hands with hers, Geraldine said in a kindly, low voice. 'I'm a good listener, Marje. What happened?'

'It's been running through my head all night,' Marje replied miserably.

'Then just start talking to me. It's as easy as that.' Geraldine's lips twitched into a small but reassuring smile. 'If you have a few facts, it's amazing how much a few words can reveal or infer.'

Such erudition from an unexpected source had Marje bewildered. Out of deference to the local man Terry Dumphy, his wife was tolerated, but she had never been accepted. She was a pensioned-off prostitute, a piece of trash who had struck gold by ensnaring a rural businessman. Marje had thought that way until quite recently.

Starting off with a stammer, Marje found it easier as she went along. She didn't stop until she had given Geraldine the full sordid story. 'Had I known what that woman was like, I'd never have let Kerry work for her. What do you think she did to Kerry, Geraldine? Just kiss?'

'I don't know much about it,' Geraldine answered evasively. Taking a cloth from the pocket of her overall, she dropped her eyes while wiping a pretend stain from the table.

'I mean, they can't do anything else, can they? They don't have ... well, you know ... No, I suppose it's just kissing.'

'I think there might be more to it than that, Marje,' Geraldine cautioned.

Marje was made uncomfortable by the tremor in Geraldine's voice. It was dawning on her that it hadn't been wise to come here. Wherever she went, she was out of her sexual depth. That kiss yesterday hadn't been so innocent. She could clearly remember the way Geraldine had looked at her when she was standing in just her bra and knickers. She sat numbly now as she felt Geraldine take her hand in both of hers. Marje felt her thumb and forefinger formed into a circle. Geraldine's right hand, big for a woman's, the middle finger long and thick, was in front of her eyes.

With her left hand holding Marje's hand, Geraldine placed the tips of two forefingers against the closed ring created by Marje's thumb and forefinger, gradually gaining an entrance.

'They do this,' Geraldine said huskily. Her blue-eyed gaze was mesmerising. Her fingers entered Marje's hand, going in, in, slowly. With a furtive glance to check the door, Geraldine withdrew her fingers, then pushed it back in; repeating this, she moved her fingers in a little further each time. Marje understood what Geraldine was simulating. She knew the crude Anglo-Saxon word for it, but couldn't bring herself to say it, even inside her head.

Mind spinning, Marje found herself enjoying the movement of the thick, hot fingers in her hand. Geraldine's hands were soft and warm, safe and comforting. For a moment she let herself be used, forgetting what she had come here for. But a glance at Geraldine's face alarmed her. Geraldine's eyes had become heavy-lidded. Her facial expression seemed to be one of pain. Needing advice on how to handle the Kerry problem, Marje was in danger of being drawn into a similar situation herself.

Fighting off the unfamiliar sensations that were thrilling her, she fought herself before snatching her hand free. Getting to her feet, she accidentally bumped the table so that tea spilled from both cups. She wanted to leave, to rush out.

Geraldine got half up from her seat to call pleadingly to her. 'Please, Marje; I was simply trying to demonstrate.'

Who else could she turn to? Your daughter having sex with a woman wasn't a subject you could discuss with just anyone. She let the begging in Geraldine's big blue eyes pull her back down into her chair.

'I can't let Kerry down.' Marje spoke disconsolately. 'I'll go up there and have it out with that woman.'

'No.'

Geraldine's words caused Marje to look at her quizzically, worriedly. 'You don't think I should tackle this Weaver person, Geraldine?'

'In your own way, Marje . . . and in your own time.' Geraldine's expression was curious, Marje thought. 'You can telephone her from here if you like. Get her to come down to your house.'

That was excellent advice. Marje realised that she must take it.

SEVEN

As far as Kerry could see, the beach was deserted. She was alerted for a brief moment by a flicker of movement in the heavy shadows an early-morning sun cast around a clump of bushes. It was just a wizened beachcomber. Bent like a question mark, he moved on to the sand to begin his searching patrol. She stood for a moment, feeling exposed. The strip of sand had no hiding places. She had been experiencing little waves of vertigo since her brother had made that awesome revelation last evening. Right now, it was as if she wasn't alone. With a check summer shirt over her swimsuit, she could have been on a catwalk with hundreds of people eyeing her, all of them knowing about her and Tinisha Weaver.

The muted lapping of tiny waves against the shore was soothing. It was really too cold to go in the water before the sun had a chance to heat it. But she would. Kerry had learned to swim before she could write her name. Whenever she had problems, ploughing through the sea with the Australian crawl she had perfected washed them away. It would take a long swim to fix what was bothering her now. Maybe she should keep going out away from the cove until she was too exhausted to get back. That would cure everything. She was tempted by the idea.

Simon was lost to her for ever. Within the next hour or so, her mother would be giving Tinisha a piece of her mind. That would bring about the end of both Kerry's employment and her love affair with Tinisha. There was a finality to that which Kerry found it impossible to see beyond.

Hearing movement on the wooden steps behind her, she turned. A squat-bodied fisherman was silhouetted, bending to his wire pots. Kerry picked a path across the loose sand, down to the waterline where the tide had packed the sand tight and firm. As tight and unblemished as a virgin, she thought wryly. Kerry still had the sensation that someone was looking at her, spying on her. It had to be her conscience reacting, or overreacting. She selected reacting. It could hardly overreact to the situation she was in.

Undoing the buttons of her shirt, she slipped out of it. Dropping the shirt on the sand. She half-turned, expecting to see someone trailing her. But there was only the beachcomber, further from her now. The fisherman had disappeared, probably having returned to the village.

Walking on, she carefully crossed a small rock barrier that was painful on her bare feet. Wading through shallow water to a smooth stone ledge. She sat down, thinking for what must have been the billionth time about the disaster that had befallen her. She had brought it on herself by taking her brother with her to the bungalow that day. But what if it hadn't happened this way? How long could she have succeeded in living a lie? It would have been terribly wrong to go on deceiving Simon. Yet it would have been impossible for her to either tell him the truth or stop her sexual addiction to Tinisha Weaver.

Head down as she sat on the stone ledge, lost in thought, Kerry hadn't heard a sound. But when she looked up, Guy Zennor was on the beach, standing in the loose sand, not more than a dozen feet away.

At first a statue, a veritable Tarzan, his brief red trunks a revealing loincloth, Guy came to life. The backdrop of the rocks emphasised the perfection of his body. Feet splashing through the water, he walked towards her with a grace any top athlete would kill for. He smiled an uneasy smile.

'Great minds think alike,' Guy said as he sat on the ledge beside her.

'I doubt that you're thinking the way I am, this morning,' a morose Kerry told him.

'I'd argue with that,' he said. 'You seem down in the dumps, and I've known better mornings.'

A silence stretched achingly between them. It was becoming too much for them both. Guy ended it. Sliding off the rock, he ran across the sand towards the comb of the waves. There was the splash of his feet as he raced into the surf, the threshing of his legs, the sharp sound of his body parting the water as he dived under, then silence until his head bobbed up beyond the swell of the waves.

What was he doing here? He seemed to be as troubled as she was. Kerry followed him, leaping from the ledge to run along the invisible trail Guy had left behind him. She dove with scarcely a sound. The cold water jolted her harshly. Struggling for breath for a moment, she then floated, feeling intimate with the water.

Guy was a good swimmer. He was going away from her, the slow strokes of his massive arms pulling him fast through the water. Sprinting after him, Kerry took a deep breath and went under the water. Seeing his thrashing legs above her, she swam up towards the surface. Grabbing both of his ankles, she held on, pulling him down. The surprise fun attack made Guy swallow water. He was coughing and spluttering as Kerry, finding that she could laugh, swam away from him.

He came after her with long strokes that quickly shortened the distance between them. Knowing that she couldn't escape him on the surface, Kerry jack-knifed her body and went underwater. Guy carried the chase below the surface. He had the edge on Kerry down there, too. She could see the bottom covered by a low jungle of seaweed. Kerry went down there and lay on the seabed. It was colder, but not unbearable. She had on a green swimsuit that camouflaged her. She blended so well with the seaweed that he passed right over her. He went by, arms moving like the flippers of a turtle as he turned his head this way and that, searching for her.

He caught her when she came up for air in the shallows. She was getting to her feet when he came streaking through the water at her. Coming up, he grabbed her and they both went under. She was in his arms when they surfaced. They floated as the waves created by their tumble flattened. Guy was laughing triumphantly, but Kerry turned in his arms. Grabbing him, she came up out of a crouch so that he went over backwards into deep water. Still attached, Kerry followed like a hooked shark breaking the surface.

They went down together. Kerry wondered how long he could hold his breath. She could hear nothing but the pounding of her own blood. The frantic motions of their legs were frothing up the water around them. It was a dangerous game. With their lungs on the point of explosion, they surfaced by tacit mutual agreement and then floated to shallow water, whereupon Guy rose from the surf. She looked up to where he stood above her. Feet still in the water, he was gazing across to where the sun was now easing the darkness of the rock formation. Different sounds told them that the village was coming to life to greet a new day. A motor was revving loudly. Ahead of the phospherent glow of its wake, a sailing craft came silently round the point and into the cove. They were no longer alone in the world.

Walking casually away, Guy bent to pick up her shirt from where she had let it drop on the sand. He held it for her as she came to him. Kerry saw the small pile of his discarded clothing lying a few feet away.

He spoke as calmly as if they were passing the time of day in the street. 'I'm planning to have a go at Trimenen Head this afternoon.'

'You can't do it alone!' she warned.

'I know.' He nodded sombrely. 'I suppose I'm really asking you to come with me, Kerry. Will you?'

Kerry heard her own voice. Seemingly coming from somewhere beside her, definitely independent of her, it said just one word: 'Yes.'

'You smell like a still.'

Guy, made cool and aloof by annoyance at Valerie having stayed in town all night, had spoken those words. But when had he said them? It had to be this morning. He had left the cottage then, saying something about climbing, as far as she could remember. But Valerie wasn't sure what this morning was. The children were noisy upstairs, as Guy's mother got them ready for whatever had been planned for this day of their holiday. The old woman enjoyed looking after the kids, a fact that took the sharp edge off Valerie's guilt. She could feel relief and tension alternating in her like a cool shower. She didn't like this. A dull headache was numbing her mind. She'd managed to have a nap in Tinisha's car on the drive back, but that had been only mildly refreshing. This had only happened to her since coming down to Cornwall. It was quite frightening. As though there were periods you should remember but couldn't. Lapses of memory for which Valerie had coined the term 'intermittent amnesia'. Could there be such a thing? If there was, then her bet would be that multiple, triple-strength orgasms were the cause.

Mechanically preparing sandwiches, she gradually pieced together the happenings of yesterday. Being drunk excused her outrageous behaviour in the hotel. But it wasn't an alibi for the thrill remembrance was bringing her. Valerie was sweating. The fact that recall was bringing her close to coming was proof that sex with Tinisha was ultra-special.

Valerie's mind was in turmoil. What was going to happen? Passing time had made her marriage the same as being single, except that Guy was with her all the time. You both lived in the same house when you were married, which was convenient. But that was where the analogy collapsed. When you were single, you could go home, or send your boyfriend home when you became bored.

If possible, she wanted to take on board Tinisha's outlook as she had expressed it on the drive back. 'There is only one sin, and that is selfishness, Valerie,' Tinisha, in one of her philosophical moods, had declared. 'Everything else is derivative. It is fine to gratify yourself as long as it is not at the expense of someone else.'

Valerie had been able to understand that, for Tinisha had not attempted to get her to do anything that she hadn't wanted to do. The difficulty came in trying to apply that tenet to other situations in her life.

Valerie felt that she could send Guy and the children home to London without her. But she had been worried, perhaps disillusioned, since leaving the motel that morning. 'Tinisha,' she'd said, her head snuggled against the other woman's shoulder, 'I do love you. And I want you all to myself. Let's you and me stay together always.'

It had devastated her when Tinisha's only response was to start up the engine of the car.

The two children were downstairs, running round the table as she packed the sandwiches. They were in high spirits, wanting to know if she would be coming with them and their grandmother to the beach, and if their father would be with them.

'Go outside and wait for me,' she told them, feeling bad about avoiding them and their questions.

Before this day was out, she needed to see Tinisha. Before she terminated her marriage, she had a right to some firm commitment from her female lover.

Though filtered into faintness by distance, the voices of the children playing outside the holiday cottage irritated Tinisha. She could never understand all the fuss made about young people. In a few years they would be old people, in their turn.

It was another hot day. Beneath the parasols of trees there was a slight movement to the heavy air, more a caress than a breeze. The smell of turpentine was strong as she worked her favourite sable brush with her fingers before putting it back in the jar. The eyes of the Ruby portrait stared at her, alive, unblinking and somehow accusing. She had a cold feeling because the picture had come to bother her so much. Tinisha felt an intuitive pressure to destroy the painting, but that would be premature as it wasn't as yet finished. Making the decision tomorrow's business brought her no comfort. Procrastination was anathema to the live-for-the-moment Tinisha.

Aware of a change in sounds that were deadened by distance, she looked down at the holiday cottage. The mother and grand-mother stood together, calling the children for the off. On seeing the young woman, Tinisha had a premonition of trouble. Great fuck though she was, Valerie had got things wrong. Reliant on the security of marriage, uncertainty about her relationship with her husband was likely to make her possessive. That was something that Tinisha shrank from. The bonus of lesbian sex was that you could fuck for fun with no risk of pregnancy. And an attempt at being sensible was the ruination of every relationship. It would be impossible to have someone like Valerie understand that.

Sex was the fuel that energised Tinisha for her painting. If you used the same fuel all the time you would never get the fire to burn brightly. The delightful Elke Fuller had been on Tinisha's mind for days. She had planned to go to the Dumphy shop today and follow up on the connections she had carefully made on her first meeting with Elke. She could tell that there was more than a glimmer of interest deep in the military blonde's ice-blue eyes.

Before that she would have to call at the Tredogan home. Kerry hadn't turned up for work today, and an over-the-top Marje had telephoned with an agitated rush of words. After doing a spot of decoding, Tinisha learned that Marje wanted to see her, most urgently.

Something must have gone wrong with the advance wedding plans. Perhaps the inane Simon Gregory had grasped what it would be like to have a mother-in-law worth fucking, and a father-in-law who needed fucking. Kerry should be grateful for a lucky escape. At least the day wouldn't come when she was standing around in a silly white dress suffering gags such as 'may all your troubles be little ones'.

Tinisha backed away a few steps from her easel, closing one eye to study the portrait. It was different. What had started out as Kerry had become the mysterious Ruby. Now the woman in the picture looked completely different. This change of direction would drive the purists mad. Perhaps she could get a good price for it. The only time an actual likeness was needed was when you intended to sell it to the sitter. She wouldn't destroy it. All it required was the background. Maybe orange. That would accentuate what Tinisha now saw as a Caribbean personality.

But a final decision would have to be deferred until Tinisha's return from the village. She had to make progress on Valerie's portrait, too. Once the passionate blonde had quelled her enthusiasm for a homosexual marriage of some description, Tinisha knew that there was considerable sexual mileage left in the petite Valerie before she went back from her holiday.

She popped the three remaining brushes in a tall vase. To avoid another zany telephone call, or possibly an even zanier visit, her priority was to put the semi-hysterical Marje Tredogan's life back in order. Then, tallyho, d'ye ken John Peel, and all that sort of bollocks, she would begin a new hunt. The quarry would be Elke Fuller. Tinisha knew that the girl would be well worth the chase. A wet cunt never lied.

It had happened, naturally and unplanned. Predestined probably, Kerry had to admit to herself in the light of what had occurred on the beach that morning. If a near disaster hadn't been averted, it would have been a non-event anyway. They had been close to the top of Trimenen Head. Projecting in such a way that it resembled an overhang, this section of cliff had few feet or hand holds. There had been a fatality last year. A Birmingham climber, young but said to have been experienced, had fallen to his death from here on to the rocks below. After this tragedy, the coastguards had issued a warning that only experienced, fully equipped teams should attempt a climb of Trimenen Head.

Guy and she had all but succeeded that afternoon, using nothing but sheer guts and enthusiasm. Kerry had decided it would be less traumatic for Guy if she didn't explain in advance about the really dicey bit some fifteen feet from the top. Here, with the cliff face sloping out so that it felt as if you were about to fall backwards, there were two footholds but only one handhold. The lightness of Kerry's body helped her. Using her left hand and pushing with both feet, she had swung up to grasp the handhold above with her right hand. Pulling herself up to the meagre safety offered by a narrow ledge, she believed that, though Guy was large and heavy, his undoubted strength would have him swing up on the ledge beside her.

'Bend your knees, Guy,' she had called down to him, 'and use your legs as well as your left arm to spring you up.'

Obeying her instructions, he had concentrated all the immense power of his body. But as he had launched himself, the pressure he exerted made his right foothold break away from the cliff. This caused his left foot to slip off of its foothold.

In slow motion, Kerry had seen the stone that had crumbled from the cliff face hurtling down. Strain on his handsome face,

Guy, holding on only by his left hand, had been kicking frantically but ineffectively with both feet against the face of the cliff.

'Don't look down, Guy,' Kerry had called out hackneyed advice.

It had been pointless in this case. Face against the rough face of the cliff, Guy wouldn't have been able to hold on with one hand much longer. The coastguard advice was sound advice, Kerry had realised retrospectively. With an iota of relief, she had seen Guy's left foot regain the foothold. This had eased at least some of the strain on him.

With her left hand gripping a spur of rock on the ledge, Kerry had leaned out over the edge. Though heights had never bothered her, the rocks and blue sea so very far below spun dizzily and terrifyingly for a moment. When her head cleared, she had stretched her right hand down. Her fingertips had reached to perhaps eighteen inches above Guy.

'Swing up and grasp my hand with your right hand, Guy.'

'I can't do that,' he had protested, his voice a hoarse whisper, as if something in his throat had been crushed.

'You can, you can make it,' Kerry had assured him.

'I can get your hand,' he had called raspingly, aware that she had misunderstood him, 'but you won't be able to pull me up. My weight will pull you off the ledge, and we'll both fall.'

'I've got a good grip with my left hand up here.'

Though she had told him that, Kerry had recognised that Guy was doubtless right. He must weigh sixteen stone or more, which would be at least double what she weighed. But it had been Guy's only hope. If many more minutes had been allowed to pass, he would be drained of the strength necessary to simply cling on.

'You've got to do it,' she had screamed, waving her right hand back and forth.

His mind made up, Guy had swung his right arm. His fingers had brushed Kerry's. She had reached further down, their hands met solidly, and they had gripped each other. The shock of his weight had come close to pulling both of her arms from their sockets. Guy had been swinging, scraping against the cliff, scrambling wildly. A seagull swooped low, coming in close, screamed its anger at them, then soared away high to tell other gulls.

Disorientated by the bird, Guy had paused for a moment. Then he had started scrambling again, and Kerry found the strain of holding him had been dragging the aching fingers of her left hand from its hold.

She had felt herself going. The scene below had begun spinning again as a blackness had started to fill her head like dense smoke. But then the fingers of Guy's left hand had got a grip on the ledge. Kerry had fallen back as he had released her right hand. With both hands gaining a scant grip on the ledge, Guy, in a magnificent show of strength, had pulled himself up to safety.

Clinging to each other, they had stayed on the ledge for a while to recuperate. Then they had made the rest of the climb easily. On the clifftop, lying in the grass, they had laughed too loudly, talked too much, the way folk do when a crisis has come and gone. Up there, they could have been the last two people on earth. An Adam and Eve in reverse. A white sail had stood out close to the horizon, its lack of movement making it lifeless. They were truly alone.

They had been lying side by side, enjoying the absolute peace and quiet. Then he had suddenly, almost viciously, wrapped Kerry in his arms and kissed her. Then, easing her away from him, he had tried a gentle kiss. 'I'm sorry. Forgive me, Kerry. I shouldn't have done that.' She had tried to stop his words with her fingers. But he had gone on, explaining. 'I just suddenly wanted you.'

Kerry had drawn him close, telling him huskily. 'Right now, you can have me any way you want.'

That was an outlandish thing for someone like her to say. It was proof that she still hadn't recovered from her trials and tribulations of late. Moving to get her back comfortable in the grass, Kerry had become a little afraid as he had loomed up over her, making her feel smothered. She felt ashamed of her little-girl voice as she heard it say, 'Don't hurt! Please don't hurt!'

It had been his turn to show fright then. Pulling a few inches away from her, his urgent hands had ceased their movements. 'Is it your first time, Kerry?'

Biting her lip had stopped her from saying, yes, with a man. Instead, she had nodded, holding him close so that he couldn't pull away further from her. They had kissed. His hands, that had previously been rough and possessive, became gentle hands in deep-searching, caressing preliminaries.

When they were both naked, Kerry had stiffened in his arms, 'There's someone coming.'

They had lain still, trying the impossible of getting down lower in the long grass. An elderly man and woman had come purposely through the grass. Each had gone down on one knee to pluck some kind of plant. The old couple had fussed around the plants they were holding, then had studied them from all angles and talked between themselves in low voices.

Then the pair had left without discovering the presence of Guy and Kerry. Guy had rolled up on to her again, rekindling their former passion in a split second. The sudden sharp finish it came to had surprised Kerry, disillusioned her. In terms of sensation, the sexual act with Guy wasn't even on the same scale as the thrills she had experienced with Tinisha. Guy stared down at her almost stupidly. Guessing that he was about to say sorry, she had silenced him with her fingers that time. It registered how much he had wanted her. In a way, it had cleared the confusion in her head over Simon and Tinisha. He could never replace Tinisha where sexual thrills were concerned, but she now saw Guy as her way ahead, her way out of the village. He was married, a family man: but all that meant in this day and age was the adjustment of a few lives.

But they were estranged now as they dressed themselves. He was slightly morose, taking care not to meet her eyes.

She took a comb from her pocket and she combed her hair, then turned away from him. She said, 'You regret it now, don't you, Guy?'

Everything, her whole future, depended on his answer, and she waited anxiously. Coming close, he held her shoulders and kissed the back of her neck. 'Of course I don't, you sweet, sweet girl.'

Smiling happily, Kerry did not try to get away. Instead she offered her neck for more kisses and caresses.

First the meeting with Marje, thought Tinisha, and then to the bank – her most recent buyer had paid a cash installment, and she hadn't had a chance to deposit the money yet. Driving by the Dumphy store, Tinisha had pulled over when she spotted Elke standing in the doorway. Elke was leaning nonchalantly, the hem of her skirt retreating up under a three-quarter-length blue overall.

The girl had come running to the window of the car as if Tinisha was Glenda Jackson about to sign an autograph for her. She was very near to Tinisha. She looked at Tinisha with narrow blue eyes.

The closeness of the girl's mouth made Tinisha quiver like the sudden release of a static charge. Elke looked cute and sharp. But her eyes weren't sharp. They looked dull. Dispirited. Army life must have shattered her psyche. And Tinisha believed that the ecstasy of woman-to-woman sex would restore her.

'I've been meaning to call into the shop,' Tinisha half-apologised. 'It's just that I've been so busy.'

Elke's nod acknowledged Tinisha's lack of time. She reminded Tinisha of the young Debbie Harry. She said, 'I was hoping to see you around.'

'I rarely come into the village, Elke. My one regular practice is a walk in the woods up at the bungalow at about eight o'clock every evening.' Tinisha had the uneasy feeling that Elke's almost child-like innocence was masquerading a highly rampant sexuality. Pointing off in the direction of the woods, Tinisha sneaked a quick look at the girl.

That was a blatant proposition. It was an invite to a picnic down in the woods for teddy bears with genitals. Bring your own honey, honey. Elke would be Tinisha's first groupie.

'I don't get up that way very often,' Elke said dubiously, but Tinisha could tell that the girl was planning to be there that very evening.

'Never mind. I'll see you around somewhere,' Tinisha said with deliberate off-handedness as she drove away.

Setting up a date with Elke was a pushover – so why did Tinisha have the sneaky suspicion that it was she herself who was being lured? But Tinisha knew that whatever Marje Tredogan wanted her for wouldn't be so easy to fix. The inner voice she should listen to more often warned her of trouble ahead.

She soon found she had been right to pay attention to that voice.

'It disgusts me,' were Marje's words of greeting when Tinisha reached the tiny stone house with its small rooms. 'I can't believe it of you, corrupting a young girl like my Kerry.'

Marje Tredogan had tousled hair, and full round hips and a mouth that could be coaxed into lewdness. She had blurted out the whole sorry story, a tragi-comedy in Tinisha's opinion. You learn not from what people say but what they don't say. Discovering that her daughter was a lesbian was a lesser blow for Marje than the ending of Kerry's marriage prospects. The Gregorys had been the jackpot; Tinisha had lost the Tredogans their ticket to prosperity. Whatever people such as the Tredogans tried, they ended up just as broke as before and eternally poorer for the experience.

The kitchen they were in was neat and clean. It looked as if it had just been dusted and swept. A few items of clothing were draped over a wire-frame airer. Owning few clothes meant that everything had to be washed and put back on daily. Hanging on the end was a pair of flesh-coloured bras, the size identifying Marje as the owner. She wasn't wearing a bra that morning. But her big beautiful tits were self-supporting inside an old summer dress of thin material. The dark patches of sweat under the armpits of the yellow, flowered dress didn't escape the notice of Tinisha.

'We mustn't get this out of perspective, Marje,' Tinisha said quietly. 'Kerry is not a child.'

'She is *my* child.'

'I understand that, but I have never made Kerry do anything she didn't want to do.'

'But –' Marje began, but she was crying. 'I just can't understand any of this . . .'

'Don't upset yourself about it. In a few days, the whole thing will have blown over,' Tinisha said consolingly.

'I don't know.' She stopped crying long enough so that Tinisha could understand her. 'This has come on top of everything else. Mr Tredogan is no help. I honestly don't know which way to turn. We owe so much money.'

She cracked up, sobbing.

Tinisha put her arms around her. There was a nice, warm-fleshed feel to Marje. She was wearing a perfume that was cheap but very effective. Her first physical contact with an older woman thrilled Tinisha.

But Marje's distress upset her. Freeing one hand, Tinisha reached to her handbag on the table. Taking out a roll of banknotes that was secured by an elastic band, she laid it on the tabletop. 'There are five hundred pounds, Marje. A little gift to tide you over.' She gave the woman a light peck on the forehead. Following up on this swiftly, she held Marje close and kissed her full on the mouth. Tinisha recognised that the lack of resistance from the other woman most probably stemmed from gratitude and fear of the money being taken back.

'You don't owe me anything, you know,' Tinisha reassured the older woman. 'This has nothing to do with money. Anything you do now, you do by choice.'

Marje kissed Tinisha hard, but then broke away. 'Wait . . .'

Still holding her tightly, the feel of the soft warm body sending dozens of little thrill waves through her, Tinisha gave a soothing, 'Shh.'

'Oh, Miss Weaver.'

Stroking Marje's red hair, lightly touching the skin of Marje's face, Tinisha carried out a test by moving her hand down to the top button of the yellow dress. Slowly undoing the button, she braced herself for a protest. She would have stopped immediately. But the protest never came – and instead Marje smiled. Holding Marje closer, able to hear and feel her heart beat beneath her huge breasts, Tinisha kissed her again. First on the forehead, then on the lips.

Pulling away, just slightly, Marje then returned the kiss, relaxing her lips. The woman's pleasure-centre was breaking through a shield of puritanical modesty that for a lifetime had protected her. She was delicately kissing Tinisha on the lips, the ears, and the neck.

To her astonishment, Tinisha was experiencing tremors that she knew would eventually lead to an earthquake of minor multiple orgasms. The fact that nothing like this had ever before happened to Marje promised much. The long-suppressed libido of Marje Tredogan was sending out rumbling but unheard and unseen warnings that it was about to erupt.

Aroused beyond belief, Tinisha cuddled the woman, desiring to feel her warmth, her softness, naked. Excitement was making it difficult for Tinisha to breathe. She felt for one of Marje's large breasts outside of her dress. The flesh was sculptured, and had a heat that permeated the thin material. As Tinisha had expected, the hard nipple was huge, in keeping with the outsized breast that it capped.

'What are you doing to me?'

Holding Marje, fingers working nimbly on her breast through the dress, Tinisha spoke words of endearment between soft kisses. She had long ago come to realise that a woman needs to hear words of love. With her kisses becoming wetter, she made silly incredible promises, spoke flatteries too wild to be believed. But, as Tinisha had anticipated, Marje Tredogan seemed to somehow melt in her arms. She was Tinisha's woman. And Tinisha, for the moment only, was hers.

EIGHT

Marje Tredogan was naked in dappled sunshine created by an elm tree, an apple tree, or maybe it was an ash outside the bedroom window. Whatever the tree was, Tinisha Weaver groaned: Marje Tredogan dapple-naked was a magnificent specimen of womanhood. Marje had a primitive quality that was galvanising. She exuded a fundamental sexiness more compelling than could ever be found in sophisticated and scented boudoirs throughout the world. It was partially concealed now by a screen of shyness as she stood with her arms folded across truly wondrous breasts. Tinisha was naked, too, but Marje kept her eyes averted. Not even curiosity had induced her to take a peep.

Tinisha unfolded Marje's arms gently and held them away. Marje didn't physically resist. And then she was in Tinisha's arms returning her kiss. Marje was strong but Tinisha's excitation gave a power to her embrace that made the large woman gasp. Tinisha felt the big breasts against her, each one an individual focus of hot arousal. They were big handfuls and Marje didn't seem to mind, no matter how Tinisha felt and fondled them. Though firm and very much a part of Marje's sturdy, muscle-thighed body, they somehow seemed independent of her. Tinisha was unable to cover them with her hands so she held them from the sides, thrilled at the long brown tips pushing out proudly to greet her. They demanded hard caresses and Tinisha squeezed unmercifully. She wondered how they could ever resume their natural shape.

Marje raised no objection, verbal or otherwise. Why did she look so bewildered? The wide-eyed expression on Marje's face baffled Tinisha. Then the answer dawned on her. Many must have wanted these ripe fruits, but this could not have ever happened before. No man – or woman, for that matter – had ever indulged Marje's beautiful breasts.

Shaping them like pears, fearing that she would either hurt them or Marje, Tinisha looked at her face. Marje still wore the bewildered expression. The flesh Tinisha had been moulding sprang back in her hands. She shaped them again and again. At last she was having some effect on Marje. The redheaded woman was licking her lips as she strained towards Tinisha. Reassured that she was not hurting Marje, Tinisha pressed both the breasts inwards and tried to cover them both with her mouth. Marje released a long, mournful cry that was more like a wail. Suddenly animated, she shoved Tinisha down on the bed, and got fully on top of her.

The seducer seemed about to be seduced. It was a nice twist that both amused Tinisha and excited her even further. She had lit the fuse and it was sizzling. The unexploded sex-bomb that was Marje Tredogan would detonate at any moment.

Tinisha was on her back and Marje was straddling her, on all fours. Marje's breasts dangled, the nipples just touching Tinisha's skin. As Marje moved downwards, the nipples delicately rippled on Tinisha's body. Marje raised her head to look at Tinisha. One corner of her mouth smiled before she lowered her red head again. Worked by some instinct that Tinisha couldn't understand, and was too worked up to ponder on, Marje moved a little sideways so that the taut nipple of her left breast traced its way down through the V of Tinisha's pubic hair. Just as instinctively, Tinisha opened her legs and the nipple entered her slit.

The warmth from the breast and the firm nipple sliding up and down her slit became too much for Tinisha. She felt the nipple go right down to become an erotic close neighbour to her arsehole. Then it was moving up with Tinisha's slippery, swollen lips clinging tightly to it. Tinisha screamed out in total ecstasy as the nipple met her clitoris. Instinct was still serving Marje well and, when she saw how excited Tinisha had become, she set her nipple to work on the clitoris.

God, this inexperienced woman knew her stuff. That was a contradiction in terms, but Marje had an innate sexual expertise. It was as if she had been programmed at birth to perform this miracle on Tinisha. Tinisha started to come. How Tinisha came! But Marje was relentless, keeping the heavy breast and stiff nipple working on her. It was unbearable.

Tinisha tried to push her lover, her tormentor, from her as she squirmed in the shrill pleasure of after-climax. But she could not dislodge Marje, who stayed with Tinisha's tense body as it subsided. Then Marje had her in thrall again, and Tinisha was screaming and creaming, and could feel how wet Marje's breast had become between her burning thighs.

Hit by a short spell of unconsciousness, Tinisha's return was boosted by an explosion of sexual energy. Shoving Marje off her so that the bigger woman rolled on to her back on the bed, Tinisha pounced on her. She kissed Marje on the mouth, sucking and biting on the heavy bottom lip. She kissed her arms and her shoulders, burying her face in the forest of red hair in the armpits. Breathing in the natural essence of Marje was like taking a drug. Driven completely wild, Tinisha licked her ears and her neck and down along her breasts. Tinisha held the huge boobs firmly together, and her head oscillated as she kissed the nipples of Marje's tits in turn. And then she went down: down she went, licking through the matting of thick, dark red hair on the stomach. Skirting past the bush of pubic hair, Tinisha slid her tongue down to big, muscled thighs. Moving Marje's legs open, she licked inside of the thighs from the knees upwards.

As Tinisha neared Marje's crotch, the hair grew thicker. Here there was more essence of Marje, but with a difference. There was more taste to it, and Tinisha wanted to linger, to relish the delight, but the nearness of Marje's distended pubis was irresistible.

Putting her head between Marje's thick but shapely legs, Tinisha pulled them up and closed them around her head. Then her tongue was in there. Tinisha's hot tongue licked, and then her teeth were gently nibbling at Marje's clitoris. Her hands were under the other woman's buttocks and she felt them tighten convulsively. She was aware that Marje's shoulders were quivering.

Marje began to make strange little noises. She was groaning, moaning, fainting, swooning . . . and she came! A shrieking orgasm. Marje's spine seemed to be on fire under Tinisha's hands. Marje's arsehole burned against Tinisha's throat. Marje's cunt ruptured gushingly into Tinisha's mouth.

The unusual force and violence of Marje's orgasm jolted Tinisha into coming again. Slobbering at Marje's vulva, Tinisha came with a devastation that knocked out all her strength. She slumped to sit on the floor, her arms, shoulders and head resting on the bed. So drained that she had to fight off sleep, Tinisha sensed that Marje was scrambling around. The other woman's movements sounded hectic.

When Tinisha had recovered enough to blearily open her eyes, she found herself alone in the bedroom. Getting into her clothes, she used Marje's hairbrush and dressing-table mirror to tidy herself.

When she went out of the bedroom the house seemed empty. She called Marje's name several times but there was no response. A bedroom door at the end of the landing was closed. Tinisha turned the handle. The door was locked and she knew. Too ashamed to face her, Marje had locked herself away.

Perturbed by this, Tinisha hesitated. Having released her sexuality fully, plainly for the first time ever, Marje would find the aftermath of such an experience traumatic. Would she be able to cope? Concern for her made it difficult for Tinisha to leave the house. But Jack Tredogan or Reggie might return if she delayed. That would cause complications, making things really difficult for Marje. Reluctantly, Tinisha went down the stairs and out through the door.

They ate on a terrace that jutted out over a sheer cliff. Below was a dizzying panorama of blue sea. The proprietor, a Greek Cypriot, who handed Valerie a red rose, told them the history of the place. Until the outbreak of World War II, an order of nuns who wore white habits had occupied the building. Then the Royal Navy had used it as a radio station, and it had become a restaurant in the late 1970s.

Relaxed and happy, Valerie looked down towards the primrose-coloured buildings clustered beside the sea. This was the town she had visited with Tinisha, but she couldn't recognise it from up here. It was early evening and there was a carnival appearance to the lights strung along the promenade. The air was warm and naturally scented by the environment.

They had eaten sea bass grilled in fennel, a delicious meal that completed the perfection of the evening. Guy's mother, with the acumen and understanding that the aged were never given credit for, had suggested that her son and daughter-in-law have an evening out together. The old lady had sensed that their relationship had been unravelling fast. Immediately she had picked up improving vibrations, she had acted as a sort of peacemaker and matchmaker combined.

Catching each other's eyes across the table, she and Guy shared a smile. It was a smile that said we've made it, we're back together. Twenty-four hours ago, Valerie wouldn't have believed that this could happen. Expecting Guy to return from his climbing expedition as unapproachable as when he had left, she was pleasantly surprised. Though quiet and strangely subdued, he had shown a need to be close to her. At bedtime, they'd had sex on a blanket on the floor to keep down the noise. It had been a passionate coupling on a par with the fantastic sex of their early days. If only she hadn't found herself thinking spontaneously of Tinisha, it would have been perfect.

Obviously popular, the restaurant was packed with diners. A girl with either a natural or contrived look of a European gypsy serenaded them with a guitar and a Gershwin song.

'I think I'm enjoying this holiday,' Guy said with a wry better-late-than-never smile.

'So am I.' Valerie smiled back. She brought the rose up to her nostrils, inhaling its delicate fragrance.

He reached for her hand, saying softly, 'You look so lovely tonight, Val.'

She let out a breath. Everything was fine. She had rediscovered peace of mind with her husband. In a way it was like regaining her sanity after the madness of seeking sexual gratification that Tinisha had caught her up in.

Tinisha was still with her, and always would be. As Tinisha had explained, they had committed no sin. All they had done was delight each other, making life more enjoyable for them both. There was no reason why they couldn't be friends, and her portrait completed. Valerie would be friendly but firm, positively firm. So far, the holiday had proved less expensive than they had feared, and Valerie considered that it might be possible, without the risk of giving offence, to offer to pay at least something towards the portrait. That way the holiday could exceed all expectations.

They lingered over coffee and brandy. Dusk was gathering and the terrace was now festooned with twinkling lights. The restaurant had an extraordinarily pleasant ambience. Music floated on a warm evening breeze, and Guy had reached across the table to take her hand in his.

'You are so beautiful,' he sighed.

'And you are so handsome,' she rejoined. 'You are every bit the Guy Zennor I once knew and loved.'

'Wrong,' he corrected her smilingly, with a slow, negative shaking of his head. Putting a finger to his lips, he looked around. 'Don't tell a soul, but tonight I'm Guy the Gorilla.'

She giggled. 'You fool, Guy. You certainly don't sound like yourself.'

'I'm not, I've told you. Though I may look myself to you, that is due to convincing make-up. Right now I might jump up on to the table, roar and beat my chest.'

'That would be embarrassing.' Valerie laughed again. 'Whatever brought this on?'

'You have. Here we sit, civilised and sophisticated, but in ten minutes' time we will be speeding along a country road on our way to an animal mating.'

'I think Guy the Gorilla is drunk,' Valerie chided him.

'He's not drunk, just incredibly randy. On the way here, I noticed a deserted spot where we can park on the way back.'

'What for?' Valerie asked, feigning innocence.

'To . . .' Guy began but looked furtively around at the other diners. Rising up out of his chair he leaned over to whisper in her ear. 'To fuck the arse off you on the back seat of the car.'

A warmth, only partly sexual, spread pleasantly through her.

Valerie gave a little giggle. 'That will be like old times. Let's give it a title – Streatham Common Revisited.'

'Starring Guy the Gorilla,' he insisted.

They laughed together, but then she went serious. 'This holiday has given me quite a scare where you and me are concerned.'

'Forget all that,' he advised, looking round for the waiter, keen to pay, to leave. 'I always say never go backwards. Why bother with yesterday when tonight is here, and love is in the air?'

'You are a complete fool, Guy Zennor,' she said. 'But you'll never be boring. With you, I never know what's going to happen next.'

'I know exactly what's going to happen next,' he told her in mock threat.

This sexual banter made her smile again. For a moment she ran cold as an image of a mildly reproving Tinisha filled her mind, and Valerie felt a ludicrous but painful adulterer's guilt over what she was about to do with her husband. It had to be a mental aberration that she regarded it as cheating on Tinisha. Then that feeling passed and her mind was filled with imagery of what was going to happen on their way back.

By the time Guy had paid the bill, Valerie was on her feet, eager to take his arm and hurry to the car.

The thick, tangled greenery of high summer made walking like a safari through an African jungle. Humming the tune of *The Teddy Bears' Picnic*, Tinisha picked her way carefully along an overgrown trail. She climbed over a dead tree-trunk. It was an old, rotting corpse decorated by a bright, fresh wreath of new vines and flowers. Taking her time, she bent double to pass under an overhang of brambles. Tinisha never hurried through the woods. There was always too much to see. In a splash of sunlight she spotted a nest on a low limb of a tree. Even on tiptoe she could see nothing, but a hungry chirping told her that the nest was occupied. A bird flew past her, going through an evasive strategy of circles before lighting on the edge of the nest. The bird was fat, its head seemingly squashed down into its tubby little body. Staying perfectly still just a few feet away, Tinisha considered that the bird hadn't seen her or, more probably, had chosen to ignore her. It had a worm in its beak. Four little squawking heads raised up jerkily out of the nest. Though the young fought ravenously over the meal, the mother bird divided it evenly so that each of her babies had an equal share.

There was a marked coolness to the evening as she walked on. The heavy foliage made it difficult to see the sky, but she was certain it had darkened. Though there had been no rain for weeks, she knew the area well enough to forecast that if it did rain it would be just a shower of short duration. The path took her to where the brook formed a pond. Fragrant bluebells, her favourite flowers, grew profusely. Tinisha felt a need to touch them, to soak up their perfume and keep it alive inside of herself. She sat at the edge of the pool. Tossing a pebble in the water, she watched the widening and overlapping ripples in fascination. Cause and effect. Just like life when one simple act spreads its consequences.

She saw Elke then, as she knew she would. Looking for the girl had unconsciously caused Tinisha to slow her blinking. She opened and closed her lids several times to cure the soreness of her eyes and clear her vision. The girl was having difficulty descending from the top of a ridge that was entangled with bramble bushes. She made it to the bottom. The striped dress that she wore made her look taller than Tinisha remembered her. A man's dark trilby hat on her fair head gave her the look of a wayfarer. On a dozen other girls, the hat would have looked stupid. It suited Elke ideally.

'Oh!' she exclaimed in surprise when Tinisha walked up to her. Again, Tinisha had the uneasy feeling that Elke's nervousness was feigned.

The dress fitted tightly around her slim waist and over her full hips. Though she had fancied Elke all along, Tinisha hadn't realised until now how lovely she was. Her full-lipped face was without a blemish, and it had a special glow, a warm radiance.

'I thought that I'd give your praise of the woods a try,' Elke said shyly. She sounded embarrassed by having come here, made awkward by Tinisha's stare.

'I'm pleased that you have,' Tinisha told her, walking off slowly so that it was natural for Elke to fall in at her side. 'Be conscious of all around you, Elke, and you'll hear the thoughts of the woods. When the woods get to know you, accept you, they will tell you their secrets.'

'That's lovely,' Elke, who seemed terribly impressed, complimented her. 'I would imagine that poets – Wordsworth, Byron, and the others – talked like you.'

'If I could write like they did, Elke, I'd give up painting.'

'Why?' The girl sounded shocked. They were going deeper into the woods as the trail swept around the bottom of a small hill. 'I was ever so thrilled when I saw your photograph, and read about you in the local paper when I came back home. I never thought then that I would ever meet you, let alone be taking a walk like this with you.'

That would have been a report on the successful exhibition Tinisha had put on in Kensington, last autumn. Tinisha was aware that caution was needed. Adoration was one thing, sex very much another. It wouldn't do to make a pass at Elke until she was sure. Well, as sure as you could ever be. A botched start could not correct itself. All that could be done then was to try new tricks to cover the first ones.

To Tinisha, the construction of a relationship was a tedious and senseless ritual. It was based on habit and tradition. Though there were sometimes catastrophic results, she liked to cut to the chase. A first-time blush accompanied by an expression of shock, and you were home and dry – or wet, rather.

'You flatter me, Elke,' Tinisha protested. 'I'm just a semi-recluse churning out mediocre paintings.'

'You're far too modest. I'm jealous of your talent, in the nicest way, and envy you your beauty, Tinisha. You can have your pick of men.'

'Men are all alike, and very dull,' Tinisha said.

If ever there was a broad hint, that was it. Tinisha awaited Elke's reaction or, more hopefully, response. A sudden flash of lightning illuminated the woods and Elke's face starkly for a split second, bone-white and beautiful.

A clap of thunder followed seconds later. Giant drops of rain began to fall. They both uttered little strangled cries and began to run. 'This way!' Tinisha called, turning left to scramble up a slope as the heavy, sloppy drops of rain quickly soaked their clothing. Stones slipped out from under their feet in a few places. These stones gathered speed and other loose stones joined them on the way down and began to roar like a small avalanche. An ear-shattering clap of thunder drowned out the roar.

Reaching out to take Elke by the hand, Tinisha went ahead of her up a flight of stone steps. The bushes flanking the steps and the grass growing up between the flaggings made passage difficult. Using her knees to knock the foliage aside, Tinisha cleared a way for them both.

They reached a derelict, tiny single-roomed house. Bushes and clinging vines and ivy hid it. But Tinisha had known it was there. The porch was collapsing. Tinisha pulled away a hand-hewn porch support that was lying diagonally across the door. Piles of leaves blocked the door. She grabbed a besom broom that was leaning against the stone wall of the house. Tinisha vigorously swept the porch as the heavy raindrops spattered against Elke and herself.

Watching her sweep, Elke burst into laughter. Bending almost double, she shouted to Tinisha, between laughs, 'Let's make it nice for them before they get back from the diamond mine.'

That was this kind of humour Tinisha appreciated. Lifting the latch on the door, she put the broom at the slope on her shoulder, like a soldier with a rifle.

'Hi ho!' she sang out; her voice rang through the rain-filled air of the woods.

'Hi ho,' Elke echoed, falling in behind Tinisha as they marched into the house, both singing 'It's home from work we go. Hi ho, hi ho, hi . . .'

A mighty clap of thunder finished their singing but not their laughter. The windows of the house had long ago been covered with vine and shaded by trees. There was little light inside. But they were sheltered from the rain. Ivy had grown in through the roof and turned white because the sun couldn't reach it.

Then the laughing had to stop.

Taking a handkerchief from her pocket, Tinisha started wiping the rain from Elke's face. Elke shut her eyes, and her lips pouted. Her facial expression appeared to be inviting, but Tinisha recognised that to accept it as such could be a mistake. Her closed eyelids were so perfectly shaped that they could have been carved. Trying to dry the girl's face was made hopeless by the handkerchief being sodden from the start. Taking a chance, under cover of an extension of their Seven Dwarfs parody, Tinisha gave each of Elke's eyes a quick kiss.

'Wake up, Sleepy.'

The Snow White reference made Elke smile. The perfection of her slender figure was shown to the full by the clinging wet dress. Being soaked to the skin brought out the womanly scent of her body. Tinisha caught her own smell. It was raunchier than Elke's because she was now all hot and sticky between the legs. She pushed things along by kissing the tip of Elke's cute nose.

Her face was still wearing a little smile. Slipping an arm around Elke's slim shoulders, Tinisha kissed her on the mouth.

A long, passionate kiss. During it, Tinisha groped one of the small, firm breasts. Finding Elke's nipple was in hiding, she released the tit and moved her hand down to feel the swell of Elke's cunt through the rain-soaked material of her dress.

The girl was shedding her passivity remarkably fast, thought Tinisha. They continued kissing as Tinisha slid a hand up Elke's thigh. Meeting encouragement, Tinisha used her hand to prise the girl's legs open a little. Tinisha got her hand inside the crotch of the panties. The sparse pubic hair was wet with rain and love-juice. Tinisha slid the tip of her middle finger into Elke, pleased to find the lips moistening and swelling as she moved her finger back and forth along the full length of the slit. She was so wet.

Then Elke did pull her head away. Her eyes were smiling as she looked into Tinisha's. She said, 'I knew this would happen.'

'Did you want it to?' Tinisha asked, moving her finger in and up, finding Elke's G-spot with ridiculous, exhilarating ease.

The girl gave Tinisha a rather piercing look. 'Yes.' Elke managed to give the one-word answer as Tinisha kissed her again and worked skilfully on her with her finger. The girl suddenly came to life. Gasping and grunting, Elke opened her mouth to permit Tinisha's tongue to enter. Her pelvic bone thrust rhythmically against the heel of the hand with which Tinisha was fingering her. Then it ended as Elke pulled her mouth away to express surprise at herself.

'Oh, Tinisha.' She began to cry, little wild animal sounds.

An understanding, sympathetic Tinisha took her hand from between Elke's legs and cuddled her. The young woman clung to her. They stood together in a state of limbo that was in complete contrast to the frantic animation they had seconds before been in the grip of.

Tinisha spoke, her voice consoling. 'I'm sorry, Elke. You're so lovely, but we can stop now.'

Shaking her head, an ambiguous movement that puzzled Tinisha, the girl said, 'It's just that I feel funny now.'

There hadn't been a clap of thunder for a long time. It had stopped raining, so they could leave the shelter of the little house. Tinisha kept a protective arm round the girl's slender waist.

'There will be other times,' she predicted.

'Oh, I know,' Elke replied. 'Sometimes the best spice is anticipation.' Tinisha looked at Elke in surprise, but the girl's blushing visage had to be proof of her innocence. Certain proof – Right?

Kerry's small bedroom doubled as a haven and a prison, depending on her mood. The room seemed crowded, like her mind. No conniving politician would chance the kind of U-turn that her mother had made. Returning from her climb of Trimenen Head, Kerry had expected a tirade from her mother, banning her from the bungalow, and putting Tinisha forever off limits.

Instead, she had been urged not to lose her job, and promised full support with whatever her future relationship with Tinisha Weaver might be. In these permissive times, a lesbian affair was hardly a scandal but, despite her encouragement for Kerry to get a job, Marje Tredogan lived back in the 1950s, when only a drunk said the word 'fuck' in public. So it was a bit of a surprise.

Kerry tried weighing up the implications of her mother's relaxed, carefree manner. The older woman had a self-confidence that amazed Kerry. With the Simon Gregory prospects at an end, Kerry's father had reverted to his habitual, drunken waster's ways. This should have driven Marje Tredogan to despair. That it hadn't done so made Kerry's mind race like a laboratory rat on a treadmill.

Sighing heavily, she searched the top drawer of her dresser. Her bedroom furniture was MFI, put together haphazardly by her mother. One day, her father was going to finish it all properly.

One day! She took out a pen and writing paper. Tonight, she felt in need of comfort and some kind of guarantee of security. The latter could only come from Guy Zennor, the man she had made love with that afternoon.

That was an exaggeration on her part. The truth was that he had made love while she had merely submitted. He had been charming. He had made it obvious that he didn't see her as an easy lay. He had affectionately, lovingly, called her 'My little-little girl'. After what she had been through recently, Guy seemed like the answer to all of her woes. Kerry had no doubts that he would leave his wife for her. Guy Zennor was her future. A future that included eventual marriage and stability. But it would still be a charade. On the way home, she had found herself comparing sex with Guy to the fantastic love-making she had known with Tinisha. Guy had come out of the comparison as a very, very poor second.

As if reading her thoughts, Guy had been in a taciturn mood on the drive back to the village. She had made two or three attempts at casual conversation, only to have them self-destruct on the launch-pad. He had stopped the car outside of the boatyard that had a spicy smell of sea-soaked ropes that Kerry found to be addictive. This was at the end of the terraced houses where she lived. It had been dark, with the moon hiding somewhere and the sun having gone to start a new day in the southern hemisphere. They had sat for a while, enjoying the peace and quiet. Kerry wondered if he was expecting to be asked in for coffee, but that was a silly thought. She had noticed that he was looking at her intently, as though he had never seen her before. When she had turned to him and smiled, it hadn't changed his expression.

But then he had kissed her.

He had been gentle, caring, but Kerry had found herself fantasising during the kiss, not only of Tinisha but others, including Valerie, and a woman who had stirred her of late – Geraldine Dumphy. Guy had got the message in her response to his kiss. He had held her tightly, painfully, his mouth becoming aggressively demanding.

Although it had been involuntary, Kerry had since regretted her coldness. It had jeopardised her chances of having him take her away from the village. Though frightened that they would be seen this close to home, she had leaned over in the car to kiss him with as much passion as she could muster. Relieved that the kiss appeared to have won him over, Kerry had looked around to see if anyone had been watching. It would be ironic if a family row ruined her fresh chance.

There had been no one in sight, but Guy had picked up on her nervousness. He had given her a kind smile. 'You'd better go.'

Guy had kissed her hand gallantly as she got out of the car. 'Goodnight, Kerry.' He had driven away. Kerry had touched her lips. They felt slightly bruised and swollen from his kisses.

She would write him a lengthy letter now. By going back to work for Tinisha, she could keep the holiday cottage under surveillance and deliver the letter when it was safe to do so. It would be great to watch his face as he read how madly and deeply in love with him she was. She would be lying, but Kerry consoled herself that it was a white lie. It was possible that she would come to love him when she was away from here. Whatever, she was determined that Guy Zennor would be taking her with him when he returned to London.

There would be upset and tears. Thinking about Valerie and the children made Kerry thoroughly ashamed of herself. Yet it eased her conscience when she realised that, by now, Valerie would have assuredly cheated on Guy with Tinisha. Two wrongs didn't make a right, but Valerie's infidelity somehow turned Kerry's love-making with her husband into a conquest.

If Kerry needed proof that Guy was madly in love with her, then she only had to remember how crazy he had been for her body up on the clifftop. But it hadn't been enough for her. Kerry wanted to be with Guy socially, to dance with him, laugh with him, for them to talk together without end. She wanted him to take her to lots of places. All of the places where she had never been. Places a woman couldn't take her to. At least, she didn't think so.

Writing the letter was no problem until she'd penned the words 'My darling Guy'. That's when the letter had lost its feel of simplicity. But it had had to be written. Kerry needed to get away from the village, away from this house. The Tredogans were on the slippery slope back into poverty. The break with Simon had been a turning point as well as an anti-climax. She could no longer endure her father's drunkenness, her mother's depression and self-degradation. She regarded her mother's present euphoria as a bad sign. It had to be evidence of mood swings that would see her spiral into mental illness.

Leaving her family would prove to be upsetting, but Kerry knew that she could handle it. Saying goodbye to Tinisha would cause her real problems. Until the prospect of going away had arisen, Kerry had thought that her relationship with the artist was solely physical. But now she realised that the strength of her emotional bond with Tinisha exceeded that of their unspoken sexual contract.

What of Valerie? It was odds-on that Tinisha and she had slept together but, nevertheless, it was plain that she valued her marriage and loved her children. Kerry pushed the thoughts from her mind. Guy had made all the running with her. If it was a case of either Valerie or herself becoming second-best where Guy was concerned, then it had to be Valerie.

Feeling suddenly sad, Kerry experienced misgivings. She was afraid that she might finish up on the wrong end of her own plan. Determined that this wouldn't happen, she concentrated on composing her love letter to Guy Zennor. The letter was genuine – only the love was bogus.

NINE

Tinisha had been painting for an hour that morning. She was too restless to go on working much longer. Valerie's final sitting had been a portraiture success but a relationship disaster. The petite blonde had made it plain that her excursion into woman-to-woman sex was over. It had been an enjoyable adventure, but it most definitely wouldn't be repeated. In the small print of Valerie's conversation, Tinisha had read that her rejection of further sex sessions was due to a rebonding with her husband.

Kerry had proved to be another disappointment to Tinisha. She was here at work in the bungalow, but as withdrawn as a nun. Putting two and two together – Kerry's climbing expedition with Guy Zennor and the way the girl continually and covertly eyed the holiday cottage that morning – Tinisha deduced that Guy was at the root of both Valerie's and Kerry's refusal to have sex with her. All of this was unsettling. Tinisha discovered that experiencing many separate emotions at one time was taxing.

Emptying the contents of a small tub into a mortar, Tinisha eased some of her frustration by working energetically on it with a pestle. It made a crunching sound like walking on frozen snow. The pestle had ground the powder fine. As she stirred to check for any large particles, the red grains and the yellow grains blended into shades of orange. The resultant product glistened until she added linseed oil. Mixing it thoroughly, Tinisha watched the shades of orange become deeper as she gave it more oil.

There was not a sound from inside the bungalow where Kerry was at work. Tinisha found herself glad when a noisy motor-boat down in the bay replaced the endless silence on her patio. She watched, heard the motor die a spluttering death, saw the little craft drifting, and lost interest.

She opened a bottle of siccative and added a few drops to the mixture. After a final stir, Tinisha tipped the paint on to a glass palette. Depositing some lead white on the side of the palette, she used a knife to create some lighter shades of orange.

As she applied the mixture to the canvas, the stench was awful. Trying to ignore the smell, Tinisha worked quickly. Valerie's portrait was enhanced dramatically by a background of light and dark fields not controlled by the lighting on the lovely face itself. Leaning back from the waist up, she studied what was a composite of Valerie – the vague collection of a thousand facets that make up that abstract thing called personality.

Inwardly, she was greatly rewarded by the work of art. It depressed her a little to consider that when the Zennor holiday ended, she would lose both the sitter and the portrait. Losing the first would be far less traumatic than losing the second. Lovers were interchangeable, instantly forgettable. This was from choice, due to her determination not to be hurt. All relationships based on sex – and that included marriage – turned ugly when familiarity made the sex uninteresting. In contrast, there had always been a profound consanguinity between Tinisha and her paintings. When autumn came and her work went off packed in wooden crates, it was as poignant as losing the family she'd never had.

Changing from a palette knife to a wide brush, she added the finishing touches. The portrait was complete but Tinisha's discontentment still troubled her. She had a sisterly talk with herself. Her immediate relationships were suspended. Tinisha could not be satisfied with any halfway things. She prescribed a placebo for herself: a drive in the Volkswagen.

She took her car from the garage without telling Kerry. The morning had turned hazily opaque. The sun permeated the overcast from above, giving it a fluorescent quality. Tinisha drove unusually slowly, admiring the flower-gardens of the isolated cottages she passed. Both colour and music are abstracts produced by vibrations at certain frequencies. At her most sensitive times, Tinisha could hear colour and see music.

Summer had bleached lawns white like an old man's whiskers. Most of the drives had either a parked Landrover or a pick-up truck. The homes of insular country folk who were neighbours for life, strangers for ever.

Closer to the village the first aroma she detected was not the sea but the mingled perfumeries of sun-tan creams and lotions. It took her a while to creep-crawl through the backed-up traffic looking for parking places along the beach road. Sometimes, when she was among all these white folk, she missed her own people terribly. That was the only profound loneliness that ever afflicted Tinisha, and fortunately it was never of long duration.

Mothers and children, clutching rolled towels and beach balls, stood embarrassed and impatient as drivers argued with drivers. For several reasons, Tinisha preferred autumn and winter, when the air was brisk and people looked as if they had somewhere to go.

She drove on by untouched, leaving the inanities of life to the inane. At the end of the rutted road she rounded the corner where the summer influx of wine-soaked, whiskey-warped drifters sat drinking, sleeping, and urinating without moving.

Making a run past the Dumphys' garage and store, Tinisha hoped that she might see Elke. It would probably be better if she didn't so soon after the incident in the woods. This was a game that required a particular expertise. Tinisha would craftily chase Elke Fuller until Elke Fuller caught her. It was paradoxical, but that was the way these things went.

An estate car on the Dumphy premises was elusively familiar. Parked outside of the shop, there was a Capital Radio sticker across the rear window. Cars are like dogs; they begin to look like their owners after a while. This was Guy Zennor's Peugeot. Identifying it, Tinisha swung the VW in on to the forecourt without signalling. Horns blew behind her and some obscenities bounced around on the humid air.

She stopped her car beside two old-fashioned petrol pumps standing hunched like ogres. Terry Dumphy approached with his rolling walk. He wore a sweat-stained T-shirt and a yellowed Panama hat; his hands were in his pockets and his eyes down the dipping neckline of her white top. 'Gas?' he asked. Dumphy went in for Americanisms.

Fill her up, buddy, Tinisha said in her mind. 'I'll have ten quid's worth,' she said aloud, getting out of the car to face the shop. The sun was too bright now and the heat came up from the tarmac so that she could feel it through the soles of her shoes.

Just then, Guy Zennor came out of the shop, wearing white trainers, white socks, fawn trousers, and a white, silky open-necked shirt. His face had the absence of expression that wearing shades induced. Looking her way, he took off the sunglasses and the idiotic look went with them. He waved. She waved back. He was striding towards her, smiling with milk-white teeth. They said hello.

Tinisha sat sideways in the driver's seat, legs outside the car. Wearing a wrap skirt, she sat carelessly. It was obvious that he couldn't take his eyes from the darkness between her legs.

'Taking the day off?'

It was like he was addressing her cunt. Tinisha answered on its behalf. 'No, I can't afford to. I just felt like taking a drive.'

'I like the car,' he said, looking the Volkswagen over in the purse-lipped style of a tyrekicker who couldn't afford to buy it. 'Going anywhere special?'

'Not really.' She shrugged. 'Are you?'

'When you're married with kids you don't "go anywhere", you just run errands,' he replied, lifting a hand to show some sweets and other items he had purchased in the Dumphy shop.

'It's a pity you don't get any time to yourself,' Tinisha said. She meant it innocently, but she saw at once how interest had quickened in his eyes. Tinisha thought what fools men were. It was true that a cunt could draw them further than gunpowder could blow them.

'I didn't know you were interested in anything but your art.'

'You know what they say about all work and no play, Guy.' She smiled. She wasn't flirting, exactly, but she was mildly curious how far he would take it. Surely he wouldn't *really* cheat on his wife for what – even with a huge ego – could only be interpreted as the mildest of flirtations.

'Exactly, Tinisha. We haven't really got to know each other, and we've been here for some time. Are you around the shops this afternoon?'

The man was unbelievable. 'No, swimming first, and then I'm back at my bungalow.'

'Well, maybe I could pop by for a while. Say, three o'clock or so?'

Tinisha was dumbfounded. 'Sure, whatever,' she mumbled. All she needed now was Guy sniffing round for the rest of their holiday, when the person she really wanted to see was luscious Valerie. Well, his puppy-dog admiration was interesting, anyway, and she wondered how far he would stray when given the chance. It brought to her mind the psychology of self-deception. If there was one thing Tinisha hated, it was self-deception. Personally, Tinisha felt that she knew her own motives inside-out.

'I'll be there,' he promised with the grin of a lecher.

'Don't expect anything other than tea and biscuits,' Tinisha warned as he walked off to his car.

He turned his head to lie. 'I won't.'

Geraldine Dumphy sauntered over as Tinisha paid for her petrol. Looking with a puzzled frown at the departing Guy, she turned to Tinisha. 'It's not often we see you during a working day.'

'It's so hot. I'm thinking of taking a dip.'

As Guy had, Geraldine gazed at Tinisha's legs. Her eyes moved up boldly on to Tinisha's breasts. Then they came up fast, hard eyes, and hit Tinisha's like a fist.

'I've got a good mind to join you,' Geraldine said, a little breathlessly. 'We're not all that busy, so Elke can hold the fort. Can you wait while I get my costume?'

'There's no need for costumes where I go,' Tinisha answered. 'I'm off out to Gallivan Rocks. It's always deserted out there.'

Eyes flicking over to where her husband was removing a wheel from a car, a dubious Geraldine made up her mind. There was a slight thickening of her voice as she opened the door of Tinisha's car and got in, saying, 'You've got yourself company, Tinisha.'

Swinging her legs into the car, Tinisha smiled a welcome. And she promptly forgot about the 'tryst' with Guy. The promise of sex had a way of doing that. 'Glad to have you aboard, Gezz.'

Despite a show of confidence, she was unnerved. Geraldine and herself had long had a tacit understanding of each other. They knew the strength of the old maxim that it takes one to know one. Both of them were aware that their relationship would have changed drastically by the time they returned from swimming together in the nude.

The sexual implications of what they were about to do didn't worry Tinisha as such. What did make her anxious was the fact that Geraldine was a little older than her, and also a woman of the world. She had known a more gracious age. A time before the anti-hero and the singer who couldn't hold a note and the non-musician and non-love sex and epileptic-fit dancing and non-trauma counselling. A relationship with someone of her generation would be a novel experience for Tinisha.

Inexplicably, Marje Tredogan didn't figure in this equation. Tinisha surmised it had something to do with intellect. Geraldine had been around more than Marje, and as a consequence was much sharper.

When the first set of traffic lights held them up, Geraldine showed that she was equally as nervous by talking too fast, coming close to gabbling.

'Is that chap you were talking to staying in the holiday cottage up near you?'

'Yes.' Tinisha nodded, moving her car away as the lights changed to green. 'Why do you ask?'

'He came on to me in the shop. He's quite a hunk. Don't tell me that you haven't noticed, Tinisha. You were giving him quite a leg show when I came along.'

'Not on purpose,' Tinisha said. 'Anyway, I wouldn't have thought that you were interested.'

'Vaguely.' Geraldine made a gesture of indecision with her hand.

'I'm still a bit "bi", and suppose that I always will be. It's not enough to bother me, mind.'

Geraldine's confessed ability to go both ways didn't bother Tinisha either. What she felt for Valerie and Kerry had to be a first cousin to love. Her interest in Geraldine was transient – the chance of sex without either commitment or regret.

They left the car on a flat stretch at the deserted end of the cove. As they climbed over the rocks, Tinisha noticed that the sounds of people far off on the beach faded away. Even the surge of the sea licking the rocks seemed muted. The world was a vacuum, with Geraldine and herself the only two in it. Tinisha had known this sort of atmosphere before. There was an eeriness to it, yet it was ideal for a lovers' tryst. They had sea and sand and sunshine. The rest was up to them.

This wasn't her first time skinny-dipping, but there was an excitement in Geraldine that said she'd never done it before. Tinisha was conscious of her own exhibitionist tendencies rising up to excite her.

Admittedly it was a biased opinion, but Tinisha was gorgeous. She was tall and with a full figure, a full figure that had barred the way to her first choice of career, as a model. The photographers in the fashion business hated big tits and the meaty swell of an arse. They didn't want womanly figures, but preferred their models to be skinny and flat, like boys. She was confident that Geraldine would desire her just as she was.

Standing on a large, flat, slightly sloping rock, she didn't keep Geraldine waiting by doing a striptease. Whipping her clothes off quickly, she surreptitiously posed naked for her. Tinisha treated Geraldine to a full view of splendid skin and flesh tones. She turned so to make the best of her firm, full breasts and her shapely buttocks. She thrust her hips forwards a little to emphasise the jet-black and curly triangle of hair at the arch of her pouting pubis.

With a lascivious smile on her face, her fair hair tousled from when she had pulled her T-shirt off over her head, fast breathing affected Geraldine's voice as she said, 'Tinisha! You are really something else!'

'I return the compliment,' Tinisha responded as Geraldine

removed her white bra to bare a massive pair of breasts that barely dropped a fraction of an inch as they were set free.

They were beautiful, crowned with nipples that were a darkish shade of pink. Geraldine had a flat stomach, and long sturdy thighs. Her hips were full and round, and when she eased her lace panties down, her fair pubic hair was not profuse: but the fact that it was straight rather than curly meant the length of it gave an illusion of abundance.

Immediately wanting Geraldine, Tinisha reached out for her with both hands. But a smiling Geraldine avoided her. Leaping from rock to rock, as nimble as a gazelle, she gained a high point and dived into the sea. Sure of her footing, lithe and well balanced, Tinisha followed her. Hearing the splash as she entered the water, a tantalising Geraldine swam away fast, gliding smoothly through the water. Tinisha took up pursuit, but Geraldine continued her teasing game by never allowing her to get within touching distance. Geraldine's athletic body moved with the effortless contortions of an eel. Each time it seemed that Tinisha was about to get hold of her, she was away again, hardly causing a ripple in the water.

Pleasantly cooled by the sea, Tinisha slowed her pace, permitting the distance between them to increase. She saw Geraldine make her way back to the rocks, fast. By the time Tinisha followed, gripping the flat rock and nimbly pulling herself out of the water, Geraldine was lying on her back with the strong sun already drying her body. She was deliberately making the best of herself. As she breathed in deeply, the uplift of Geraldine's ribs put her breasts temptingly on display.

It was too much for Tinisha, who was standing pushing her wet hair back with both hands as she looked down at Geraldine.

Lowering herself to her knees, she bent over to press her lips against the soft skin of Geraldine's left breast. Moving her head slightly, she took the rigidly erect nipple into her mouth. Cushioning her teeth with her lips, Tinisha lightly bit and teased at the nipple. Top lip moving back from her long white teeth, marking her arousal, Geraldine put her hand between Tinisha's thighs. Palm upwards, she bent the thumb so that the knuckle was in the slit and pressing against the clitoris, Geraldine found and entered Tinisha's anus with her long middle finger.

They stayed in that position, working each other up into a state of ecstasy, for some minutes. It was Geraldine who ended it, suddenly and semi-violently, by pushing Tinisha away from her. Undaunted, Tinisha straddled the white woman high, her knees under Geraldine's armpits.

Placing her hands on Tinisha's thighs, Geraldine put out a pink tongue with which she parted the black pubic hair. The tongue had entered the slit, causing Tinisha to give a shudder of delight, when Geraldine again broke off contact. Easing Tinisha up off her, Geraldine sat up.

'Someone might see us,' she said, her eyes made heavy lidded by sexual arousal, but an expression of worry on her face.

'There's no one within miles.'

Looking at the distant cliffs to their right, Geraldine was cautious. 'There could well be somebody up there with a telescope or binoculars.'

'Fuck them!'

'You may not be worried, Tinisha, but I'm a married woman with a reputation to protect.'

Recognising both the hypocrisy and the logic of this, a disappointed Tinisha knelt without saying a word as Geraldine stood between her and the sun, getting into her clothes. Bounding from the flat rock, Tinisha landed lightly on her feet. Bending to pick up her clothing, she swiftly dressed. Now there was distance between her and Geraldine, the urgency of her desire had eased. Nevertheless, she still felt the pain of unfulfilled sexual arousal. Maybe she should give Valerie a call. Or Kerry. Maybe both. She had an irritating feeling that there was something she ought to recall, but for the life of her she couldn't remember what. It made her grumpy when her usually razor-sharp mind let her down. Ah well, it was nothing a little sex wouldn't cure. She'd give Valerie a call as soon as she had a chance. Fuck, but she was horny.

Geraldine spoke, then, showing that she, too, was suffering. 'This is only a postponement, Tinisha. I need you really badly.'

Nodding, Tinisha agreed. 'The sooner the better.'

★

Daylight makes things different. Valerie Zennor's bad dream had loomed monstrous and misshapen in the night. But the cold steel of dread it had put in her had melted away before breakfast. Everything was too familiar for it to survive – the children's laughter, her mother-in-law's bossiness, and Guy's good-morning kiss. In the dream she had become separated from Guy in a sultry rain forest. Battered by the slashing rain and winds of a tropical storm, she had called his name over and over again. She still hadn't found him when fear had awakened her. There was a vestige of that terrible sense of loss in her mind now. Could it have been a prophetic dream? Though it felt as if she and Guy were close again, it worried her that he had not yet returned to the cottage. She was probably worrying unnecessarily. Having found something wrong with the car, he had gone into the village to get it fixed before driving them all to the nearest town to do shopping. With it being such a small village, Guy had probably had to go to the town for spares. When she thought of it that way, he wasn't really all that late.

Valerie had to admit to being a little impatient. She was really looking forward to the shopping trip. Top on her list – though she hadn't written it down because it had to stay a secret – was a present for Guy. As it was to mark their coming back together, it had to be something special. Though she had a few ideas, Valerie had not decided on anything yet.

She had quickly got used to Tinisha's style of life, in a way, though not in the way she thought. But how could a woman even contemplate living without a man? That made it easier to break away. It was odd to think of comparing anyone with Guy. She had been his wife for many long years. He was the dearest thing she had ever known. Until lately.

She glanced at her watch, then at the glass that held the watery grave of her forgotten drink. She leaned on the windowsill to look out. The children were playing happily while their grandmother dozed in a deckchair. Valerie intended to get a gift of some kind for each of the children, too. They wouldn't know why they were being treated, but Valerie would. Buying them a present would serve to appease her conscience, even if only fractionally.

Valerie had distanced herself from Tinisha, but hadn't been able to free herself from the wisps and torrents of erotic thought. How long would this haunting, this plaguing, go on? Last evening while preparing supper for her family, Kerry had come into her mind. Losing control of her imagination, she had found herself watching mental images of Tinisha and the girl deep-kissing. She had seen them making love the way Tinisha and herself had made love. Highly aroused, she had wanted sex with each of them separately. Then she had been overwhelmed by an urge to have sex with both of them together.

Once in the bedroom last night she had given herself to her husband, not as a wife but as a charlatan. While she was in Guy's arms, an hallucination had changed him into Tinisha. The black woman had strapped on the huge rubber dildo she had promised to use on Valerie. To Valerie's chagrin, she'd had an immediate, mind-shattering orgasm. Guy had proudly claimed her response as his doing. Valerie couldn't disillusion him. Valerie hadn't wanted to disillusion him.

Sanity had at last returned to her when she had hit the high spots of her orgasm. She had reverted to being herself then, and hadn't suffered even the tiniest of relapses since.

Thinking that she heard a car approaching, she went to the far window. Hoping that it was Guy returning, her spirits slumped when she saw the road twisting away down from the cottage was deserted. Yet another mindshift disturbed her. From the moment they had arrived, all the Zennors had been in agreement on the loveliness of the area. But suddenly the environment seemed squalid and she felt enormous physical sensations of pride that this was not her home. She was living here by accidental choice and only for a short time.

The telephone rang, startling her. It had to be Guy explaining why he was late. She hurried to pick up the receiver, so confident it was her husband that she just said, 'Hello.'

'Valerie. Oh, I'm glad that I found you in.'

It was Tinisha. Valerie found that her palms had begun to sweat. The hand holding the telephone was in danger of becoming stuck to it. Though unsure of what to say, she tried to speak. But her vocal chords were paralysed.

'Hello? Are you still there, Val?'

135

The familiarity in the shortening of her name caused Valerie a fleeting dizziness. Feeling foolish, she fought for and found her voice. 'Yes. What is it, Tinisha?'

'I've finished your portrait, but that's not why I rang. I wouldn't disturb you if it wasn't important, Val. I wonder if you could pop up to the bungalow. I'd really like to see you.' Tinisha's voice had become enticingly seductive.

'I can't really,' Valerie faltered, looking at her wristwatch. It was fifteen minutes to three. Guy should be back soon.

'I bet you'd like to see me, too.'

Hearing children's voices raised outside; the voices of her children, Valerie found courage. She felt controlled enough in her emotions to handle the situation. 'I've told you that I don't want us to be anything other than friends, Tinisha, so there wouldn't seem any point in me visiting you.'

'Oh, Valerie,' Tinisha said with what sounded like an apologetic, perhaps even sympathetic, little laugh. 'I'll invite Kerry as well. Maybe. Safety in numbers. What do you say?'

'Well,' Valerie, weakening, said doubtfully.

'Come up right away, Valerie.' Tinisha's voice was low and urgent.

Hearing a voice echoing in the room, Valerie knew that it had to be hers. She listened to it say, 'OK, I'll come up.' She already felt wet, but she told herself that that element of her relationship with Tinisha was over. So why did she feel so aroused?

'Great.' Tinisha sounded relieved – and excited. 'I'll give Kerry a ring right away.'

'I'll be up there soon,' Valerie said, then put down the receiver, her breath already coming quickly.

Her walk was measured, unhurried. In her school days Kerry had learned to pace herself in life. That was why she looked and felt fresh and cool even on the hottest days. And this day was oozing with wet heat. On finishing her work at the bungalow, that morning, she had left while Tinisha had still been absent. Kerry hadn't expected to be called back that day. She hadn't wanted to be called back.

After she had heard Tinisha's car drive away, that morning, she had seen Guy fiddling with his car at the side of the holiday cottage. Using the edge of the woods for cover, she had slipped down to the cottage. Watched by a jerkily suspicious squirrel, she had stayed behind the trunk of a giant oak for what must have ebeen three minutes, but had seemed like three hours to her. She had been just a few feet away from the unsuspecting Guy. For hours during a practically sleepless night she had rehearsed this moment. The time when she would pass Guy a letter, the words of which ran constantly through her brain and had become etched on her heart. She had put everything of herself, probably even her soul, down on paper for him. There was such an awesome finality, a frightening point of no return to giving him the letter, that she had been frozen immobile behind the tree.

But being that close to him, needing him to rescue her from the biggest crisis in her life, had been impetus enough to get her moving. After a quick check that there was no one else around, Kerry had stepped out from behind the oak.

Guy's alarmed expression had swiftly changed to one of puzzlement. When she held out the letter, his hand came out automatically to take it. Kerry hadn't said a word, hadn't been able to say a word. Feeling infantile, idiotic, she had melted back into the woods.

In the letter she had asked him to meet her. Not knowing what he had planned with his family that day, Kerry had been accommodating. She had suggested that he meet her outside of Dumphys' garage at either five, six, or seven o'clock. She could even give Guy some leeway each side of the hour by having a cup of tea in the café. From there she could watch for him through the window.

Kerry had to get away from the village. Either things at home were worse than they ever were, or it seemed that way because they had for a short time been better. The bills were piling up again. Mostly they didn't get opened, now. Poverty has its own symbols. It shows in the way people walk, the state of their shoes, how their hair looks, and the kind of shopping they do.

When things were bad, it first registered in her mother. The glowing Marje Tredogan of the evening Simon had come to dinner was no longer. The mass of red hair was the same, but the woman had changed. Her eyes were older and more tired. Her generous mouth wasn't young. She held herself tighter, and she could no longer look Kerry straight in the eye.

It perturbed Kerry that she wasn't anxious about her mother, but she was irritated by her. Kerry blamed this on too many years spent in an unhappy home. Her mother's distress meant no more to her than hearing of the illness of a distant relative or a neighbour. Neither could Kerry feel untowardly guilty over her attitude. Her mother was despairing; her father was back to his old wastrel, argumentative ways. She found herself cutting off all conscious feeling for her parents. When she did think of them she thought of a woman dejected in life and a man rejected by life, troubled people drowning in a sea of problems – too far out to be saved.

Out of habit when leaving to walk to the bungalow, Kerry had pecked her mother on the cheek. As she'd started to step away, Marje's strong hands had embraced her, drawing her close. One hand had pounded on Kerry's back as her mother had wept, loudly and mournfully. Swaying her shoulders from side to side, she had spoken not a word, only wept.

Fearing contamination, of being afflicted by the disease that had her parents live together in what seemed to be a hatred never fully or properly expressed, Kerry had tried to break away. But, feeling her own abysmal lack of emotional balance, she had stayed until the storm of abject unhappiness had abated. When her mother's fingers were no longer digging into her, Kerry had freed herself and walked out of the house without a word.

Whatever Tinisha wanted now, she had promised that it wouldn't take long. From experience Kerry knew that she shouldn't take that assurance at face value. Tinisha was sweet, but Kerry wanted to keep her job and her sex-life at opposite ends of her consciousness.

It was reassuring to know that Valerie Zennor was also going to be at the bungalow. Or so Tinisha had said. Whether Valerie was there or not, Kerry was confident of being back at Dumphys' by five: the first of the times she had offered Guy. With some astute, unobtrusive questioning, she might even learn from Valerie just when Guy would be free.

Kerry was not fully deluded in all this. Sex was the foundation of her incipient relationship with Guy, and that never lasted for long between any man and woman. There was the complication of his wife and family, too. Yet if she could hold him with what she had between her legs, the way Tinisha controlled her with a throbbing wet cunt, then at least he would take her away from here. Though still with more than a touch of romance in mind, the mercenary side of Kerry regarded Guy Zennor as a ticket to London and a new life. You never knew what might happen. And it was a good thing most of the time that you didn't.

Seeing a figure climbing the slope to her left, Kerry's heart skipped a beat as she identified it as Valerie Zennor. It was time to stop thinking and start acting. A show of friendship was vital. Mind whirling, Kerry practised what she would say to Valerie. A sick-scared feeling came over Kerry turning her ice cold, like the sun had gone out.

Exaggeratedly wiping her forehead after her climb, Valerie stepped up on to the path. Her eyes met Kerry's. They were like a couple of boxers before the first bell had sounded. Though showing mutual respect, they both sensed that they could seriously damage each other.

Valerie hesitated.

Kerry could have sworn that Valerie's pupils were dilated in arousal: could even swear that she could smell the moist fresh scent of a juicy cunt. I must be imagining things, Kerry thought, as Valerie smiled and they both nodded silent hellos.

'How are you, Kerry?' she asked.

Kerry replied that she was fine, everything was just fine – but she was curiously nervous, apprehensive.

'Have you any idea what this is about?' Valerie asked.

'Not a clue. Tinisha was careful not to say.'

'She was the same with me,' Valerie said with a pensive little smile. 'I don't know Tinisha as well as you do, but she strikes me as being full of surprises.'

'She certainly is,' Kerry said flatly.

Letting that pass, Valerie said, 'I hope she's got plenty of that lemonade of hers. I'm dying for a long cool drink.'

They walked on together towards where the bungalow nestled in its idyllic surroundings. Kerry found herself thinking of the wolf in *Little Red Riding Hood*. The better to eat you with, she thought, and then blushed.

TEN

'Shouldn't we be in the bedroom?'

Shaking her head, Tinisha deliberately cursed her faulty memory. Typical that randy Guy would show up just when she'd finally arranged a possible threesome with Valerie and Kerri. And, far from being interested in his psychological behaviour, she now fervently wished him far and long away. Oh, well, she would flirt innocently, and give him to understand that he had completely misinterpreted her interest in him. Which was the absolute truth. She would try not to injure his masculine pride when she rebuffed him, but she had to admit that she was not exactly in the right frame of mind to assuage his ego. Not when Valerie and Kerry could be coming along in a couple of minutes.

Keeping her distance, detached from him by a total lack of desire, she thought Guy a pathetic creature. She watched him shuffling from foot to foot, in the grip of a myriad emotions, all obviously with their own elements of excitement. An immense feeling of pity for him rocked her. She found that she could pity him. The prospect of sex with an 'exotic' woman was reducing this man to something like a gibbering idiot. If he had a pedestal under him as a husband and father, he was about to kick it away. Now I know the answer to my question, anyway, thought Tinisha. The man has no resistance at all.

141

'Guy, I'm sorry, but I've got other plans. You're going to have to go.'

A noise broke from Guy's throat. Sounding like a word, although it wasn't, it had surprised him as much as it had Tinisha. He paused for a moment, head on one side, as if listening for more self-created noises. The way he was looking at her was degrading. It was degrading for both of them. There was a crudity to his lust, a baseness. Tinisha momentarily reflected on her own seduction routine. In their different ways, the pair of them were down to animal level. And not just them: come the revolution, they and just about everyone else in this crazy world were ready to slip back to apehood.

But it wasn't always coarse. On a night that Kerry had stayed over at the bungalow, they hadn't made love. Turning their backs on each other in bed, they had lain with soft buttocks against soft buttocks. That had been a highly erotic and profoundly spiritual experience.

Guy still hadn't spoken; he just looked her straight in the eyes.

'Guy, I'm serious. You really do have to leave.'

Then, to Tinisha's mortification and embarrassment, Guy brusquely grabbed her and kissed her. She could feel his cock hard against her body. She attempted to pull away, but his hands held her hips tightly. She braced her hands against the tabletop, gingerly succeeding in pulling away – though his hands were still placed lightly on her hips – when she heard the scream. It was a woman's scream, but she was unable to tell whether Valerie or Kerry had uttered it. It didn't matter. She felt him instantly release her and move away.

The cavalry had arrived. Right on time, just like in the old western movies. What a mess.

The sunshine in the room was dull. It was early-day sunshine shredded through venetian blinds. Marje Tredogan tried to relax in the clasp of the black plastic chair. She was pleased that she hadn't been made to wait in the front part of the bank. It had been busy out there, with people coming and going. There were some that she knew, but who didn't want to know her. Nothing scared folk more than a neighbour in trouble. Watching the tellers, Marje had wished that money could stop being money for her, as it had for them. To the bank employee, it was just something to be counted and sorted and balanced up in the books. She took the thought further. It would be nice to have the people who surrounded you each day stop being people, in the same way.

The money Tinisha Weaver had given her had settled some debts, but had done nothing more than delay the inevitable. These were desolate days – as desolate as the sunbaked leaves that had begun to fall, brown and dry and brittle, breaking under your feet like ancient, forgotten bones. There was a toxic, numbing dread in her body. It had seeped slowly into bone and tissues, making her feel terribly old. As much as possible, she had been avoiding going out in the day. She waited to slip out hurriedly, furtively, when all of the doors were closed, and all of the people back in their houses. It was said that money isn't everything. But those who had it appeared to be a lot happier than the mid-poor and the poor.

But a fragile hope had arrived with news that old Ned Grover was retiring and wanted to sell his fishing boat. Being bigger and better than the boat Jack Tredogan had gone into debt to buy as a young man, it would bring in more money than the Tredogan family had ever known. Marje knew that her husband could really make a go of his business if he bought Ned's boat. It was when the situation was hopeless that Jack Tredogan went off the rails. Give him an opportunity and he would work as good as, most probably better than, the next man.

But, as Marje and Jack had always known, it took money to make money. Buying the bigger boat was impossible.

It was Geraldine Dumphy who had suggested that Marje applied for a bank loan. She had stressed to Marje that buying the boat for Jack would mean the end of the Tredogan financial problems.

Geraldine, who had even made this appointment for Marje, had been very convincing. She had resuscitated Marje's ego and boosted her self-confidence, but the feel-good factor was draining away fast now that crunch-time had arrived.

It was good to be here in the back room. There was just a secretary, polite and pretty in one corner of the small room. An aroma of furniture polish blended delightfully with the smell of percolating coffee. The girl in the corner had brought Marje a cup

of coffee. She was a cute little bundle, too young for the engagement and wedding rings on her finger. She had uptilted breasts,
tousled hair, and pouting red lips that smiled at Marje as if she was
a much-valued customer.

The girl's polite, considerate attitude did nothing for Marje's
nervousness. Approaching a bank manager for a loan had her feel
diminished, ashamed. The bank hadn't gained much from her. She
had opened an account with a ten-pound win the second week
after the National Lottery had begun. Three modest withdrawals
just weeks later, and her balance had gone down to one pound.
That single pound was enough, Geraldine Dumphy had advised
her, to form a base on which a request for a loan could be made.

'You're not lowering yourself, not begging,' Geraldine had
stressed. 'Banks make their money by lending money. The manager
probably needs your business as much as you need his money.'

Accepting that as well-meant propaganda, Marje was crushingly
aware that she hadn't thought this through. She hadn't thought it
through at all. Bank managers weren't fools. This one would soon
spot her aura of destitution. Marje had to admit that if she were to
change places with the manager, she wouldn't advance money to
someone like herself. Yet she had to force herself to go through
with the application. The Tredogans were in a desperate state and
could only be saved by an advance from the bank.

Marje had taken a long time to select a dress from her wardrobe
of threadbare clothes. It had been a difficult choice. She wanted to
create an impression of cleanliness and orderliness while not appear-
ing to be too well-off.

She'd had it up to here with poverty and the belittling business
of wagging her tail. In a few minutes she would be bowing and
scraping to someone she had never met. A man in a good suit who
knew only affluence, and considered it the needy's fault that they
were poor.

Reggie needed new trousers for going back to school. Long
ones, now, which hiked up the price. She had gone into Matthew
Crane's place. The tailor's shop had been as soundless and musty-
smelling as a church. Crane had been as immaculate and sophisticated as ever. With the help of a time-slip, he could have been

Cary Grant's father. The thick lenses of his glasses had magnified his disapproval. Marje had put humility into her look.

'I know we have a bill,' she had begun, apology in her voice, begging in her eyes. 'But you have been awfully kind.'

He had smiled back unctuously. 'Perhaps if you could pay just a little off what you already owe?' he suggested, knowing that she couldn't. He had been demanding her subservience rather than payment. Taking out her account, he had teetered back and forth on his toes, thin lips pursed, playing judge and jury to her need. He knew that he had the power to get the money at some time. But he had been feeding his self-satisfaction on her begging. He had let Marje have the trousers, and she knew that he would be happily carrying his generosity home that night, while burdening herself with more poverty.

She found herself thinking of sex. Of late, sexual daydreams had diverted her from her misery. Sex was no longer a taboo subject since Tinisha Weaver had introduced her to its heady delights. She had been waiting for the artist to come back for more. Tinisha hadn't yet done so, but Marje still lived in hope. While waiting she had been relieving herself by hand.

Taking her break at her desk, the secretary sipped coffee, cup to her lips, smiling at Marje round the rim. Biting into a cream doughnut, her face flushing a little in embarrassment, the girl smiled again, self-consciously this time. There was cream on her lips.

Cream that Marje suddenly found that she wanted to lick off. It was the wrong cream, the wrong lips. Tinisha had come into Marje's mind again. She was longing for her touch, her kiss. This raunchy thinking made her feel guilty, of course, but it was a less harrowing guilt to that inflicted by the family's financial problems.

A murmur of voices came through the closed door that carried a MANAGER nameplate. Unable to hear what was being said, Marje could pick out cool, firmly official tones asking questions in cadence with excited, quavering answers.

Some other beggar had come in off the streets. It was the human equivalent of a slaughterhouse in which animals were harried through, rolling-eyed and frightened, not expecting the bludgeoning hammer that was supposed to dull their senses, but often increased the terror instead. Sometimes they struggled, fought and tried to escape, screaming out their fright.

The door opened and a small man came out. He had the devastated, lost look of one for whom the last chance, abject grovelling had failed.

'You may go in now, Mrs Tredogan.' The secretary smilingly pronounced what had the sound of a death sentence.

Standing on legs that were trying for independence, Marje soundlessly crossed the thick carpet. Her hand froze an inch or two from the door handle, as if to touch it would trigger off an explosion.

Conscious of the secretary's puzzled eyes on her, Marje took a huge, shuddering breath. Turning the handle, she went in through the door.

The grey sky was greasy with leftover night. Unable to sleep, Valerie Zennor had awoken early in a bedroom dimmed by drawn curtains. The cottage had had a muted feel, as if pressurised into quietness. It was too strange to be waking up there at that hour. For a moment she hadn't been able to think where she was. She had stirred and the movement brought it all back sharply.

Not wanting to get up and face all the hurt and bewilderment over again, she had forced herself out of bed. She had to get out of the cottage, to be on her own. While the long walk down to the sea might not produce a cure for what ailed her, it should clear her mind. Windows of houses stared blank-eyed at her. The village still slept with all its bare bones showing. She passed where other wives lived with their husbands. Homes that housed their own secrets and sorrows, their own frustrations and problems, boredoms and hatreds. All at once she felt too tired. She'd come all this way from the cottage, and now she wanted to go back. But to do so would be a mistake. More talk with Guy would solve nothing. What was hardest for Valerie was hiding from her children and mother-in-law that something was wrong.

Her mind was going like there was a video recorder in the back of it someplace, doing a rerun of yesterday afternoon. She saw Guy kissing Tinisha. A woman who was her lover. Did that make it better or worse? It certainly made maintaining her anger with Guy difficult, because she'd even had sex with Tinisha.

She went slowly out along the creaking wooden stage that had steps leading down to the beach. The light-fawn sand had black patches where shadows hid, waiting and wondering why she was there. At her back was a life that until recently had been uncomplicated. Boring perhaps, but safe and secure. Now all was different. She had been taken to the heights and plunged to the bottomless depths.

A rising sun was stitching thousands of twinkling sequins on to the surface of the sea. Valerie was crying. She didn't know that she was crying really, except in the corners of her mouth there was a salty taste that she kept licking at.

Guy had half-awakened in the night. His arm had gone round her. Out of a habit of long standing she had buried her face in his chest. As if everything was still all right between them, his hand had moved slowly to stroke her hair.

'Val,' he'd said. 'Val . . .'

'Oh, Guy,' she had whispered. 'What has happened to us? What will happen to us?'

Some kind of hurt had wrenched through him. His fingers had closed tightly, spasmodically tightly, in her hair. 'God!' he said, and it had been a terrible cry.

Her arms had gone around him, holding him – holding them and their marriage in an act of desperate loving. 'It's all right,' she had whispered.

'It's not!' He had pushed her from him, knuckling his fist against his forehead. 'God in Heaven!' he'd choked. 'What's happened to our marriage?'

That had been her opportunity. Valerie could have, should have, told him then that he'd done nothing to her that she hadn't previously done to him. Even less, really. Yet she couldn't say words that she didn't really believe. She had behaved badly with Tinisha, and she regretted it. All he had done was steal a kiss, really. She had been about to say that she loved him when he had moved further from her in the bed. There he had lain rigid in self-rejection.

Two fishermen appeared now on the beach as if from nowhere,

over by the rocks to Valerie's right. There were manhandling a rowing boat towards the water. Spotting her, one stood upright, shielding his eyes with both hands, puzzled as to who she was and why she was there so early in the morning.

Turning, Valerie walked back along the rotting wooden stage. A cold loneliness had descended upon her. In need of comfort, she considered going back to the cottage before the others were up and about. There she would offer Guy a peace pact. But it wouldn't work. It would be a farce that had no trace of comedy, a charade of necessity.

She would not get the human warmth she needed so badly from her husband. There was only one special person she could turn to for that. Her pace quickening, Valerie went back through the village. Finding a purpose had eased the tension from her, settled her mind.

Determined not to let anyone down, she would return to the cottage and cook breakfast for them all. When it was over, and the dishes washed and dried, she would take a walk up to the bungalow.

ELEVEN

M r Ganderton wasn't anything like any one of the hundred Dracula-like bank managers Marje had created in her mind over the past few days. He was a charming gentleman, portly, fleshy, and florid, with twinkling green eyes and a ready, cheerful, chesty laugh. He had a happy face, a bulbous nose, a huge paunch, and a bald head of pink skin. With a set of whiskers and a red suit he could have been a stand-in for Father Christmas.

Shaking her by the hand, ushering her into a seat on the opposite side of his desk, he had said something into a machine that she was in too much of a state to catch. Then, obviously waiting for something, he had leaned back in his tall swivel chair. Hands together in front of him, he made a steeple with his fingers and talked over it. He commented on what a pleasant morning it was. Marje agreed, although she couldn't remember what it had been like outside. The room seemed to be getting smaller, and she was finding breathing difficult. She shouldn't have come here. Mixing with the mighty was too traumatic.

The door opened and the secretary came in. Carrying a blue card folder, she still had a smile for Marje. Knowing that the folder contained her file, her dismal banking record, Marje was incapable of smiling back. When the girl had left and the door had closed behind her, Santa Claus in mufti opened the folder. Marje saw something change in his eyes, as if some inner light had gone out.

His lips formed a goldfish O below a brow that went into deep corrugation. Mr Ganderton remained silent. It was a silence pregnant with squalling dismay.

She knew the worst. How could she have been so foolish as to come to a place like this?

He looked up, and it was as if he was seeing her for the first time. Marje had been a person on entering his office, but now she was an extension of the unadmirable banking record on his desk.

'Your account is far from impressive, Mrs Tredogan,' he intoned as gravely as a judge imposing the death sentence. She had been found guilty of being poor: a heinous crime in a money-orientated society.

'I know. You see . . .'

Marje had begun to explain, but gave up. If he bothered to listen he wouldn't believe her.

Putting down the pen he had been holding, the bank manager pushed up from his chair. Perplexed, he paced, fingering the heavy gold chain hung across his waistcoat. Shaking his head, apparently in answer to a mental question he had asked himself, he went to the window. Standing for some time looking out, he spoke to the view outside rather than to her. 'You are asking for a considerable amount of money, Mrs Tredogan. You should present me with a credible business plan. As it is intended for an enterprise of your husband's, Mr Tredogan should ideally be here. If not in your place, then I would certainly expect him to accompany you.'

'Jack . . . Mr Tredogan is very much an outdoor man. He's good at his job, but he's not a person who can put things properly into words.'

Marje's spirits flagged. She'd blown it. If it meant having Jack come here to the manager's office, then he would have to have a drink first – Dutch courage – and that would be an end to it. A little dizzy from disappointment, she was ready to leave.

But he turned away from the window and back to face her with a smile strictly confined to his mouth. His eyes remained bleak.

'Normally in these circumstances, Mrs Tredogan, I would be forced to reject your application out of hand,' he said. 'But you are fortunate in having good friends.'

'I don't understand, Mr . . . er . . .'

Marje had forgotten his name, and he didn't rate her interesting enough to remind her of it. Picking up two letters, one in each hand, he swung his head slowly from one to the other before speaking again. 'Mrs Dumphy and Miss Weaver, both customers that the bank holds in high regard, have petitioned me on your behalf.'

Shaken by this, moved by it because the two women – who she couldn't really describe as friends – had put themselves out to support her. Ganderton was looking at her, waiting for her to speak, but she had no idea what to say. She managed to utter, 'I see . . .' but could not get her mouth to form any further words.

The manager glanced irritably at his watch, and took command of the drifting situation. 'As these two ladies speak so well of you, I am inclined to grant your application for a loan,' he said in the same self-satisfied tone Matthew Crane the tailor had used. Marje was encouraged by what he had said, but resented being used for a power-trip. 'What I must stress – and I can't emphasise this enough, Mrs Tredogan – is that neither Mrs Dumphy nor Miss Weaver have gone so far as to offer to act as guarantors. That means that the onus is on you. Should you default on payments, you will not only be letting down the bank and your two good friends, but you will be letting down yourself, very badly.'

'I understand that, Mr Ganderton.'

Marje could remember his name now that she was about to get his money. Not that it really was his money, although he acted as if it was.

He was speaking again, saying words that she had never expected to hear. 'I'll authorise the counter to advance you whatever you need in cash, and issue you with a cheque book for when Mr Tredogan and yourself are ready to purchase the boat.'

Returning home along the scorching pavements of streets heavy and lethargic in the heat, optimism had Marje feeling better than she had for years. She would go to see Geraldine Dumphy, to thank her, right away. Then she would seek out Tinisha Weaver. She was indebted to the two women for helping her secure the bank loan. She owed them everything. It wouldn't be overdramatic to say that she owed them her very life.

★

The Reverend Anthony Scollop had been gardening or, as he put it, 'Just having a little potter around,' when Tinisha had stopped her car outside the Vicarage. He went into the house before her, dropping his hat on the sideboard and wiping his forehead. His hair was thin on top and greying at the temples. His face had the parchment look and sharp lines not of age but of someone who had spent a lot of time under a tropical sun. His tan was the permanent kind that is kept through summer and winter.

They were in more of a den than a room. A well-filled bookcase took up one wall. There was a roll-top desk cluttered with papers, and an oak table that was equally overloaded. With a smile – he smiled so often that Tinisha didn't know whether they were warm smiles or a contrived I'm-a-nice-guy image – he used an arm to bulldoze a space for her on the table.

'Thank you.' Tinisha wondered why strange houses always smelled odd. She put the framed painting she'd been carrying on to the table.

'Oh, my giddy aunt!' Exclaiming at the sight of the painting, the vicar clapped his hands together like an applauding seal in a circus. Jumping back a couple of feet, he clapped his hands again, excitedly. 'Oh, my word! My word!'

A long time ago, just out of art school and struggling, Tinisha would have basked in this rapturous praise. The reflections thrown by the window on the painting enhanced it. Doing the colours justice, it gave the work a completeness she hadn't seen at the bungalow. It depicted the local bay but in another age. There were sailing ships at anchor; men in eighteenth-century clothes rowed boats ashore. Other sailors of a distant era carried kegs of whiskey up the beach on their shoulders.

'Oh, my word! This will sell some tickets,' Scollop enthused, with another girlish clap of his hands.

Every year Tinisha donated one of her paintings to be raffled at the church fête. They always raised a considerable amount of money. She was confident that this year would be even better. This painting was one that would be popular with locals and holidaymakers alike.

Ushering Tinisha into a comfortable chair, Scollop settled into a swivel chair in front of the desk. It squeaked harshly when he

hadn't known that Marje had lost her job. That single factor could well deter the bank manager.

The suggestion brought an unexpectedly animated reaction from Scollop. He wagged an encouraging forefinger at Tinisha. 'Now that could be fruitful. Despite her current difficulties, I regard Mrs Tredogan to be a very able woman.'

You can say that again, Vicar. Tinisha chuckled inside of her head. She felt foolish then, remembering how she'd been gripped by irrepressible giggles in church as a little girl. Her present covert behaviour was barely more adult than that. She was ashamed.

The Pop In café had been unusually busy that lunchtime. Normally the customers were folk wandering up from the beach to explore the village. The café did better on wet or windy days, but there hadn't been many of those lately. But just before noon today a coachload of trippers had arrived like an invading army. Elke and Geraldine had found themselves struggling with a long queue of people clamouring for different meals at the same time. There was the shop to see to, as well, but somehow they had coped. It was mid-afternoon now. Needing something cool, ice-cool and sooth-ing, Elke made herself a strawberry milkshake.

Not many of the hard red chairs were occupied now, giving Elke the opportunity to wipe the surfaces of blandly red tables. Two young guys in flowered shirts and knee-length shorts played the jukebox. They laughed a lot, touched each other often. A woman sat in one corner, agitatedly drawing on a cigarette, regularly smacking her two unruly children round the head between puffs. It looked as if she had a black eye. She was telling everyone prepared to listen, and those who didn't want to, what a selfish swine her husband was. 'He's in the bloody pub now, when he promised these dear little children he'd take them on the beach,' she squalled, wiping her nose on her bare arm. 'I'd like to kill the bastard!'

Running a cloth over a counter that was covered with some kind of everlasting synthetic that looked like wood but wasn't, Elke saw Marje Tredogan come in the door. Without a glance at Elke, the big, deep-bosomed, broad-hipped woman – wearing a smile that was a stranger on her normally worried face – crossed the tiled floor to where Geraldine was refilling a vending machine. Head close to Geraldine, the Tredogan woman looked as if she was relating a dirty joke, but Elke knew that wouldn't be so. Geraldine was attentive, plainly very interested, giving serious nods at well-judged intervals.

'Tea, please.'

Although she was keenly interested, Elke's attention was distracted by a customer. A white-haired professor type stood across the counter from her. He had a solemn spaniel-face.

'It's hot,' he commented in educated tones as Elke turned a handle and the stainless steel urn let out a Concorde-like roar.

'It is in here,' she agreed.

'You could do with air-conditioning.'

'There's lots of things I could do with,' Elke pointed out, sneaking a look at Geraldine and Marje. The two of them were still smilingly wrapped up in a happy discussion.

'I guess you're right,' spaniel-face agreed.

As he paid, took his tea and walked away from the table, Elke noticed Geraldine slant a look in her direction. They had become pretty close since Elke had been working here, their relationship more that of two friends rather than employer and employee. Several times, Elke had been on the point of telling Geraldine about her crush on Tinisha Weaver. On each occasion, something had stilled her tongue. Uncertain why she couldn't speak of the incident, Elke suspected it was because, despite being a little bewildered and scared at the time, the thought of being the one who was seducing Tinisha – rather than the other way around – was an exciting one. That was something she had difficulty in admitting to herself. She could never confess it to Geraldine.

Maybe soon, when the memory of their kiss and Tinisha's arousingly probing finger weren't so vivid, and didn't bring an immediate reaction between her legs, Elke would be able to confide in Geraldine. That way if her boss, who was as honest and straightforward as the day is long, asked questions, Elke wouldn't have to protect herself by giving lying answers.

She saw Geraldine impulsively grip Marje in a one-armed congratulatory hug. Smiling wildly, Marje Tredogan embraced Geraldine briefly in both her arms. It was a sight that alarmed Elke.

Though she was very fond of Geraldine, she just couldn't take to Terry Dumphy. Though something of a lecher, he hadn't bothered Elke in that way. Probably that was because she had never provided him with the opportunity. But he was a nastily jealous man who even begrudged his wife female companionship, unless it was under his control. If he should as much as glimpse this display of friendship, he would be very angry.

Elke saw spaniel-face grimace as he settled uncomfortably on one of the hard arse-hurting chairs. He voiced protest when the woman with the black eye slapped one of her kids again, knocking him off his feet. The woman told spaniel-face to 'Get fucked!' Disgust on his drooping, mournful face, the old man moved to a table further from her. His new seat had him closer to the jukebox. The two guys in flowered shirts put on another disk. They did some crazy psychedelic dancing, facing each other, smiling at each other. Looking even more disgusted, spaniel-face changed tables again.

With Geraldine leading the way, she and Marje went into the little storeroom where they kept the towels, toilet rolls, and the cleaning gear. Elke saw the door close behind them. The music ended and Elke could hear the clock behind her ticking. It sounded too loud.

'What ice-cream have you got?'

A man with a boy by the hand had come into the café and up to the counter. Elke reeled off the different flavours, taking a malicious delight in going too fast for the guy. The Marje Tredogan thing was bugging her. The simplest explanation was that Geraldine was going to give the woman a cleaning job. If so, it would be unnecessary employment, as Geraldine and herself had no problem getting the place clean before they opened each morning. Perhaps there was another, more interesting reason.

'Two cones – vanilla.' The guy with the kid took the easy way out.

Holding two empty cones up to the machine, Elke happened to glance out of the window at the garage. Terry Dumphy was coming out of the wooden shed that was his office. He had a large banknote in one hand and was pointing to the café as he made what looked like an arm-waving apology to a man standing beside a car. Elke knew the worst. Dumphy was heading her way to get change.

In a rush, she overflowed the cones. Pushing the messy ice creams towards the man, she snatched his money. Tossing the change on to the counter, she checked out where Dumphy was. He was halfway between the petrol pumps and the café. Under the angry glare of a disgruntled customer, Elke ran to the storeroom.

'Terry's heading this way for cha–' she began as she pulled the door open. Her words switched off, and she froze into immobility.

Both the women in the small room were unaware of her presence. Marje Tredogan had her back against the rack of linen shelves. Geraldine was holding her, astride one of Marje's thighs, working herself against it. They were kissing passionately, heads twisting this way and that to wring every ounce of pleasure from each other's mouths. The top of Marje's dress was open. Her left breast, a huge swell of naked flesh, was held in Geraldine's caressing right hand.

Stunned, Elke didn't know what to do. Who could have guessed that this little Cornish village was as much of a lesbian hotbed as the army? Her first inclination was to join in. Then she remembered Terry Dumphy, advancing in his rolling gait. Heading for what would have to be the biggest shock of his life. Elke couldn't abandon Geraldine.

Mind made up, Elke called in an insistent hiss, 'Geraldine! Terry's coming to the café for change.'

Jerking away from Marje, Geraldine turned an alarmed face to Elke. Marje still lay back against the shelves, eyes heavy-lidded, lips wetly parted. She seemed to be close to orgasm. Perhaps too close to stop. Geraldine, hair awry, scooped the big breast back inside of the dress. Marje, coming to panicky life, tried to do what Geraldine had already done for her, and the tit fell out again. They worked together to put it away, buttoning the dress. Geraldine called to Elke.

'For God's sake, Elke, stall him.'

Fast as Elke was in going back to the counter, Marje passed her. She hit the doorway at a run. About to enter, a startled Dumphy had to stand back to let her by.

'She must be on a promise from Jack,' Dumphy joked as he

reached the counter. He held out a banknote. 'Give me change for fifty, Elke.'

Opening the till, Elke found it difficult to concentrate. Everything that had just happened pushed up inside her. It had been too long since the woods. She brushed her hand over her short hair. The jukebox was playing again. The music was winding around her like grey ribbons of fog that blurred everything. There was a high note singing in her ears, and her hands felt stuck to the drawer of the till so that she couldn't move them.

'Hurry up, girl. I've a customer waiting,' Dumphy snapped at her.

Geraldine was coming calmly towards them. Elke almost collapsed in relief. Her boss had quickly tidied herself so that nothing about her, even her hair, was out of place. Elke gave Dumphy the change he wanted. He winked smilingly at Geraldine and hurried off.

There was a hitherto unknown awkwardness.

'I'm sorry, Elke,' Geraldine said contritely.

'You don't have to apologise to me, Geraldine,' Elke replied, using her employer's full name instead of the now customary 'Gezz'. She was unsure how to react to what she had witnessed. Should she admit how much it had turned her on? How she used to do exactly the same thing to her former commanding officer? It had left her unsure about everything.

'I suppose that I've shocked you?'

How could she truthfully reply to that? Elke didn't know, so she delayed her answer. She felt strange, distant. It was not like being drunk, but similar to how she'd felt when a group of her comrades in the army had persuaded her to have a drag of a spliff. She was so sexually aroused. But she wasn't about to admit that to Geraldine.

'Not shocked, not really.' Thrills rippled through Elke as Geraldine moved closer. She could feel the woman's body-heat, breathe in the natural perfume of her as Geraldine's fingers lightly held her chin, turning her head so that they were face to face. There was something in Geraldine's eyes that Elke found difficult to decode.

Geraldine said softly, 'You're just a little girl sometimes.'

Moved by an enlargement, an enhancement, an increase of the

feelings Tinisha Weaver had unleashed in her, Elke felt anything but a little girl. But that was something she was going to keep to herself for the time being.

As though from somewhere else, far away, Valerie heard the sounds of a shower. For a moment the surroundings, Tinisha's bungalow, had faded away. But now she got her mind back into gear. Calling to be told by Kerry that Tinisha had gone down to the village and wouldn't be long, Valerie had accepted an invitation to sit in the lounge and wait. She found that she liked being with Kerry. There was a serenity about the girl, a soothing tranquillity that Valerie welcomed.

Kerry had finished her work and had been about to take a shower. But Valerie was bursting to tell someone her troubles. The trouble shared, trouble halved proverb had much appeal for her that morning. Kerry, having been with Valerie when she had walked in on Guy and Tinisha, knew most of the story. She had proved to be a good listener, and had consoled Valerie when she'd said how her relationship with her husband was irreconcilable. She had nodded wisely when Valerie had explained that Guy and herself had agreed to put a bold front on it for the sake of their children. Though now poles apart, they were going to stay *together*, at least until they were back home in London.

The discussion had brought the two of them close. Valerie had been aware of an exacerbation of the physical attraction Kerry had held for her from the first time they had met, and she sensed that Kerry had noticed it, too. In addition, some kind of an asexual bond had formed between them in the short time they had sat together talking.

Hearing the shower turned off, Valerie was astonished to find herself hoping that Kerry would appear clad only in a robe. But the girl, hair wet, had put her striped dress back on. However, some kind of auto-erotica had stirred Kerry in the shower. Face unsmiling, she came to sit on the settee beside Valerie, slipping an arm around her shoulders.

Her body came to Valerie's, her hand cupped Valerie's chin, and her mouth opened on Valerie's mouth. She smelled of shower and perfume and body lotion.

Stirred by Kerry's velvet lips, Valerie responded passionately. They touched tongues, exciting each other. Kerry's hand came up to the back of Valerie's head, and she eased herself up over Valerie.

But Valerie found that her problems had more energy than her libido, right then. Taking her mouth away from a disappointed Kerry, she apologised. 'I'm sorry, Kerry. I like you, like you a lot. If I'm honest with myself, I've wanted you since the first time I saw you. But today, with what's happened with Guy and . . .'

'I understand,' Kerry assured her, then it was her turn to be apologetic as she said. 'I know this is selfish of me, Valerie, but I'm so worked up over you. Can I touch you?'

Nodding, Valerie's expression changed and she opened her legs. Kerry's hand went up between them sensuously. Valerie was wearing a skimpy pair of French knickers that offered Kerry no opposition. Her hand was on Valerie's mound, parting the soft and curling pubic hair. It was a one-way exercise that was marred by a distinct lack of response on the part of Valerie. Kerry's finger found the slot, the tip of it causing pain because Valerie was so dry. Jerking, uttering a little cry, Valerie settled down again as Kerry felt and caressed her.

The slit was greasing up. As her finger began to move easily along it, Kerry then entered the cunt that became increasingly wet, increasingly hot. The long finger slid inwards and upwards.

Valerie began to breathe heavily. Eyes half-closed, she begged, 'Kiss me again.'

This time, the kiss was shared and fired by passion. They writhed together, adding wetness and heat to the kiss as Kerry worked her finger in Valerie's cunt, and Valerie worked her cunt on Kerry's finger. Then they jerked apart, their mutual sexual excitement murdered by the sound of an approaching car. Tinisha Weaver was coming home.

Valerie and Kerry sat apart, tidying their hair, straightening their clothes. Valerie reached out a hand to Kerry, and whispered a promise. 'Some other time, Kerry.'

She knew, and she was aware that Kerry knew, that this promise was unlikely to be kept. No matter how much they wanted each other, they probably wouldn't ever find themselves alone together again.

Tinisha half-stood, half-sat on an awkwardly tall stool at the scarred counter. With a combination of direct viewing and use of a large mirror on the wall behind the counter, she had a constant, uninterrupted view of Elke as she served customers. The girl's black waitress's dress was form-fitting to magnificent perfection. A tiny white apron added a French-maid, porno movie touch that Tinisha appreciated.

Elke had been polite but cool and distant when Tinisha came in to order a coffee. In Tinisha's opinion, Elke's aloof manner was part of a protective strategy against any mention, or possible innuendo, about what had happened on that rain-soaked evening in the forest.

Tinisha had broken the thin layer of ice between them by inviting Elke up to the bungalow one evening. You used money to appeal to the greed in people, and flattery to entice their vanity. By hinting that Elke's looks were such that she should be painted, Tinisha had won the girl over.

It was true the artistic proportions of Elke's young body were magnificent: no sharp angles, nothing overdone or underdone. The beauty of her, the want of her, nearly made a cry of delight break from Tinisha's throat.

Coming alone behind the counter, Geraldine Dumphy gave Tinisha a heavy-lipped, white-toothed smile that covered remembrance of what had happened between them and what was still to come. Geraldine enquired cheekily, 'You slumming?'

'Just seeing how the other half lives,' Tinisha drawled laconically. She was watching Elke bend over, the tight dress clearly embossed by the outline of her bikini briefs.

'If I were Clement Freud . . .' Geraldine mused.

'You'd cook me a meal.'

'I was about to mention psychiatry.'

'Then you want Sigmund Freud,' Tinisha lazily advised.

Unabashed, Geraldine laughed, her merriment genuine. 'No matter how I try, my conversations are a balls-up. I learned some Latin phrases to impress, but I always use the wrong ones.'

'Whatever.' Tinisha shrugged. 'I'm ready to be psychoanalysed.'

The conversation was postponed while Geraldine served two elderly men who had come to the counter close to Tinisha. They were ugly and smelled of garlic and decay. Tinisha moved to the next stool, sliding her cup and saucer along the counter.

'I was going to comment,' Geraldine came back to say, 'that the way you are looking at my assistant says much about you.'

'Does it make you jealous?'

Geraldine shook her blonde hair. She spoke banteringly, asking, 'Of her or you?'

'You remember those lesbian separatist badges you used to see in the old days?' Tinisha smiled sweetly. 'They said, "I don't give a fuck".'

'And that's your answer to my question.' Geraldine laughed.

'Exactly.'

'I know something that would interest you,' Geraldine said teasingly.

'Marje?' Tinisha was unable to conceal her curiosity.

Geraldine nodded. 'She got her loan. She was really grateful when she came to see me. My old man would have caught us together, had it not been for Elke.'

'What, here in the café?' an incredulous Tinisha asked.

'Right here,' Geraldine grinned. 'Me and Marje, quite literally, came out of the cupboard. Like I said, she was very grateful.'

'I suppose she was. After all, we saved her from jumping off the Bristol Suspension Bridge, or wherever it is they leap from these days,' a detached Tinisha remarked. 'When are you going to see her again?'

'I didn't have a chance to fix anything up. She ran out of here like a fresh-fucked cat,' Geraldine replied. 'I was going to suggest to you that we make it a threesome.'

'Do you think Marje would go for that?'

'I'm sure that she will. I'd say she'd be ready right now, if you can spare the time, Tinisha?'

'Not at the moment I can't. You arrange something for tomorrow, or whatever,' Tinisha said as she eased herself down off the stool. 'I think I may have a visitor waiting for me up at the bungalow.'

'Someone a bit on the gorgeous side, I bet.'

Making a circle with a thumb and forefinger, Tinisha bestowed an elaborate kiss where they joined. 'The best!' she said fervently.

Jack Tredogan had a hard-on! Marge thought it so momentous an event that it should be marked on the calendar. He had come home that afternoon a bit earlier than usual, not quite so drunk as always. That hadn't been through choice, but because of their low financial state. Jack had been sober enough to rejoice at her good news, and to make a solemn promise that he would give up the drink and devote himself to the fishing business. He wasn't who Marje really wanted to make love to her, but he could give her sex. It would be a relief valve after the dramatic tensions of that day. She had sent him off up into the bedroom to await her. Marje wouldn't – she couldn't – keep him waiting for long. Relieved of the immense burden of money worries, she was ready for anything.

Taking her clothes off in the kitchen, she was stirred by hearing a football kicked against the wall at the back of the house. That would be the neighbour's boy who had masturbated in front of her. Naked, she caressed her breasts with both hands, teasing herself with the thought of what seeing her naked like this would do to young Adam Croad.

Reminding herself that she didn't have to make do with fantasy, because the real thing was there for her, she dabbed perfume behind both ears. As an afterthought, she scented her breasts with it. Then, after a pause, she hopefully prepared for the ultimate by applying a few drops of perfume to her stomach where the softer down of hair merged with the coarse bushing triangle of pubic hair. Satisfied that she was ready, Marje did a half-run up the stairs.

There were beer fumes on the landing but she resolved not to let that put her off. Jack had got himself naked, as she had asked him to do when he had been downstairs. The sight of him initially sent a tidal wave of sexual desire through her. But then she half-collapsed, falling back against the bedroom wall for support. Her husband was asleep. A mighty snore assaulted her ears; his prick, as limp as a bloodhound's ear, insulted her eyes.

Suddenly unable to hold back the tears, Marje staggered towards the bed. But, terribly distressed though she was, she couldn't bring herself to lie beside her pig of a husband. Falling to the floor on her knees, Marje wept in anger, in self-pity, but mostly in frustration.

Then anger boiled up in her like lava. At the back of the house, the thud of the football reached the volume of cannon-fire. Throwing her head back, Marje wanted to scream. She suffocated the scream with her hands because the neighbours would hear. She looked around to find a way to soothe her hurt. The mirror looked back, and she decided to regain her self-confidence with a reminder of how good her body was. It didn't work. Her reflection in the mirror mocked her nudity. The proud thrust of nipple had disappeared and her breasts seemed to be sagging as she knelt. The mirror was imprisoning her, ridiculing the way she looked, tears running down her face, her hair dishevelled, her face ashen and twisted.

She cried out the names of the only two people whom she thought loved her: 'Tinisha! Geraldine!'

Disturbed by her voice, Jack Tredogan stirred in his sleep. He moved a little, mumbled something, farted raspingly, and then recommenced his snoring. Leaving the bedroom in a shambling, staggering run, Marje went down the stairs. She felt old, drained and old, a thousand years old and so very tired. She sat down in the living room. It was unlit by the sun, the shadows huddled in the corners of the room, waiting. She sat stiff and straight, as cold as a Bedouin in a blizzard. Still naked and shivering, Marje went over to where she had dropped her clothes in joyous anticipation of sex. The anti-climax of it all hit her like a sledgehammer. Agonisingly frustrated and disappointed, she moved to stand in the window so that the boy with the football could see her.

She saw Adam Croad's eyes widen. She could both see and sense what the sight of her naked was doing to the boy. But her exhibitionism didn't have the effect on her that she had wanted. Feeling incredibly stupid, disgustingly dirty, she stepped away from the window.

Marje Tredogan started weeping again. Eventually she stopped crying and narrowed her eyes. Things were going to change around here.

TWELVE

Giving Valerie one last quick kiss, a loving rather than a sexual kiss, Kerry stood up from the settee. She knew that she had to get out of the bungalow at once. She heard the engine of the car switched off in the garage. If she didn't get out before Tinisha walked in, then she doubted that she could leave. Her lust for Tinisha Weaver had total control over her, and she could only break the invisible chains that held her by not being in her presence. Life devoid of sex with Tinisha would be despondently dull, but that was a price that Kerry knew she was most willing to pay.

First she must get out of this bungalow, and then she must escape from the village. The romantic dream of going away with Guy had smashed into smithereens so completely that Kerry could scarcely remember dreaming it. Kerry was in lust with Tinisha, but there was more to it than that. Kerry was uncomfortably aware that what she felt for Tinisha had to be close to real love.

That was what confused her right then. Kerry was uncertain as to why she felt a need to protect Valerie from Tinisha. Was it because she wanted either, or both, the women for herself? Though she quizzed herself over and over again, Kerry could not come up with an answer.

Concern for Valerie made her turn back in the doorway. Valerie was still seated on the settee, looking much more like a teenager than a married woman, a mother of two.

'She'll be here in a minute or two,' Kerry said in a low voice. 'Come with me now and we'll both avoid her.'

Looking at Kerry for a long moment, Valerie moaned miserably. 'I can't, Kerry! I just can't!'

Kerry followed the path along the side of the bungalow. The woods were quiet in the afternoon heat. The wildlife was taking a siesta. If only the birds would sing. Any sound would be a friendly thing.

She couldn't tell if she would make it to where the pathway forked down to the village before meeting Tinisha on her way in from the garage. Heart missing a beat and having difficulty in regaining its rhythm, Kerry saw Tinisha come round the corner and come towards her in her graceful walk. The rubber-soled shoes Tinisha wore were as soft and silent as feline paws. She was holding her head proudly; her hair was loose, falling down over her shoulders, the dark beauty of her face a compelling mesmerism. The white princess-line dress did wonders for a figure that didn't require any help. Tinisha looked confident but soft and yielding. Aware of Tinisha's strength and firmness, Kerry had long ago accepted that this was the root of her desirability.

Tinisha smiled, moving close to Kerry, breathing warmly on her as she spoke. 'Now aren't I the lucky one, having a lovely woman come to meet me?'

Smiling weakly, insincerely, Kerry couldn't stop herself from sucking in air to catch and savour Tinisha's sweet breath. Their bodies were already breast to breast, hips pushed forwards so that they were pelvis to pelvis. The special erotic scent of Tishina filled Kerry, and Kerry knew that she was lost. She avidly inhaled Tinisha's aroma. She wanted to taste her.

'Don't I get a kiss?' Tinisha murmured. Her eyes were slitted. She was an enchantress who dealt in love-magic.

Shamed by her own weakness, while at the same time aroused to fever pitch, Kerry ran a moistening tongue over her lips ready to give her mouth to Tinisha.

Pausing just before their lips made contact, Tinisha asked, 'Is Valerie here?'

Kerry, frustrated by being kept waiting, despite it being only for a split second, answered, 'Yes, in the house.'

'Good!' Tinisha said. 'Give me one of your long, lovely kisses, then all three of us will party.'

The two men somehow wrapped her living room around them. Marje felt intimidated and deprived of space. She was used to Mr Galton, who called as regular as clockwork in the afternoon once a week. In better times, she always had the book and weekly payment ready for him on the table. In recent weeks, she had made more excuses than payments. The fact that he had the other man with him told Marje that trouble was afoot.

'This is our Mr Bascombe, Mrs Tredogan.' Mr Galton introduced his older companion with a smiling display of ridiculously even and white plastic teeth.

Mr Bascombe was a tall, lean man with silky white hair luminously brushed. He wore black-rimmed spectacles and had eyes so pale that the pupils seemed non-existent. Though every inch a gentleman, charming and polite, he was to Marje the epitome of the nameless, faceless individuals who had harassed her down the years. He looked friendly, harmless.

Yet Marje was on her guard. People you owed money to only appeared to be friendly and harmless. When evolving, civilisation had been unable to leave the savagery of the jungle behind. It existed in the world of finance. She wasn't particularly worried about this visit, as she had enough money upstairs to appease their avarice. Marje couldn't really enjoy the feeling of not having to worry because she could pay these men. Years of avoidance or making excuses were etched on the memory too deeply to be shrugged off in hours or days.

'I hope that we can expect a payment this week, Mrs Tredogan,' Mr Galton said, airing his plastics in a smile that was poised to become a sneer.

'And a little something off the arrears,' Mr Bascombe prompted.

'Yes.' She nodded, facing them squarely. You could face anyone squarely when you had the strength of money behind you. Marje had already calculated what she could manage for Mr Galton the tallyman. 'I can pay you today. I'll pay whatever the arrears are, too.'

The two men exchanged the kind of snide looks of disbelief that belonged in a pub when someone is telling a tall story. Mr Galton went to open the book that he carried but Mr Bascombe took it from him. Toady Galton relinquished the ledger without a murmur of protest.

'I'm afraid it amounts to a little over sixty pounds, Mrs Tredogan,' Mr Bascombe said despairingly, like he was announcing the National Debt.

'Right. Give me a moment and I'll settle that.'

The shock on their faces gave Marje a reason for a secret smile as she hurried up the stairs. Paying someone who expected you to default damaged their sense of superiority.

Opening the drawer she reached in, filled with an immense satisfaction as her fingers contacted the packed feel of the plastic wallet full of money. Seventy pounds would get the two men downstairs off her case, while hardly making a dent in what the bank had advanced.

She felt dizzy with triumph as she went back down the stairs. The two men stood waiting, hiding smirks. Having judged her earlier willingness to pay as yet another way of stalling, they waited for some ingenuous excuse from her.

Savouring the moment, Marje permitted herself to smirk as she handed over the money to the astonished men. Though she had been born fifty years ago, Marje Tredogan felt at that very moment as if she had entered the world for the first time.

Kerry was proud of having turned down Tinisha's invite to join her with Valerie in a threesome. But there are degrees of self-discipline, and Kerry didn't have enough control over herself to turn away from what was going on, to leave the bungalow. Having to be content with a semi-victory over herself, she stood propped against a switched-off radiator as Tinisha sat herself on the settee beside Valerie. The heat returning from the village in her car now brought out perspiration to add a sheen to Tinisha's dark skin.

At first made tense by Tinisha being so close to her, Valerie then relaxed, shifting her position, drawing her legs up under her bottom on the settee. Tinisha stretched her left arm along the back of the settee behind Valerie, fingers touching her hair, toying with it. Kerry both envied and pitied Valerie as she saw her lean back to rest her neck in the palm of Tinisha's hand. The black woman was irresistible, and an honest Kerry admitted to herself that, in Valerie's situation, she would be wanting Tinisha every bit as much.

Never before having played gooseberry, Kerry cringed in embarrassment as she watched Tinisha use her hand to draw Valerie closer to her. Their faces were almost touching. Valerie's lips parted and Tinisha twisted her body to accommodate her. Their first kiss was long and passionate. Seeing the two women holding each other tightly, longing for both of them, Kerry felt a sexual stirring that began in her groin and spread hotly throughout her body. Tinisha's hand was on Valerie's upper back, her fingers busily undoing the buttons of Valerie's dress.

Knowing all along that this was Valerie's reason for coming to the bungalow, Kerry was still amazed. The elegant, ultra-respectable Valerie was as uninhibited as a total slut at a rave.

Twisting her slight, slender body, climbing into Tinisha's lap, Valerie was kissing her again. The shoulders of her dress were loose. They fell away, and the watching Kerry came close to choking as she caught her breath. Though not large, Valerie's naked breasts were excitingly vulnerable and beautiful in Tinisha's gently manipulating hands.

Guided by something intangible, something that didn't come from practice, Valerie shifted her body just enough to permit her to get her hand under Tinisha's white dress and up between her legs. As she suddenly jerked into animation, Tinisha's long hair sprayed out across her shoulders, hiding her face; she bent dominantly to Valerie's mouth.

Unable to see the kiss, Kerry was not thwarted because her imagination ran riot. Reaching up to push her own hair back from her forehead, she found that her hand was shaking.

After what seemed an eternity, Tinisha raised her head. With a jerk, she cast her hair back from her face. Cupping Valerie's face in both hands, she moved herself to adapt to Valerie's posture, allowing the blonde's hand access to the deeper regions between her thighs. Scarcely breathing, Kerry split her attention between

Valerie's hand lifting the white dress, and Valerie's face. Always getting a buzz from it herself, Kerry waited to see the lightning bolt of pleasure on Valerie's face on discovering that Tinisha was not wearing underclothes. Not even panties.

Far from disappointed, Kerry had to put her hand on herself outside her dress as she watched an electrified Valerie lift the white dress higher. It was hiked up enough for Kerry to see Valerie's hand at work between Tinisha's thighs. With a similar unaccountable expertise as she had shown before, Valerie quickly stimulated Tinisha so that the black woman's legs splayed wide open.

It was a marvellous sight. Blood racing through her veins and her mouth going dry, Kerry slid her own hand up between her thighs. Pulling the crotch of her panties aside, her fingers slid over cream-soaked hair. She found her target and parted swollen, drooping lips to slide in a finger.

When she looked again, the white dress was gone and Valerie was shrugging out of her dress, letting it tumble to the floor and stepping out of it. Then Tinisha took command. She rolled Valerie on to the floor. Both naked on the thick-pile blue carpet, they went at each other, ferocious as wrestling bears.

Eyes wide, Kerry was caught and held by the mind-blowing scene. With her breath tight in her chest, finger busy alternately with her clitoris and sliding in and out of her vagina, she had an overwhelming desire for something else. For something more. Yet she couldn't bring herself to join the naked bodies writhing together on the carpet.

Kerry had become aware of the deep and disturbing feelings toward Valerie. Sex played a prominent part in these feelings, but there were also other emotions mixed in. They were profound but delicate, so tender, so fragile that Tinisha could easily shatter them.

A desperate cry from Valerie jolted Kerry from her reverie. Disentangling herself, Tinisha was getting to her feet with a sinuous agility. Valerie's body was threshing from side to side. Lying on her back, she was jerking her pelvis up from the floor and letting herself drop back – thrusting, thrusting and thrusting.

'Don't leave me, Tinisha,' she called tearfully. 'Come back to me. I love you. I need you.'

Ignoring Valerie's appeals, Tinisha crossed to a small table.

Standing in sweat-shining nakedness, long black hair wild, pubic hair uncurled and made lank by vulva-juice, she opened a drawer and took out a vibrator. Long and sleek, silver and black, battery-powered, it had a hybrid magnificence. It had the incongruous appearance, more of an aura, of a cross between superb engineering and an oversized erect penis. The overall effect of the vibrator was one of fantastic erotica.

Standing with feet apart, Tinisha could have been an Amazon ready to spring on to a horse and ride into battle, or the perfect earth-woman about to engage in a sex session with an ancient god. Looking down at Valerie she slid her right hand through the strap of the vibrator. She switched it on and a little motor hummed enthusiastically. Running the tip of the instrument across the knuckles of her left hand, Tinisha gave a little smile of satisfaction and then lowered herself to the floor, close to Valerie.

She started with Valerie's breasts; the tip of the vibrator barely contacted the skin. But Tinisha was artful, skilful, gentle and very patient. The throbbing of the vibrator jiggled at the nipples of each of Valerie's breasts in turn. It went along her ribs and made small circles on her flat white stomach. Then it dipped in between Valerie's legs, circumnavigating the labia, ignoring the clitoris. It went down and under, touching and exciting the base of the spine. Then it moved a little to allow Tinisha's tantalising machine to move in.

Shivering and moaning, Valerie at last screamed, 'No more! Oh, Tinisha, no more!'

Unrelenting, Tinisha brought the vibrator up. Kerry gave a small cry of pleasure herself as she saw the rounded silver end of the vibrator part the thickened lips of Valerie's cunt, to move slowly up and down the slit. Tinisha had Valerie sobbing, rolling from side to side, trying to escape the ecstasy of the vibrator, while at the same time attempting to get even more sensation from it.

Expertly planning every move, accurately aware of each response she got from the threshing Valerie, Tinisha slid the vibrator gradually up until it met Valerie's clitoris, making her release a scream that rent the air. It could have been mistaken for the scream of someone being murdered, but in reality it was the frenzied cry of a fully aroused, highly sexed woman.

Wriggling her body as Tinisha continued to titillate her clitoris, Valerie half sat up; wrapping both arms around Tinisha's right thigh, she hugged it, kissing the skin, sucking at the skin, biting the skin.

'Come over here, Kerry,' Tinisha called. 'Kiss her while she comes. Hurry up!'

Seeing Valerie's slack lips slobbering at Tinisha's thigh, Kerry was sorely tempted. But though she knew how tremendously rewarding a kiss from Valerie in that state would be, she couldn't do it. Kerry wanted Valerie, but she wanted her for herself, not to share her. She didn't move, and Tinisha shouted at her.

'Come on, for fuck's sake! You'll be too late.'

There was no time. Even if she'd had a change of mind, Kerry wouldn't have made it. In different circumstances, Valerie would have been judged to be in the grip of insanity, the way she was behaving. Kerry had seen Tinisha in the throes of mighty orgasms, but never anything to equal this. For a moment she was filled with a fear for Valerie. It didn't seem possible that anyone in this state could ever return to normality.

But then it ended. Collapsing on to her back, Valerie lay inert. Taking the vibrator out from where she had been thrusting it vigorously up Valerie's cunt, Tinisha backed away. To the amazement of Kerry, a recovering Valerie rose up to move with Tinisha, as if there was an invisible tow-rope between them. As she reversed towards the settee, Tinisha slipped her hand from the strap and adjusted the vibrator between her buttocks. Holding it upright on the settee, she slowly and carefully lowered herself on it, feet on the floor, knees spread wide.

The purr of the motor muffled by her body, Tinisha, her wide-open cunt fully exposed, moaningly beseeched Kerry. 'Please, Kerry. I need you to finish me.'

Tinisha's cunt was wide open, her protruding clitoris as erect as a saluting soldier. Wanting to go to the imploring Tinisha, afraid to disobey her, Kerry found herself unable to move. In her first venture into voyeurism, she had already experienced a series of low-key orgasms. Now, battered by the gales of erotica that were sweeping the room, she could feel herself building up to a mighty climax. But unseen manacles and fetters held her.

She saw Valerie, her beautiful face contorted by lust into a loveliness that could only be paradoxically described as awesome, sink between Tinisha's knees. The noise of the vibrator motor escaped to buzz on the air when Tinisha moved slightly. But then the small sound was muffled as Tinisha pushed herself down harder on the vibrator. Mouth open wide, Valerie engulfed Tinisha's fully aroused, spunk-pumping cunt.

Valerie's hands were tight on Tinisha's dark thighs. Her tongue licked. Her lips sucked. She gobbled, bit, nibbled, slobbered and slavered. The watching Kerry thought how Valerie's jaws must be aching. But she wouldn't know. When you were engaged in this highly charged kind of sex personal discomfort, pain even, went unnoticed.

'Oh, oh, oh, oh, Valerie, you are wonderful!' Tinisha was moaning, her droopy-lidded eyes and the loose-lipped look on her face bringing Kerry to the cliff-edge of a climax.

Kerry both shared and wallowed in the pleasure of Tinisha and Valerie. She again tried to move. Her limbs gradually, too gradually, began to carry out her instructions. The kneeling Valerie's naked bottom was facing her. The buttocks were spread apart. Peeping invitingly at Kerry, Valerie's cute anus was puckered. The coarse hairs lining the bottom of the canyon formed by the parted cheeks of her bum glistened wetly. Everything, including the heavy-lipped, gaping cunt drooping below, was ripe for licking.

For Kerry, it was a heart-hammering, nerve-screeching, cunt-tingling, jiggling, vibrating, excruciating temptation that she couldn't resist. She just had to bury her face, her eager nose, her salivating mouth, between the cheeks of Valerie's bottom. Kerry's legs worked, weak and wobbling, but they worked. Pushing herself away from the radiator, she started across the room towards the settee.

She hadn't reached halfway when Tinisha and Valerie came simultaneously. It was a cataclysmic event that must have registered about eight on the Richter Scale.

Staying for a moment, slobbering and blubbering with her head between Tinisha's legs, Valerie then moved up. She and Tinisha held each other, sharing a slow, tender, post-sex kiss. It was a prolonged kiss.

Made to feel alone, isolated and mortified, Kerry ran out of the room, out of the bungalow.

Geraldine Dumphy let the estate car coast silently over the rough surface of the pull-in at the side of the country road. Elke braced herself in the front passenger seat. The suspension of the heavily loaded vehicle jolted over the ruts. The greenly smooth hills rolled and tumbled away on both sides. It was late afternoon, but still very hot. Geraldine wound down the driver's window. She smiled at Elke and Elke smiled back. There was little uncertainty in Elke, but she found it amusing to pretend this was the case. Things had moved too fast for her and in an unexpected direction.

Today was early closing day for the shop and Geraldine's afternoon for going to the cash and carry in town. There had been little trade in the café and, to Elke's surprise, Geraldine had closed it early and taken Elke to town with her. It had been fun. Geraldine had been great company, and Elke had seen another side of her. Having always thought of Geraldine as tarty-looking, in the nicest possible way, the attention the men at the cash and carry paid the older woman made Elke realise that Geraldine was stunningly attractive.

Elke also appreciated how Geraldine showed how much she relied on her, by asking her for suggestions on what to buy. Elke had greatly enjoyed herself, welcoming the change to humdrum routine. And now that they were stopping here was exciting, to say the least. This little ingenune role had its benefits. They had driven off the main road on to what was little more than a dirt track.

Then Geraldine eased Elke's worry by reaching into the back and breaking one can of Coca-cola free from a plastic-wrapped cardboard tray. 'Phew! It's hot!' she exclaimed. She pulled the ring and Elke heard the short, hissing escape of air. The single can puzzled her, as it wasn't like Geraldine, who was generous to a fault.

Elke stopped pursuing her unfounded worries. Even puzzling situations eventually explained themselves, just as this one was sure to.

Smiling at her again, from under her eyes this time, Geraldine rolled the can from side to side across her forehead. 'It's still icy cold from the fridge,' she said.

Elke nodded. When was she going to make a move?

Geraldine laughed. 'You think me a tight-fisted cow, don't you?'

'Of course I don't,' Elke said stoutly.

The two of them sat silently watching a hawk hovering up ahead, honing in on its prey. The bird waited patiently, needing only an occasional light flap of its wings to keep it airborne. Just when Elke was thinking it would never move, the bird did a swooping dive into the grass. Nature in the raw. A tasty tea for one creature, a painful death for another.

Elke considered that Geraldine was affected as much as herself by the little drama that had been played out before them. Though she tried to be tough with a sort of gangster's moll style, Geraldine was really a sensitive person.

She spoke now, holding up the can of drink. 'It's more fun sharing.'

Putting the can to her mouth, Geraldine tilted her head back to drink. Cheeks bulging, she reached out to put a hand behind Elke's head, bringing her forwards. Elke had never really been with older women. In the army she had always felt older, much more mature than the girls of her own age (with the single exception of her commanding officer). In contrast Geraldine, a fully-fledged woman, made Elke – especially in *different* situations, such as this – feel like a silly, gangling girl.

Now Geraldine was looking into Elke's eyes. It was a peculiar sensation for Elke, as if she were becoming a part of the older woman. Still bemused, she was conscious of Geraldine's lips against hers. Not realising for a moment what was happening, Elke then understood. Geraldine was feeding her Coca-cola, warmed after being inside her mouth. It was truly an awakening. After the clandestine army life, it was also a revelation for another woman to openly acknowledge lust. More than that, it was a physical revelation that brought into dynamic play centres deep inside of Elke. They were sexual centres that she hadn't known she possessed.

Sensing what Geraldine expected of her, Elke didn't swallow the drink. Washing it around in her mouth, with Geraldine's lips still against hers, she returned the Coca-cola to Geraldine.

They continued this, sometimes swallowing. On those occasions, Geraldine would replenish the drink. At last the can was empty. By that time, they were both at a high peak of sexual arousal. Kissing replaced the exchange of drink. Deep kissing that involved darting, probing, delicious tasting tongues. Elke thrilled at the feel of Geraldine's large hand clasping her breast. Emboldened by this move on the part of her employer, Elke didn't break off responding to hot kisses as she put her right hand tentatively on Geraldine's left breast. Geraldine fumbled hastily at her blouse. Elke's hand trembled as it felt the velvety skin and heat of a breast that had been bared for her. She teased Geraldine's nipple the way she played with her own breasts, exciting herself while in bed.

Then Elke suddenly went cold as Geraldine moved away from her, back into the driving seat. To Elke's immense disappointment, it was all over. Geraldine was cupping her own breast to put it back into the bra. Elke stopped Geraldine with a hesitant plea. 'Can I kiss it?'

Geraldine gave a short laugh that was made explosive by her high level of excitement. 'Listen to you, Elke. You're certainly coming out of your box.'

'I . . .' Elke began, blushing, feeling incredibly stupid. Maybe she should tell her the truth.

Leaning over, Geraldine kissed her lightly and quickly on the lips. 'That was crass of me, Elke. I didn't mean to embarrass you.' With her breast still bare, she offered it up. 'I'd like you to kiss it.'

Bending over, Elke kissed the breast and pressed her nose against the skin to inhale the scent of it. Then she started licking it all over before reaching the ultimate goal of the prominent nipple. As Elke flicked her tongue across that exquisite nipple, Geraldine let out a groan of pleasure and grabbed Elke's head with both her hands to keep Elke's mouth on it. Elke sucked and occasionally covered her teeth with her lips to give soft little bites. As she continued sucking, Geraldine's moans became choking sobs; then the older woman started squirming.

Taking one hand from where it had held Elke's head, Geraldine put it between her own knees, then moved it up under her skirt. It took a little while for Elke to realise that Geraldine was frantically feeling and fingering herself. The realisation brought an excited giddiness to Elke as she sucked at the big nipple. A little later, Geraldine's body shuddered and she released a small strangled cry.

Gently moving Elke's head away from her, Geraldine replaced the breast inside her bra and did up her blouse. She found it amazing that a sexually experienced woman could reach orgasm swiftly and simply.

Tidying herself, leaning to look in the rear-view mirror and pat her hair, Geraldine asked solicitously, 'Will you be all right, Elke? You know what I mean?'

'Yes, I'll be fine.'

'Good. There'll be other times,' Geraldine assured her. 'Plenty of them, now that we've got to know each other.'

It wasn't until Geraldine had driven them to rejoin the main road that the penny dropped for Elke. Geraldine had felt guilty because she had come and Elke hadn't. She had been enquiring if Elke wanted to be brought to orgasm before they left the isolated area. Realising this made Elke understand what she had got herself into. This wasn't like the fumbles of the army. This was really adult stuff. It frightened her in one way, and excited her in another.

Elke thought it provident that tomorrow was her day off from work. A period of time between Geraldine and herself meeting again would be mutually beneficial. Not only would it cushion any embarrassment caused by their intimacy; it would also afford Elke the chance to decide what to do.

She found it difficult to concentrate on her work. Alone now, Tinisha had brought the Ruby portrait out on to the patio, intending to add some enhancing touches. But she felt restless. Ridiculous though the thought was, she could feel animosity from the mystery woman in the portrait. That was probably due to some chemical imbalance in her brain. A growing sense of dissatisfaction had become a tight band across her temples. The sex with Valerie had been hot and satisfying at the time, but in retrospect there was a sameness to it that was boring. It would have been very different if Kerry had joined in. That would have been something novel.

That girl was becoming a problem. Kerry had turned into a sulky party-pooper. The time was fast approaching when Tinisha had to decide whether to give Kerry the sharp shock treatment to bring her back into the fold, or give her up as a lost cause. At the moment, the latter appealed to Tinisha, but judgement on these matters was always flawed in the wake of an expenditure of sexual energy.

Below her, the bay seemed to be fashioned out of a rainbow stolen from the sun. The phenomenon intrigued her. The colourful kaleidoscope fascinated her as an artist. Some of the rainbow had spread to the cliffs and the hills to act like flowers. It was a wondrous mirage, but an illusion nonetheless. This visual miracle could neither be captured by a brush on canvas nor stored in a human memory. As fleeting as it was rare, it was an experience not to be missed, but one that left you wanting to be more familiar with things spiritual. Maybe it was even some kind of an invitation from God. Half-past seven for eight, dress optional! If that was the case then Tinisha was neither ready nor worthy to accept it.

She looked again at the canvas propped on the easel before her. Were she an author, then she would be suffering from writer's block. Could it be that sex was channelling her talent along a different route? Beethoven could write wonderful music but he couldn't fuck. Perhaps that required rephrasing – Beethoven wrote wonderful music *because* he couldn't fuck. What if her talent, her ability to create, was dribbling away out of her cunt?

It would have to be a psychological rather than a physical thing, as both Kerry and Valerie had swallowed so much of her spunk that they each should be able to turn out a masterpiece that would wipe the smirk off the face of Mona Lisa.

Boredom was taking over, the way a migraine does. Suddenly holding great appeal for Tinisha was the idea of taking her boat out. The spluttering roar of the outboard motor would be preferable to the silent loneliness of her cottage. But she liked to swim when out in the bay, and it was late in the day now. The water would still be warm but, by the time she got back into the boat, the chill of evening would be uncomfortable. Tinisha postponed the notion until the morning. It would be something to look forward to. The sparkling blue sea would wash away her ennui.

She forced herself back to her painting. She started fussing with her paintbrushes. There was a stiffness to some of them, a warning that greater care was needed in cleaning them. Brush poised, she studied the painting on the easel. It was a lovely face marred by an indefinable hardness, an implied cruelty and a tacitly ugly selfishness. The eyes were compelling. They were bright, almost too bright. She stared into them, and they stared back. In the end, it was Tinisha who had to look away.

Rattled by this, she stood with her brush poised ready to add lines, to regain control of her own creation. Without consciously relaxing her grip, she dropped the brush. It clicked against the easel and danced on the patio before falling over sideways. Seized by a sudden anger, Tinisha picked up the brush and threw it into the bushes. Wiping paint off the flagstones, she whistled tunelessly.

Somewhere on high, a bird forgave her childish tantrum, picked up the tune joyfully and sang it back to her. Others echoed it all around, but lost Tinisha's melody on the counterpoint. After some faltering chirping, the birds returned to the familiarity of their own song.

Tinisha was really bothered by the portrait. It was an abstract as anonymous as the Unknown Soldier. Any artist, if he or she stared hard enough at a human face they had 'designed', should be capable of identifying the subject. She concentrated until her mind drifted like a fortune-teller's at a crystal ball. She experienced a mental exercise that was the equivalent of rubbing a hand over a corroded tombstone and seeing the name of the deceased gradually appear.

With a feeling of icy water running down her spine, Tinisha discovered the truth. What she was looking at was a self-portrait. But it was a self that had hitherto been hidden from the world. Tinisha Weaver had painted her own alter ego.

THIRTEEN

Was it possible to sometimes have thought-control over people? Tinisha Weaver was convinced that morning that it was. Not the common 'test' of staring at the back of someone's head until they turn to look at you, but control from a distance. Maybe it was a kind of unconscious arranging of situations in an unseen world that then occur in the material world. Any doubts she might have had were swept aside by a prescience that this day, the hottest day of the year, would hold wonders for her.

With vestiges of her bad mood of the previous evening still darkening her mind, Tinisha's thoughts had been on sex as she had driven down to her boat. But her thinking was in some undefinable way very different that morning. Coming face to face with her own dark side had been a traumatic experience. Not only had it shamed her with an insight of her true nature, but also it had painfully highlighted the way she had unconsciously mistreated others. *Know yourself* was the message of just about all the great thinkers. Tinisha Weaver vowed that she would really get to know herself, and be a better person for it.

Last night she had been close to despair when all of her conquests had done a parade of defeat through her mind. But help had come from somewhere inside herself. Celibacy had no place in her new order. There could be nothing sinful in sex between consenting people. It was possible that she had unknowingly used people in the past. The difference in future would be that she would *know* in advance that she was not taking advantage but was partaking in a shared pleasure.

An image of Geraldine Dumphy had tightened Tinisha's nipples and warmed her between the legs. The brassy but undeniably attractive Geraldine knew what she had it for, and would be capable of using it to best effect. This diversion had restored Tinisha's sex drive. And a vision, sharp-focused and perfect, of Elke Fuller brought Tinisha instantly back to what she enjoyed the most and what she was best at – teaching. The girl had been a little scared out in the woods, but not unresponsive. Whatever her heterosexual experiences, if she had any, Elke was a virgin by lesbian standards. The fact that Elke had pretended disgust at the soldier-girls who had attempted to get into her knickers made the seduction of her a challenge that Tinisha could not resist. But she would determine that her search for sexual gratification would be altruistic.

It was when she was running those hot thoughts through her mind that the mini-miracle happened. In front of her, heading for the beach with a rolled towel under her arm, was Elke Fuller. She had the walk of a person in touch with every inch of her body. That pleased Tinisha. A woman had to know how to pleasure herself before she could please anyone else. The girl was wearing a white lace top that came down just far enough to cover the blue bikini that showed through. Pulling her Volkswagen in close to the kerb beside the girl, Tinisha leaned across the passenger seat to wind down the window.

'Great minds think alike,' she called, holding up a towel. 'Hop in.'

A frowning Elke stood undecided.

The girl was as jumpy as a bird you tried to feed in the woods, wanting what you had to offer but afraid to close the final distance, Tinisha thought.

It was only some three hundred yards from here to the beach, which was closer than a walk from the car park would be. Obviously, the girl could see no logic in the lift that Tinisha was offering.

Elke looked confused. 'I'm only going down to the beach for a swim.'

'I'm going to the jetty,' Tinisha said enticingly. 'It's a great morning for taking the boat out for some real swimming in deep water. You're welcome to join me.'

It was an offer that Tishna figured Elke couldn't refuse. Getting into the car, she smelled sweet and clean. Now they were heading out across the bay in Tinisha's round-bottomed rowing boat. The inside glowed with new varnish and a short pair of oars was fastened to the gunwales. It had slat seats with leather cushions. The chrome outboard motor focused the sunlight blindingly. The noisy motor shook the boat, and speed raised the bow. But Tinisha handled the controls competently. They passed two fishermen who waved from their rowboat. A porpoise passed them, rolling round-backed, boasting to them of its prowess in the water. Otherwise, they had the bay pretty much to themselves. It was too early yet for the two pleasure boats that gave holidaymakers trips round the bay.

Putting her feet up on the seat in front of her, Tinisha's face was hot and she could feel her skin beginning to burn. Holding the tiller with one hand, she cooled her other hand by trailing it through the water. They were doing ten knots, and as yet there had not been the slightest splutter from the tiny carburettor. It had given Tinisha a lot of problems on other occasions.

Elke had taken off her top. She had a deep tan rarely seen on a fair-skinned person. Her long legs made her seem taller than she was. They were full, shapely legs, firm and strong-looking. She'd obviously been a little afraid when she'd stepped into the boat, and her jerky motions had made her flesh vibrate a little. It had turned Tinisha on to watch.

Still nervous at being in the boat, she seemed to be losing her fear of Tinisha. When Tinisha gave her a smile now, the corners of Elke's mouth twitched. With a little encouragement, Elke would become friendly. Some extra encouragement, and who knew?

'This is great.' The young woman suddenly smiled, leaning back, arching her breasts. 'I feel daring enough to skinny dip.'

Elke wasn't going to be really hard to get. She was either incredibly naïve or up for it. She guessed that Elke was a clever game-player. At poker, she would win every time. Whichever it was, Tinisha felt confident. She was benefiting now from the reunification that had taken place during the night between her and the other self she had painted. The portrait no longer disturbed her.

'Wait until we're a few miles further out,' Tinisha advised. 'The villagers have powerful binoculars, long tongues, and a lot of them drool excessively.'

'I'll wait.' Elke laughed.

Rapidly gaining confidence, she stretched her hands to the sides of the boat, rocking it back and forth. 'This is really something, Tinisha. Can't we go any faster?'

'We can, but if I rip the arse out of the motor we'll have to walk back.'

'We should have brought Reverend Scollop with us.' Elke laughed, the little etchings at the corners of her mouth dancing into an even pair of dimples.

'I doubt that he's reached the walking on water stage, Elke.'

'Probably not. Most of them seem to be a bit kinky.'

'You're quite a woman of the world.'

'I did serve in the army,' Elke reminded Tinisha.

'Where you hated the girls who tried to get into your bed,' Tinisha reminded Elke.

'Did I say that?'

Tinisha cut the motor. They were so far out that the shoreline was a just a smear on a very distant horizon. Out here the water was a darker blue. There was a slight swell that rocked the boat. Standing up, Elke spread her legs for balance. Her thighs twitched in an involuntary nervous rhythm.

'I've never swum in water this deep,' she said.

'The only difference you'll notice is that it's a bit colder,' Tinisha explained.

'Which can't be a bad thing on a day like this.' Elke grinned happily. 'I'm going in.'

'What about going naked?' Tinisha enquired jokingly, although she feared being disappointed.

Hesitating for a short while, head bowed, Elke then gave a positive nod as if having reached some kind of agreement with herself. Facing Tinisha, she reached behind herself and unclipped her bikini top. The areolae of her small but full, uptilted breasts glistened pink in the bright sunlight. Though never one to take anything for granted, Tinisha was more than half-convinced that this young girl was getting a kick out of stripping for her. There was the hint of a promise in the sea air.

Elke eased the bikini bottom down over her hips with an unnecessary wiggle. The narrow fuzz of pubic hair gleamed blonde. She grinned. 'Your mouth is open, Tinisha.'

Tinisha closed her mouth.

The boat rocked as Tinisha wriggled out of her one-piece costume.

Elke's eyes were hotter on her than the blazing sun. Tinisha grinned. 'Your mouth is open, Elke.'

A blushing Elke closed her mouth.

Elke poised on the gunwale of the boat, posing provocatively for a moment. It was a clean dive. There was scarcely a splash to trace. Tinisha began to worry when Elke failed to reappear. Holding the side of the boat, she leaned over to peer into the deep blue sea. Then the water broke close beside the boat. Elke's head came up in a swift continuous motion in which she took a breath and disappeared again.

How long could Elke hold her breath?

Raising her arms, Tinisha arched herself over the side of the boat. She went deep. The sun permeated to a depth of about twelve feet, turning the water a translucent green. Tinisha's range of vision was good. She could see various species of fish, and the porpoise from before did a shadowy leaping further away. But there was no sign of Elke. Tinisha came up for air. The water beside her rippled. Elke's head appeared, delicately spouting water.

'Were you looking for me?' she cheekily asked.

Elke took a breath and went under again, to come up on the other side of Tinisha, who asked complainingly. 'Don't you ever swim on top of the water like normal people?'

Laughing, Elke raised a hand to wipe water away from her nose and mouth, push her hair back from her brow. 'I've been swimming all my life. I found that the more time you spend in the sea, the less interest you have in the surface.' Stretching out her hand, she patted Tinisha on the head. 'Come on; let's see how good you are.'

She swam off with long, powerful strokes. Going after her, Tinisha caught up with Elke and they swam side by side. Matching each other's timing, they moved gracefully through the water. Heads turning to breathe simultaneously, their arms were perfectly synchronised. Like an offshoot from an aquatic display team, they swam in a wide circle before coming back to the boat.

Clambering aboard before Tinisha, not caring that she put her naked cunt and arsehole on clear display as she threw a leg over the gunwale, Elke reached out a hand to pull Tinisha into the boat.

They dried themselves vigorously. Aware that Elke was slow in putting her bikini back on, Tinisha realised what had been going on from the moment they had swum in unison. They were playing the game, stalking each other like predatory animals. Though each of them was ready for sex, they were able to back out at the last moment and claim misinterpretation.

Finesse was an essential. Elke was very different to the uncomplicated Kerry. A sustained campaign was required. After coming up with a reason for sending Kerry home early, Tinisha would invite Elke up to the bungalow that afternoon.

Starting up the motor, Tinisha brought the bow of the boat round to the shoreline. There was a little headwind on the way back that blew salt-spray into their faces. It was cooling, pleasant. Tinisha called to Elke above the roar of the motor. 'Do you have the whole day off work?'

'Yes.'

'Come up to the bungalow this afternoon.'

'I wouldn't want to impose.'

'You won't, Elke, I assure you.' The girl's answering look was disconcertingly innocent.

For a seaside summer show, it was probably remarkably good. The performers and the television has-been they supported gave their all. But Valerie was unable to take much of it in. Being an afternoon performance, the show was poorly patronised. The audience was made up of families, with parents vastly outnumbered by their offspring. Beside her, Guy laughed as often and as uproariously as the children in the audience, including theirs.

Valerie had never subscribed to the theory that men have a superior sense of humour to women. The truth was that on average men were very much more childish than women. Right at that moment, Guy's infantile behaviour sickened her. Yet to be fair – which was difficult, in her situation – before all this she would have loved the effort Guy was making to have their son and daughter enjoy themselves.

Valerie was finding it difficult to think straight. In fact, Valerie was finding it difficult to think at all.

Gloom filled her mind like a cold black fog. Her marriage to Guy was over, that was for sure. Whether that was due to what had happened here on holiday, or the holiday had merely accelerated the rate of decay in their relationship, she didn't know. It didn't really matter. The effect overshadowed the cause.

A troupe of girl dancers on the stage exacerbated her problem. A week or so ago, she would have felt jealousy over what the sight of their flashing long legs would do to Guy. But now the girls were getting to her. Accepting her arousal, although she would have not so long ago suspected insanity, Valerie was comforted that in modern times lesbianism qualified as 'normal' behaviour. Normal was an abstract term. Yardsticks certainly existed, but they covered too wide a range to be reliable. To be classed as 'average' meant falling within a certain scale. The fact that she enjoyed sex with a woman did not make her abnormal. This reasoning brought Tinisha into Valerie's mind. In some ways, Tinisha was the bravest person she had yet met – because Tinisha was completely honest about her desires and didn't really give a damn what anyone else thought. That was interesting, thought Valerie. If Tinisha could live openly, then maybe she could, too. It was something to consider, anyway.

Valerie's portrait was finished, but Tinisha had yet to present it to her. It was obvious to Valerie that the artist was withholding the painting as a passport to one last sex session with her before she went back off holiday. Valerie accepted that what had gone on between them justified Tinisha's expectancy. This would involve Tinisha wearing the dildo, the gigantic erect cock attached to

187

bright yellow straps. The thought of that happening had tantalised Valerie since the time Tinisha had given her a glimpse of the sex toy, although to Valerie the long, thick rubber dildo defied the description of a 'toy'.

Not doubting that Tinisha would give her a good time and she would be taken to the verge of utter madness with Tinisha on top of her, fucking her with that magnificent instrument, Valerie had hatched a plan of her own.

Since the breakdown of her marriage had clearly become irreversible, a worry had mutated into a terrible dread inside of Valerie. As an only child, her husband and children were now all the family she had. A year after she had married Guy, her parents had died within six weeks of each other. The cause of their deaths remained a mystery. But they had both died soon after returning from a holiday in the Middle East. The family doctor saw that as too much of a coincidence, and believed that Valerie's parents had picked up a lethal bug while abroad. To Valerie, it was all academic. That her mother and father were dead was enough. Why they had died didn't seem important.

What was important to her was the fact that, when she separated from Guy, she would be entirely alone in the world. To Valerie, that was too daunting a prospect to be contemplated even for a split second. For her to be alone would be unbearable. But then again, Tinisha was 'alone' and she managed to do just fine. And maybe she could get custody, too. It was food for thought.

There was no reason for Valerie to leave Cornwall and return to London. It would be heartbreaking to let her children go even temporarily, but at least she would have a firm base here in the West Country, and could travel to London regularly to see them. They would both be ecstatic about spending school holidays down here with her. And in the long term . . .

All of this depended upon Tinisha. She loved Tinisha and Tinisha loved her. It would be perfectly natural for her to move into the bungalow to live. Tinisha and herself would thoroughly enjoy living together. Maybe even happy ever after was possible, but that was a prognosis that had always made fairy tales incredible for Valerie. She would keep the idea in cold storage until the next time Tinisha made love to her. In the throes of the wild passion she was capable of, Tinisha was certain to agree.

The show was ending. Valerie came fully back into the present to see the full cast on the stage. Arms linked, they swayed from side to side singing the Maori song *Now is the Hour*. The entire audience, such as it was, joined in lustily. Everyone in the theatre was singing, except for Valerie Zennor. But a knowing, slightly mysterious smile was creeping over her face, all the same.

At first when the telephone at the bungalow wasn't answered, Marje had feared that Tinisha was out. Then she remembered that Kerry was at work, so she would pick up the receiver if her employer wasn't there. It was stifling in the public call-box. The heat was drawing up an acrid stench of urine up from the floor. A handkerchief held to her mouth didn't help. Then there was a click and a voice said, 'Hello.' It was Tinisha's voice.

Marje's nerve fled; her voice deserted her for some awkward seconds. Then she recovered sufficiently to say what she wanted to say, but not so clearly and in the order that she had planned and hoped for. She explained that the bank had granted her a loan, and that she was ringing to express her gratitude to Tinisha.

'I'd really like you and Geraldine to call, sometime, so that I could thank you both properly.'

The long pause at the other end suggested that Tinisha suspected that there was a hidden agenda in Marje's invitation. This made Marje consider the same possibility. Until that time, she hadn't doubted her motive, but now she wondered if she could trust herself. As her financial difficulties abated, so sex had occupied her mind more frequently. Having had erotic daydreams about both Tinisha and Geraldine, she could be fooling herself over why she wanted them to visit her.

'It's not necessary to thank me, and I'm sure that the same goes for Geraldine.' Tinisha's voice broke the telephone-line silence. 'But it is very kind of you to ask us to your house. Next time I'm down in the village I'll pick up Geraldine and we'll call on you.'

'I look forward to it.'

'I'll let Kerry know when it will be,' Tinisha said helpfully.

Marje blurted out quickly – too quickly, 'No, I don't want Kerry to know.'

Marje's own words made it clear to her why she wanted the two women in her home. She realised that she must also have just made it abundantly clear to Tinisha.

There was a detectable tremor in Tinisha's voice as she gave Marje her assurance. 'Don't worry, Marje. Kerry won't hear about it from me.'

'Promise?'

'I promise, Marje,' Tinisha said, and hung up.

'I'm on my own here all day.'

Geraldine hadn't had a minute to spare since opening the shop and café that morning. The world and his wife seemed to know when it was Elke's rest day. Each time when she passed where a persistent Guy Zennor leaned his muscle-packed arms on the café counter, he chatted her up. She was interested, flattered, and highly aroused by the attention the hunk was paying her, but had no time to reciprocate or enjoy it. Giving her a cleverly disguised version of the my-wife-doesn't-understand-me routine, Guy was trying to persuade her to drive out to somewhere quiet and meet him that afternoon.

Someone had put an old number on the jukebox – Carole King's *Will you love me tomorrow?* This was one of Geraldine's favourites from the past. Music had a powerful effect on her emotions. Guy Zennor would never know it, but if he got what he wanted from her, then a lot of his success would be due to a 1971 song.

'This evening, then,' he suggested, pretending to drink from a teacup that had been empty for the past half hour.

Filling ice-cream cones from a machine, Geraldine asked, without looking in his direction. 'What shall I tell my husband?'

'You'll think of something.'

Guy Zennor knew that she would, and she knew that she would. Having his eyes on her as she moved about had worked her up. Terry was a sucker for a reasonable-sounding excuse, and she had a few hours to make one up. There was a roaring in her head that would vanish with the climactic ending of her lust.

Next time she was within conversation distance of Guy, she had a question for him. 'How well do you know your way around here?'

'I don't.'

A self-diagnosis Geraldine had done as a teenager came up with nymphomania. Nothing had changed since. At times such as this, sex filled her world. Everything else was a fake, a sham. This was the real thing. You couldn't even find words to do it justice. Any description was too tame. Unfair though it was, she blamed Tinisha Weaver for her present condition. Out on the rocks at the edge of the bay, the artist had started something that she should have finished.

Mind busy now as she served a family with pie-and-chip meals, Geraldine selected the spot on high where she had stopped with Elke. It was deserted enough up there to do it in his estate car, or even for an *al fresco* fuck. Maybe it was the heat working in the café, but she was gagging for it.

Pausing as she passed him to go to serve a customer in the shop, she gave Guy instructions how to get to the spot, making the time of their meeting a question: 'Eight o'clock?'

'Eight o'clock will be fine,' he said with a satisfied smile.

Things were much easier at home for Kerry. Being owner/skipper of a bigger and better boat had her father so absorbed that he hadn't bothered with drink. With her mother having shed something like twenty years overnight, Marje was even fun to be with now. But it wasn't enough. Kerry had known improvements before – admittedly not on this scale – and they hadn't lasted. She had no faith in this turn for the better lasting, and was still determined to leave home.

Parents were dead selfish. They acted like you owed them everything. But it was the other way around. It was they that brought you into the world, so they owed you – big time! She'd had enough of the lot of them and of this village of insulated residents and lobotomised visitors. Kerry was still agonising over Tinisha, too, and was puzzled by her recent behaviour.

It was as if Tinisha had squandered her sexual desire for the next year in that torrid session with Valerie. Since that time, Tinisha had not mentioned sex with Kerry. Neither was Tinisha in the sulky mood that was normal for her when her rampant sexual appetite wasn't being satisfied. She was treating Kerry better than when they had been at each other daily, sometimes as much as three times a day, for every conceivable kind of sex. Tinisha was now so nice that Kerry was feeling uneasy, if not outright guilty, about her plan to leave her employment and go away.

Tinisha had come back to the kitchen after taking a telephone call. Absently looking out of the window, she had bounced a quick glance off Kerry, and had then stared out of the woods again as she said, 'You can finish up there and take off, Kerry. It's a lovely day and winter will be here before we know it. So go out and make the most of this weather while it lasts.'

That had been extraordinarily lenient for Tinisha, who paid good wages but insisted on getting an adequate return for her money. Thinking about the new, undemanding Tinisha as she walked slowly away from the bungalow, Kerry looked down at the holiday cottage. She was disappointed not to see Guy's car there. That was silly, because Guy Zennor was a childish dream that she believed she had laid firmly to rest. On her own now, Kerry accepted that she had to make her own decisions, and depend entirely on herself once she had made them. In a weird way, Tinisha's sometimes infuriating independence was inspirational, for it proved that Kerry could be independent, too. Last night, it had come to her that joining the armed services was one option open to her.

As she walked down a long slope cropped to a mossy smoothness by sheep, the curving downland gave solitude a meaning that was almost oppressively mysterious. Tinisha's reference to the coming winter had depressed Kerry a little. In summer you carried the blue sky about with you, but when darkened by autumn or winter it was different. Then the sky met you on its own terms as part of the moody uncertain world in which you lived.

Needing to know some certainty before the days of early dusks came, Kerry decided to call on Elke Fuller. She didn't really know Elke, because the other girl had mostly lived away from the village, but they always greeted each other in passing. Elke would be able to tell her a lot about being in the army. She would be able to list the pros and cons that would permit Kerry to decide whether service life was for her.

Crossing the road to avoid the winos that the seaside attracted in summer, she made her way along to Dumphys'. The whole place had a slightly tumbledown look. The woodwork needed paint, and weeds grew knee-high in the little patches that were once gardens. Kerry hesitated, almost coming to a halt as she saw Guy Zennor's car parked outside.

Then she carried on. Why should she avoid people? She had done nothing wrong. The whole Zennor family was probably inside, and Kerry looked forward to seeing Valerie. Opening the door, she went in. Blinking for a moment to get her eyes adjusted to the dimness of the café's interior, Kerry gave an involuntary shudder as she saw Guy Zennor at the counter.

Heads together, faces serious, the big man and Geraldine Dumphy were talking in the close, intimate manner of lovers or would-be lovers.

'I've often wondered how you got this so-complete sun tan. It's amazing how it stays just right, never becomes any darker.'

Sitting on the bed on which Elke lay, Tinisha began to work the scented oil into the girl's skin, over her abdomen and sides. They were both refreshingly naked at the peak of a scorchingly hot day.

'It wasn't easy getting started.' Elke stretched and closed her eyes. 'I always burn a lot at first. You should have seen me then, when I was about sixteen.'

'I would have liked to have seen you.' Tinisha carefully poured more oil, working it over her hips and her legs. She smoothed the oil between Elke's thighs. With the oil and the sunlight coming in through the bungalow window, Elke began to shine like a sleek animal.

'I blistered and my skin went all flaky,' Elke continued, oblivious to Tinisha's hands. 'The man next door worked at Boots and I asked his advice. He wanted to take a look and, like a fool, I showed him. I was innocent then.'

'But you're not innocent now?'

'More innocent than you think I am.'

'How do you know what I think?' Tinisha smiled, pouring more oil on her stomach, a lot of oil.

'I have special powers. I can read minds. Crikey, this is relaxing! It makes me feel so good.'

Using her hands to move up the excess oil on Elke's stomach, Tinisha massaged the younger woman's breasts with both hands.

Elke's eyes opened and she caught her breath.

'I don't think that I agree with you.' Tinisha picked up the bottle and dropped some oil on the two nipples.

'Don't tease me. I'm a bit scared.'

'Of me?'

'No, of myself.' It was true. Elke was overcome with lust. She'd have to play her cards very, very carefully, thought Elke.

Elke's eyes closed again and there was a deep purring in her throat. Tinisha worked the oil in ever narrowing circles. With Elke on her back, it didn't seem possible that her breasts could stand up like this unsupported. The tips were enormous, unbelievably long. She poured the last of the oil on. It made little sucking sounds as her hands worked it into the skin, and Elke's tiny excited cries were keeping time with it. Her body began to tense and relax and each time she tensed her muscles it was with greater abandon. Elke murmured, 'You're taking advantage of me.' It was clear to them both that she wasn't.

'You can read minds; I can read bodies,' Tinisha told her. 'I can tell exactly what you want.'

'Prove it,' Elke said challengingly.

Pleasantly surprised by this response, Tinisha looked down. Elke's lips were opening and a wet pink tongue thrust out at her. Feeling herself pulled down, Tinisha opened her mouth to accept Elke's tongue.

As they kissed, Tinisha traced the smooth skin from Elke's knee to the crease where her body began. The kiss ended, leaving Elke gasping. Tinisha bent to take the left nipple lightly between her teeth. It was a slow beginning, but Tinisha had big plans. She gave Elke a quick kiss, then stood to walk across the room. Opening a drawer, she stood with her back to Elke. Undecided for a moment, her hand rested on her super vibrator strap-on made for two. Tempted to use it with Elke, she recalled that she had promised herself that Marje Tredogan was to be the first with this special dildo. Her hand moved to grasp it.

This had been meant to be Valerie's treat, but the blonde holidaymaker was already slipping into history. Elke was here, young and vibrant, ready for it. As Tinisha placed the dildo on full display, she was rewarded by Elke's reaction. It may have been excitement, or more likely trepidation that widened Elke's blue eyes as she saw the stupendous size of the dildo. Not knowing which it was – and observing how Elke reached her arms out for a new embrace – Tinisha was somehow convinced it was the former.

FOURTEEN

Tinisha held Elke close and never once stopped talking in the special language lovers used when they communicated. She stroked Elke's hair. She put her lips lightly against Elke's mouth and said. 'I want you and I'm going to have you.'

The blood-coursing state of arousal that Tinisha had got Elke into made her not want to miss one thrill that this lovely woman was capable of giving her. It was such a luxury to be seduced. She allowed Tinisha to push her down on to a bed that was warm with body heat and had a strange, pleasant, piquant odour. Elke heard herself give a low moan of pleasure as Tinisha's lips travelled over her neck and down her shoulders. Eyes closed in ecstasy, Elke moved her hands over Tinisha's arms and back. She explored skin that had the texture of satin. Tinisha's body was an exquisite sculpture of planes and surfaces.

The lips moving down over Elke's breasts were soft, languorous, moving downwards, slowly over her stomach, on down to the insides of her thighs. Elke consciously made the movement that brought her the touch of Tinisha's tongue. And she was glad that she had when she was able to work against the thrust of the older woman's tongue and lips. Stirred beyond anything she would ever have imagined, she wanted Tinisha on top of her, kissing her, in between her legs, entering her with the long thick dildo that lay on the bed beside them. That would be an extension of Tinisha, and she desperately wanted Tinisha deep inside her.

Crying out softly, she tried to pull Tinisha up. But her lover fought her off, pushed her hands away. Tinisha's mouth was demanding, a torturous alternating pressure of soft and hard. Then suddenly Elke knew that she was coming. There was the flood of release and her scream was piercing as she held Tinisha's head tight against her.

When Tinisha raised herself to kiss the girl, to stifle her sobbing, Elke tasted herself, bittersweet, on Tinisha's lips.

Lying partly on top of her, Tinisha licked Elke's ear. Her right hand passed down along Elke's body: over a hillock of firm breast, along the plateau of a flat belly, and into the lush valley between her legs. Moaning softly, Elke became aroused again. Tinisha's middle finger found the slot, slid in, slid up to her erect clit and deftly titillated it.

'Just keep doing that, Tinisha – just keep doing it.'

'Most of us love a good fuck,' Tinisha breathed against Elke's mouth before tongue-kissing her.

Oh yes, thought Elke.

Elke's breathing grew more spasmodic as Tinisha's hand worked more swiftly in her crotch. Saying something that neither Tinisha nor herself could decipher, Elke's body arched up. Her thighs trembled and her buttocks tightly contracted; she shivered, jerked, twitched and cried out in the ecstasy of her second orgasm.

Lying still for a moment, Elke then reached down to grasp Tinisha's wrist and take the older woman's finger from her vagina. Bringing the hand up, Elke kissed it, then licked at her own juice. She could see that this action had really turned Tinisha on. Her eyes were brimming, her thick top lip was drawn back from long white teeth. Elke looked down at the long, wet straggling black hair round Tinisha's cunt.

'Do you want me to go down on you now?' It was a blatantly sexual question. Elke laid her cards on the table. Either Tinisha accepted her as the experienced, sexual woman she was, or she didn't accept her at all.

Making no reply, Tinisha moved up to straddle Elke's head, a knee on the bed on each side of her. Using both hands, Tinisha opened up her cunt, spreading her sex-folds open wide. Elke's sweet little tongue avidly played up and down the smooth mother-of-pearl inside of Tinisha, titillating her clitoris unmercifully.

With this stimulation threatening to bring her to full orgasm, Tinisha moved back without warning. Her cunt came away from Elke's mouth. Collapsing on Elke, Tinisha lay there for a while, holding her. They were bonded by their mingled perspiration. There was now barely a trace of perfume from the oil on Elke's body. The air was filled with the smell of their sweat, the scent of their womanhood, the tangy odour of sex.

Elke, her face suffused by rampant desire, turned to look as Tinisha lazily rolled off the bed and stood up. Lazily she watched the black woman cross the room. Then she gripped the bedding with both hands, thrilling in anticipation as she saw Tinisha strapping on the massive dildo. Tinisha deliberately turned sideways on to Elke so that the younger woman could appreciate just how long the rubber prick was. Then Tinisha came back to the bed, lying down beside Elke.

She gave Elke a long, sucking, sensual kiss. Then Tinisha whispered, 'I've got to get you nice and wet.' She slid down on Elke yet again. Elke began to writhe slowly in response to Tinisha's oral expertise. But the tongue in her was like a whiplash. It was too much. Elke felt herself rising to Tinisha again. Another orgasm was building. Elke could tell that the power of it would dwarf her previous ones. Her hands pulled at the hair of Tinisha's bobbing head and Elke started up cries that rapidly became screaming.

But Tinisha was a veteran in the love game. She knew when to stop. She moved up, her lips and all round her mouth wet and shining. She spoke without smiling. 'I know that you like the taste of your own cunt, Elke. You like the taste of cunt. I suspected it all along. And don't act so innocent. You know what I'm talking about.' Then she kissed her.

Tinisha was up on Elke. Her body was over Elke's, her tongue in Elke's mouth as she kissed her – Tinisha was some lover, a remarkable lover. She was becoming urgent as her long-fingered hands gently stroked Elke's body. Elke's groans were smothered by Tinisha's hungry kisses. She sucked on Tinisha's tongue, got Tinisha's heavy bottom lip between her teeth and lightly nibbled it. Elke was totally lost to feelings, oblivious to everything except the magic of the moment. It was only when she felt the big knob of the dildo entering her that she came back to reality.

She could feel every one of Tinisha's movements. Elke felt the lips of her cunt close over and grip the bulging end of the dummy prick. As Tinisha moved it in and out, Elke could hear the sucking, slurping noises that her greedy cunt was making. Surrendering to another hot kiss from Tinisha, Elke felt the prick going further up her with each measured thrust. It was stretching her, filling her, thrilling her.

Then her mind seemed to detach itself from its body that had writhed in pleasure. There were two women on the bed; one black and the other white, and she was watching them through an observer's eye. She saw two sets of arms and two sets of legs moving in urgent search of more gratification. She could actually hear the two bodies, damp with perspiration, beat against each other. The sound they made was rhythmic, hollow. The whole scene had a dynamic effect on her. Watching seemed to be even more arousing than participating.

Elke returned as quickly and unexpectedly as she had left. Tinisha was moving violently on top of her, her face earnest, her breathing heavy. As Tinisha thrust deeper inside her, Elke responded. The fact that Tinisha's pelvis was tight against hers was evidence that she had the whole dildo up her, every fraction of an inch of it deep inside of her. Panting, lips close to her ear, Tinisha said, 'Wherever you go, whoever you're with, Elke, you'll always remember how good it was to be fucked by me.'

Then Tinisha kissed her hard, capturing her tongue, pumping faster. Elke could feel the end of the dildo moving high up inside her. She was aware of Tinisha sliding her hand beneath her buttocks and squirming a finger into the tight hole of her anus. Elke felt as if she would explode with the intensity of the sensations that rocked her. She did explode. Wave after wave of pleasure washed over her. Her muscles contracted and her body convulsed uncontrollably.

Tinisha cried out, too. She was ramming at Elke's groin as if trying to get something of herself into the deep, wet chasm between Elke's legs. Then she subsided on top of Elke.

They lay like that for a while, lightly holding each other, getting their breath back. Then Tinisha rolled to one side. The rubber penis slipped out as she did so. Elke felt like she had been unplugged. She felt a wetness flowing so strongly out of her that she feared she was urinating.

She put a testing hand down. It wasn't urine. She lay quietly, the heaving of her chest gradually subsiding. Tinisha had her back turned to her. Elke suddenly felt very alone, very frightened. It was as if Tinisha had coaxed something from her that Elke herself didn't know she owned. Whatever that undefinable thing was, the absence of it left Elke feeling dangerously exposed, and not just because her 'cover' was blown. Recognising this as an understandable reaction to a mind-blowing new experience, she needed Tinisha to turn to her, to hold her lovingly, to say nice things to her. But Tinisha was unmoving. Elke waited expectantly but, just when she was about to despair, with relief she found herself being taken tenderly and lovingly into Tinisha's arms.

They lay unspeaking, communicating through the silent, mystical and indescribable post-orgasm closeness of lovers.

After a few minutes had gone by, Elke, needing some assurance, asked quaveringly, 'Will I see you at the church fête tomorrow?'

As soon as the words were out, Elke knew that it had been a crass thing to say. She must have sounded like a silly schoolgirl trying to ensure that her first date would one day marry her. Shame at her own childishness was lessened by Tinisha stroking her hair and reassuringly kissing her on the forehead. She felt for the first time, entirely grown up. And Tinisha seemed to like her just as much without the subterfuge. Well.

Tinisha Weaver sat with Geraldine Dumphy in the vicarage gardens. They were apart from everyone else, cooled by a slight breeze that escaped as the last ray of sunlight was dragged over the horizon. Bursts of azaleas rimmed the area, wisping like coloured smoke in the twilight. The village's big day was at an end. As such events go, which was a matter of viewpoint – something that Tinisha lacked, in this case – it had apparently been a huge success. All the silly games were over; even the echoes of the excited squeals of raffle winners had long ago died away. Now the flames of the barbecue danced bravely in a new darkness. The aroma of scorched meat had attracted a long queue for hot-dogs and hamburgers. Folks still milled around, reluctant to let an enjoyable day end. They gave off squealing 'Oooohs!' as fireworks and rockets burst sparklingly and noisily in a display supervised by school headmaster Gerald Delroy. Tony Scollop, who always flapped under pressure, still dashed about, smiling and answering questions that no one had asked. For a reason that Tinisha couldn't fathom, the vicar was wearing Levi's, a plaid shirt and Western boots.

She had seen Kerry several times during the day. The girl, tight-lipped and stiff as a steel girder, had barely spoken. An astute Tinisha was convinced that Kerry had decided to leave home and her job. So sure was she of this that she had already given Elke the opportunity to fill the housekeeping vacancy that Kerry would leave. A wavering Elke had murmured that she was content working with Geraldine Dumphy, but Tinisha was confident of changing her mind.

Not for the first time that day, Geraldine brought up the subject of Marje Tredogan. 'Honestly, Tinisha, Marje is a different woman. She has Jack on the straight and narrow, and he looks like staying that way. It seems that he brought in one of the biggest catches known in this area, and Marje was able to double the repayment the bank requires.'

'That's good news,' Tinisha said. 'I'm glad that you and me didn't give up on the Tredogans as everyone else did.'

'Let's be honest.' Geraldine studied Tinisha's face in the fading light. 'Would either of us have helped if we hadn't fancied Marje?'

Made a little uncomfortable by the question, Tinisha replied, 'I'd like to think that we would.'

'So would I, but I don't like lying, even to myself, Tinisha, so I thought that I'd double-check with you. Marje has asked us both round to her place. What if we don't go?'

'I don't think that would prove anything about us, one way or the other,' Tinisha answered, pretty sure that she had helped Marje regardless of her dynamic sex appeal, and also being sure of Geraldine's generous nature.

'I think I agree, and she really wants us to call,' a thoughtful

Geraldine said. 'Can you make it tomorrow morning, Tinisha – say, ten o'clock?'

'Could you make it eleven, Geraldine?'

'No problem,' Geraldine assured her. Then she groaned, speaking *sotto voce*. 'Oh, no! Here comes Billy-fucking-Graham.'

Still in his semi-cowboy gear, the Reverend Anthony Scollop was heading their way, his portly wife, Grace, at his side. Tinisha stood up to greet him.

'Good evening, Tinisha, and good evening to you, Mrs Dumphy,' he said with an elegant bow. 'There is no way to express my gratitude to you, Miss Weaver – Tinisha. Your painting made an absolute bomb. Now we'll be able to afford a new church for the roof.'

Throwing his head back, he laughed loudly, the fillings in his back teeth shining like glass. Tinisha and Geraldine laughed with him, falsely.

'Seriously, though,' he continued, 'it raised the most money here today.'

'I'm so glad.'

Scollop turned to look at a passing couple. It surprised Tinisha to see that the couple was Kerry and Simon Gregory.

'Young love,' the vicar remarked with a smile. 'I do hope it comes to something. One day, Kerry might be mistress of Laurel House.'

Tinisha thought of the Gregory home. The grandest house in the area, it stood on a plateau high on East Cliff over the cleft through which an insipid river flowed to the sea. The front of it clung dramatically to the brink of a steep drop. The rest of the house was cantilevered over it, suspended a hundred feet or more in the air. She commented, 'A great place for anyone contemplating suicide.'

'That's a peculiar thing to say.' Scollop frowned.

Tinisha, who didn't know why she'd said it, shrugged. She attributed it to an onset of depression after having seen Kerry with Gregory, who in male terminology was a two-fingered wank. She tried to excuse herself. 'I say peculiar things at times.'

Geraldine remained sitting and, under the cover of dusk, put her hand up between Tinisha's legs from behind. It went higher, gently taking the weight of the crotch of Tinisha's panties. Then Geraldine's big fingers tugged the nylon crotch down a little and went inside.

'Yes.' The vicar smiled, as if accepting that lots of people said peculiar things at times. 'Whatever, we shall be eternally grateful to you, Tinisha,' Scollop said with a wide smile. His wrinkled face looked like an ordnance survey map in the poor light. 'Your place in heaven is assured.'

'Is there any chance of you fixing up things for me down here?' Tinisha asked, the twinkle in her eye going out as Geraldine's finger entered her.

'Not under my jurisdiction, I'm afraid,' Scollop laughed, enjoying Tinisha's joke, but not so much as he had his own. 'But there is an idea I'd like to put to you.'

'Anything to help,' Tinisha offered, finding it difficult to stand still because Geraldine was furiously fucking her.

Her jerking body had the clergyman and his wife puzzled.

'Are you feeling all right, Tinisha?' he solicitously enquired.

Transforming her sexual reactions into a shiver as best she could, Tinisha smiled. 'Yes, thank you, I'm fine. I just suddenly felt a little cold.'

'I noticed this breeze isn't as warm as it might be,' Grace Scollop agreed.

Geraldine's finger had located Tinisha's G-spot and was making the most of it. Suffering an excruciatingly delightful torment, Tinisha fought for control of herself as she faced the vicar and his wife. She was silently wishing them away, and for the second time in a couple of days, her thought-control system proved that it worked.

'What was it you wanted to discuss, Tony?' she asked, wondering if they had noticed the tremor in her voice.

'I was wondering if you could paint the church at some time, Tinisha. It is of historical interest, and I thought if we had postcards made from the painting they would sell well. But we'll talk it over some other time. There's still a lot of people here, so Grace and I had better circulate.'

'Just as you wish, Tony,' Tinisha said as the couple walked off. Then, as Geraldine's finger continued to do its work, she hissed at her, 'You absolute bitch! I hope we're going to go somewhere you can finish what you've started, Geraldine?'

Swiftly withdrawing her finger, Geraldine said cruelly, 'No, I'm going to let you stew in your own juices – that's a good choice of words – until tomorrow. We're going to see Marje, remember?'

Tinisha certainly hadn't forgotten.

The day had turned out better than Kerry had dared hope. She had found herself closer to her parents than she had ever been. Kerry found it easy to be in her mother's company. Marje Tredogan had suddenly become much more open. She was no longer a prude who avoided the topic of sex at all times. For Kerry, it was like having a big sister, and she really appreciated the new woman that her mother had become. Though she wouldn't have believed that anything would weaken her resolve to leave the village, Kerry discovered that the new and apparently permanent harmony within her family was doing just that. Maybe it was as well that she hadn't yet found the nerve to tell her mother that she was leaving home. As Simon spoke at her side, she had to drag herself out of deep thought.

'All of what happened between us was my fault,' Simon was saying. 'I was being as narrow-minded as the people in this village.'

'You mean that you don't . . .?' Kerry began, a little afraid to enjoy the relief that was filling her. She wouldn't have to plan; she wouldn't have to think for herself. She sucked air hard into her lungs, willing them to fill up. Holding it down there, closing her throat so that it couldn't get out, she waited.

'No, Kerry, I don't mean that I am prepared to accept that kind of thing,' Simon said, disappointing Kerry so that the air escaped from her lungs in a long sigh. 'What I'm saying is that you are under the influence of a strong and particularly nasty woman.'

About to protest that Tinisha was not 'nasty', Kerry held her tongue. Her mind was a mess. She felt as if she was at a crossroads: one way would mean easiness, complicity, an uneventful life of acceptance and no worrying self-questioning. The other way was less certain: independence, an uneasy trek, the possibility of social rejection – but perhaps more personal happiness . . .

They passed the end of the boat slipway. A man and a woman standing at the bus stop said, 'Goodnight.' Simon and Kerry answered in unison. It felt good to Kerry to be one of a partnership again. This is how it feels to be normal, she told herself. Think of what you'll be giving up.

'I'm leaving the village on Saturday,' she said, sounding positive although she had half-changed her mind, an additional influence being meeting Simon again. 'It's just that there's nothing here.'

'Where are you going?' Simon asked sadly.

Kerry shrugged. 'London, possibly.'

'Is this because of me, Kerry?'

She gave a second shrug. 'Partly, I suppose.'

They were entering the poorly lit, dead-end street where Kerry lived. Her rented home was a hundreds-of-years-old fisherman's cottage. Kerry knew that flocks of visitors came to admire the cottage, judging it to be wonderful. But they would soon change their minds if they had to live in it.

'Then you mustn't go,' he implored.

They were in the dark alcove beside the cottage. Here they had said hundreds of fond goodnights. It was not a lovers' playground but their own holy ground. 'Are you asking me to stay, Simon?'

'I am,' he assured her, bending for her kiss.

In that kiss, all of Kerry's problems of recent times faded away. If anything, his kissing was more ardent than when they had been together before. That was a good sign. Christmas was still a long way off, and an engagement then could be back on schedule.

Simon's breathing became ragged, laboured, frightening her. Then his hands perturbed her by groping her breasts. Kerry used both hands to force him away. Then his hand was down on her hip and, when she went to move it away, she gave a little cry of pain because he gripped her fingers so tightly. For some reason, Simon's unforgivable behaviour brought the scene of Guy Zennor and Geraldine Dumphy together vividly and sickeningly into her mind.

'Simon, please: you're hurting me!'

He released her, but stared at her with cool eyes. 'Come on,' he said calmly. 'I don't want anything from you that that bitch up in the bungalow hasn't already had.'

I could have this, Kerry thought. But I don't want it any more. She somehow found the strength to walk slowly away from him, until she went round the corner. Then, sobbing, she ran to the front door of the cottage. Her final tie with the village had just been broken. With his hissed comments still echoing in her ears, she unlocked the door and hurried in. She would start packing tonight.

'I don't know why you just don't pack your things and move in with her up at that bungalow,' Terry Dumphy said angrily.

Boiling milk at the stove for their cocoa, Geraldine didn't answer him. Coming home later than expected from the church fête, she had told her suspicious husband, truthfully, that she had been with Tinisha Weaver. He would have accepted that as a defence had she not used Tinisha as an alibi, the previous evening, when she had driven out to meet Guy Zennor. That had been another episode to add to the long list of regrets in her life. As they had left their cars to walk through the copse together, Geraldine had wanted to ensure that she would retain her dignity by explaining herself. It had long been her hope that she would find someone who would sympathise with her libido affliction, and honour her. She had hoped that Guy would be that gallant knight. As much as she wanted sex with him, she would have preferred his respect.

But a sudden wild flurrying had startled them as a partridge had flown off, her wings troubling the air around them as she went off squawking. Frightened, Geraldine had welcomed Guy holding her hand. They had entered a narrow defile through some rocks that burst into the bright open again. There had been tall grass that was both comfortable and concealing. With scarcely a rustle, they had been lying face to face. Around them the woodlife had noticed and chattered and watched in excitement. When it came to a sudden, sharp finish, she had burst into tears.

Geraldine felt a little like crying now as she routinely put a mug of cocoa in front of her husband and completed the boring nightly ritual by joining him at the table. But she cheered herself with thoughts of the morrow. There would be no tears, only thrills, when she and Tinisha paid a visit to the luscious Marje Tredogan.

★

A smiling Marje Tredogan met them in the hall. Her bright appearance astonished Tinisha. Marje's batteries had been fully recharged and she was buzzing with what Tinisha picked up as powerful sex vibrations. Looking at Marje was evidence that no matter how much resolve, how much glow a woman has, she cannot glow indefinitely in the face of bitter disappointment. Money was said to be overrated, but lack of it had drained Marje of all the vital juices, and the loan from the bank had fully restored her. No, restoration was too mild a word. Marje Tredogan had been resurrected.

Though far from smartly dressed, the gorgeous Marje was wearing a tight sweatshirt of thin material. The garment showed off the large, firm breasts so that they filled Tinisha's mind, taking up all available space, forcing out all thoughts other than her need to have this unconsciously provocative woman. Marje's worn dog-tooth skirt was so tight and short, that though Tinisha's hands were at her sides, clutching at air, they seemed to be feeling Marje's big buttocks. Beside her, Geraldine's breathing had quickened and from the corner of her eye Tinisha was aware of the blonde's breasts heaving.

Marje stopped smiling. Her voice was husky when she spoke. 'I owe the two of you so much. What could I do to repay you both?'

No one could be that naïve. Marje knew why she had invited them to the house, and was aware why the two of them had accepted her invitation. An innate shyness, genuine modesty, and sexual inexperience was holding back, but not stunting, Marje's needs and urges. Not suffering from any of the three things afflicting Marje, Tinisha stepped forwards to put her arms round Marje and hold her tight.

There was a nice smell from Marje, a blend of cooking and sweaty woman. Tinisha could have dropped to her knees there and then to savour Marje's hairy cunt. Tinisha started to kiss the soft skin of her face. Then she moved her mouth down to Marje's neck. As she kissed and sucked at the sweet skin, Marje's head went back and her eyelids drooped sensually. The red-headed woman's instant arousal set off a chain of sexual events in Tinisha's body. She reminded herself that she had to stay cool to get the best from what was certain to be a hot session.

Marje began to shed her inhibitions. She said huskily, 'Let's go up to the bedroom.'

'Are you sure about this, Marje?' Tinisha asked anxiously.

As much as she wanted Marje, and was excited about a three-some that included Geraldine, Tinisha didn't want Marje to get involved in something she would afterwards regret. The new life that the advance of money had given Marje could be ruined just as easily and swiftly as it had come into being. With her parted lips resting lightly against Marje's soft cheek, Tinisha awaited an answer.

'I want you both,' Marje said in a voice strangled by desire.

Geraldine slipped an arm around Tinisha's waist. Together they watched Marje's wonderfully swaying buttocks until they disappeared out of the door.

Drawing Tinisha to her, Geraldine stroked her hair. She held Tinisha close, and she could hear Geraldine's heart beat beneath her full bosom. Geraldine's hands moved across Tinisha's shoulders and down her back. She kissed Tinisha first on the forehead and then on the lips. The kiss, gentle rather than passionately demand-ing, formed their signatures on the unspoken contract they had made when naked out on the flat rock.

Then their open mouths were wetly together. Geraldine's tongue went into one corner of Tinisha's mouth, then travelled along between her bottom lip and her teeth. Reaching the other side of Tinisha's mouth, Geraldine brought her tongue up to make a similar, slow, saliva-collecting probe between Tinisha's upper teeth and top lip. This simple but highly arousing act caused them both to utter little squeals and gasps. Their breath was hot and coarse as they kissed wetly.

But the thought of the tasty Marje waiting for them made them pull away from each other by mutual tacit consent. Sharing one sucking kiss as they went, they headed for the stairs.

When they went into the bedroom, a slack-mouthed, steaming Marje stood up from where she had been sitting on the edge of the bed. Tinisha and Geraldine went to her. They kissed and felt her, kissed and felt each other. They stripped Marje naked, both of them crazy with lust. They stripped themselves naked and man-handled Marje on to the bed.

'Do whatever you want to me,' Marje groaned. 'I want everything.'

'We're going to ravish you,' Tinisha promised, her own words and Marje's reaction to them lifting her up on a sexual high.

'We want to taste every inch of you,' Geraldine murmured as she put her tongue between Marje's legs.

At first kissing Marje's mouth while Geraldine lapped at her exposed cunt, slurping at her juices, exciting her clitoris, Tinisha then moved down behind the kneeling Geraldine. Parting Geraldine's buttocks, Tinisha held them open while she pressed her nose and mouth in, probing both of Geraldine's holes with her tongue, avid for the scents, tastes and juices that were available in that wet and hairy valley. Geraldine was making little thrusts back, and Tinisha gauged exactly when she was coming, and slid her tongue deep into the vagina from behind as Geraldine had her first orgasm.

Jumping from the bed, Tinisha got her vibrator from her handbag. She had brought the sex instrument with her in anticipation of something like this happening. The full length, from the tip of one knob-end to the other, was more than eighteen inches. Geraldine was still performing cunnilingus, but Tinisha rolled her on to her back. The apparatus consisted of two phallic-shaped vibrators joined in the middle, where there were raised pieces to work against the clitoris when the shafts were deep into two women. An oblong switch dangled on thin wires, capable of controlling the vibrators independently.

Kissing Geraldine, Tinisha worked one of the vibrators right into her vagina. Marje, lying on her back, legs open and her face contorted by lust, watched them. With the spare vibrator protruding from Geraldine like an erect penis, Tinisha gestured with her head to Marje, telling Geraldine, 'Give her a really good fucking.'

Marje opened her arms for Geraldine as she rolled up on her. Breasts pressed hard against breasts, they kissed. Dropping on to her knees beside the bed, Tinisha looked in to where Geraldine was using movements of her hips to thrust the vibrator a bit at a time into Marje. Then the two bodies of the women were tight together, threshing together, sweating together. The vibrator was right in Marje, with Geraldine bringing it out about an inch each time before thrusting it back home again.

Reaching for the controls, Tinisha switched on the vibrator that was inside Marje. She couldn't hear the motor, but Marje yelled out. First she uttered intelligible words. 'I'm coming . . .' But then it was so pleasurable that she gave a roar like a bull.

Delaying a few seconds, Tinisha then pressed the button that controlled the twin vibrator she had fed into Geraldine's body. This time it was Geraldine who let out a crazy-sounding cry. Pushing her head in under them, Tinisha licked at both their oozing cunts as Marje and Geraldine hit a series of orgasms that ended with a shared come that shook the bed and threatened to suffocate Tinisha.

Totally spent, Geraldine collapsed on top of Marje, who seemed to have fainted. Rolling Geraldine off, letting her fall limply back on the bed, Tinisha pulled the vibrator out of her. After licking the glistening moisture of Marje and Geraldine from each of the vibrator's simulated penises, Tinisha worked one of them up herself. Then she mounted the inert Marje, slapping Marje's face until she came round to peer bleary-eyed up at Tinisha. Tinisha didn't attempt to enter Marje until she had her conscious enough to respond hotly to kissing.

A French-kissing, eager, grunting Marje was ready again, and Tinisha moved her hips to fuck her with the vibrator. Tinisha was so worked up herself that she couldn't wait. Switching Marje's vibrator on first, she enjoyed the craziness as Marje writhed around, kissing her open-mouthed and wetly, biting her lips, thrusting her hips up off the bed in time with Tinisha's downwards thrusts. Switching on her own vibrator at just the right moment, Tinisha brought them both to a shattering orgasm.

Tinisha rested on top of Marje for a minute or two, then got off, pulled out the vibrator, wiped it on the bedclothes and put it in her handbag. She dressed quickly, worried – now that she was no longer under the control of rampant sexual desire – that either Jack Tredogan or the boy would come home unexpectedly. Kerry was safely employed up at the bungalow.

Rousing Geraldine was difficult, but she eventually got her on to her feet. Geraldine looked across at the seemingly unconscious Marje.

'Oh, fuck! Is she all right, Tinisha?'

'Yes,' Tinisha replied, although she was herself concerned. 'She's not out, just exhausted. She'll come round in a short while.'

They waited, worry for Marje overcoming the impatience they both felt. It would be a traumatic time for all if a member of the Tredogan family arrived to find them in the bedroom with a naked and unconscious lady of the house. Then Marje came partially round, reaching for them, wanting more. Avoiding her exploring hands and kiss-seeking mouth, they helped her into her clothes. Despite their eagerness to get away, first Tinisha and then Geraldine enjoyed a long, tonguey kiss with Marje.

'We have to go,' Tinisha told Marje as she and Geraldine made for the door.

Calling pleadingly after them, Marje said, 'There's no need to go yet. Please stay for a while.'

'We'll be back, some other time,' Tinisha assured her. Marje winked at her in response.

As they went down the stairs, Geraldine spoke in an awed voice. 'That was my best fuck ever, Tinisha. That's one wicked machine you've got there. I'd like to borrow it, because I think I might get Elke Fuller to come across.'

'You're welcome to borrow it,' Tinisha said generously, then smiled. 'But you're too late with Elke Fuller.'

FIFTEEN

Kerry discovered that Sergeant Petters was an Army recruiting officer and a lecher. One was his vocation, the other his avocation, but with her present he didn't know which was which.

Once a confectionery shop, the place was now an Army Careers Office. Even so, it still looked like a shop. Neither it nor the sergeant was what Kerry had expected.

Elke had been helpful but careful to remain neutral on the subject of the army. 'I had some good times and I had some bad times,' she had said ambiguously.

'More good times than bad?' Kerry had enquired hopefully.

A candid Elke had replied, 'It's difficult to answer that, Kerry, as you tend to remember only the good times and forget the bad.'

That hadn't been reassuring, and neither was Sergeant Petters. She estimated that he was around thirty years of age. Tall and slender, he had black hair and dark eyes. Now his dilated pupils merged with the irises and appeared to be as black as his hair, either due to drugs or sexual excitement.

Whatever the cause, Kerry didn't want to know. Combined with his attitude, which veered between bullying and what he probably regarded as seductively cajoling, the sergeant had unwittingly convinced Kerry that the army was not for her. She knew that she should have deduced that from what Elke had told her, but she had hoped it would work out. By enlisting she would have had somewhere definite to go, with bed and board guaranteed.

'I don't think that I'm interested,' she said, getting up from a chair with a canvas seat.

'At least think about it,' Petters insisted, picking up pamphlets one by one from the desk, like a croupier dealing in reverse. He thrust the pile of pamphlets into her hands, trying to touch her hands with his as he did so. 'Take these with you and study them.'

'No, thanks.'

Tossing the pamphlets back on to the desk, taking a delight in scattering them and all the others that had been neatly laid out, Kerry left the office. In spite of feeling good about putting down the obnoxious Petters, Kerry wondered if she was making a mistake in passing up a chance to join the army.

As she was closing the door she heard the sergeant mutter, 'Fuck you, then, you miserable cow.' That convinced her that she had been right to leave the office and the chance of a career in the army. It meant that she would need to find lodgings on going to London, and the prospect of that did worry her quite a lot.

Kneeling on the bed with Tinisha behind her, Valerie was aware of two things: one, of how much she liked the thrilling sensations Tinisha was giving her, and secondly, she had included Tinisha in her plans for the future. They were both naked, apart from the dildo that Tinisha had strapped on. She was holding Valerie with a hand on both hips and fucking her deeply with the long rubber prick. Each time Tinisha drove it right home, Valerie let out what sounded like an anguished cry, but it was really an aural signal of total pleasure. Moving tight up against Valerie's hot bum, Tinisha gave short, rapid strokes, while reaching forwards to hold each of Valerie's suspended breasts. Swinging her head violently from side to side then in a circular motion, Valerie reached a shattering orgasm.

Absolutely spent, Valerie began to lower her body away from Tinisha, but Tinisha's hands were back on Valerie's hips, holding her firmly in position. When Tinisha spoke, her voice was a rasping whisper. 'Be a shame to waste it now that it's all slippery, Val.'

With that, she withdrew, and Valerie gave a mighty sigh as the lips of her cunt closed with a little wet smacking sound. But Tinisha had moved the knob end of the dildo up to Valerie's anus. Gently but with determination, using Valerie's own lubrication before it had chance to dry, Tinisha fed the full length into Valerie. With her right hand going down and under to find and play with Valerie's clitoris, Tinisha began short strokes that brought Valerie off again in a dynamic climax.

Tinisha delayed withdrawal and Valerie turned her head to say gaspingly, 'I want to talk, Tinisha.'

'We'll talk, honey. We'll talk in a little while,' Tinisha promised as she withdrew and unstrapped the dildo.

Valerie didn't resist as Tinisha rolled her on to her back and lay on top of her, between her legs. Pressing her lower body rhythmically against Valerie's, Tinisha kissed her passionately. Wanting the woman's mouth, Valerie opened hers. They kissed for a long time while Tinisha kept her body movements going. Aware that Tinisha was building up to an orgasm, Valerie felt her own body reacting yet again. Just when she was about to hit the peak, she was disconcerted by Tinisha getting off her. Reversing herself on the bed, Tinisha straddled Valerie, facing her feet. Moving up backwards, Tinisha lowered her spread-open buttocks down to sit lightly on Valerie's face. Feeling Tinisha's hands go in between her legs and start working her, Valerie bent her arms and put a hand on each of Tinisha's buttocks. Steadying her lover's body, Valerie then licked and sucked, her stroking, darting, probing tongue soon driving Tinisha over the top of a magnificent orgasm.

Dropping tiredly on to the bed beside Valerie, a sweating Tinisha held her in a one arm-embrace. 'I'm really going to miss you, Val,' she said pantingly.

This was her cue. Knowing that, Valerie cleared her throat as she gathered her nerve. A truly beautiful woman smiled out at her from a silver-framed photo on the dresser. She wondered who the woman was, and felt a sharp pang of jealousy. Then she found her voice.

'I've decided not to go home tomorrow, Tinisha.'

Jerking her arm from around Valerie, Tinisha propped herself up on one elbow. Breasts resting on Valerie's shoulders, she was frowning. 'That's a drastic and sudden decision.'

It wasn't sudden to Valerie, as the end of her marriage had been a more than half-formed fact in her mind for some time. It had been confirmed last night when Guy had come back after spending some unexplained hours out on his own. Something had changed his whole attitude. No longer caring that he was about to lose her, he had declared how much he was looking forward to the freedom of being single again. Valerie had detected a woman's perfume on him, but had been unable to identify it. All she knew was that it was neither Tinisha's nor Kerry's.

'It may be drastic but it's not so sudden,' Valerie explained. 'I've been thinking about it for days. Guy and I have nothing now. Everything I want, all I ever wanted, is down here in Cornwall. I want to stay here with you.'

As she spoke, Valerie had reached to catch hold of Tinisha's hand. Tinisha snatched her hand away, an action that chilled Valerie to the extent that she felt goose-pimples standing out all over her body. Then she had to strangle a sob at birth as Tinisha got off the bed and walked towards the bathroom.

At the door, Tishina turned, leaning nonchalantly against the jamb, her face hard as she addressed Valerie, her tone sad. 'I'm sorry if I inadvertently led you to believe that ours was to be a long-term relationship, Valerie. We've had fun, but everything has to come to an end. We both have our memories, and let's hope that we'll meet again some day.'

'I feel very foolish, Tinisha,' a red-faced Valerie confessed humbly.

'Don't feel that way because of me,' Tinisha said with a kind but unhappy smile. 'I need to put some finishing touches to your portrait. Call for it in the morning before you leave. We'll say goodbye then, Val.'

Valerie had considered that she might need to argue a little, press her case for staying here with Tinisha. But she hadn't expected such a chilling rebuff as this. Getting off the bed, she scrambled frantically for her clothes. She wanted to get dressed and leave before embarrassing herself further by breaking down in tears.

★

Tinisha's bungalow wasn't in this direction, but Kerry had changed her mind. She decided that she thought too much of Tinisha to risk seeing her again. There was no way she could achieve a clean break with the area if she didn't overcome her strong feelings for Tinisha. The sadness of leaving was like a lead weight in her chest. It became dark and cold as she walked into a grove. Rarely did the light or heat penetrate the green awning here. She barked her shin lightly against a fallen branch. The pain was intense. Everything that had happened had made her ultra-sensitive. Her feet felt heavy so that it seemed she was dragging them along. Her head ached with an awful dread that she was doing the wrong thing in going away. Kerry searched her mind in vain for a reason to stay, but couldn't come up with one.

All around her, the wood was peaceful and quiet. There was not a sound to be heard. Kerry strained at listening, just to be certain. There was a faint singing up ahead where the brook flowed. Here in the densely packed trees, humidity raised a steamy mist about a foot from the ground. Kerry found herself pointlessly kicking the low-lying fog away as she walked.

Coming to a wide section of the brook that had a fallen log for a bridge, she crossed. On the far side she sat on the end of the log and picked up a few pebbles, thoughtfully toying with them. The pebbles were making her fingers gritty. Kerry threw them one at a time into the brook, fascinated by thick widening and overlapping ripples of water that spread shimmering in the sunlight. The surface of the brook was once again smooth and flat until she dipped her hand in to wash her fingers.

That was when Kerry heard the sound. She became instantly alert. Distance deadened sounds and Kerry knew what it was she had heard. Only high frequency echoes came through, and this was the snapping of a twig coming to her like the whisper of a faint breeze.

Partially concealed behind a tree, Kerry waited. The wood was quiet again. There was no warning of anyone approaching. Suddenly a dark shadow moved fleetingly across her sight and was gone again. Moving out a little from her tree, Kerry saw a figure moving as graceful as a fawn. Her heart skipped several beats. Tinisha moved that way in the woods, silently blending, creating a scene so enchanting that she would disappear to leave you wondering whether or not she had ever been there.

Though she hadn't wanted to go to the bungalow, Kerry would not avoid Tinisha out here in the woods. She stepped out into the clearing, clapping her hand to her mouth as she saw that it was not Tinisha.

On one knee in the grass picking flowers close to a large tree, was Valerie Zennor. She was wearing a long black embroidered skirt and a white V-neck jersey top. With the grass around her alive with yellow and white flowers, Valerie could have been in some overcolourful scene from a cartoon movie. But there was no fantasy in Valerie's reaction to Kerry's sudden appearance. Her alarm included a scream that she never uttered, and she was still shaking when Kerry walked up to her side.

'What are you doing out here all alone, Valerie?'

'I could ask you the same question,' Valerie countered, getting to her feet. She gave a little laugh that lifted nothing of her unhappy air. Her delicate, regular-featured face had the kind of opaque whiteness that is brought on by either terror or tears. Kerry was certain that in this case it was tears. Valerie averted her face. 'Please don't look at me like that, Kerry. You embarrass me.'

'I'm sorry. I didn't mean to be rude.' Kerry reached out to stroke Valerie's bare arm. 'Has something happened to you?'

With a wry, humourless grin, Valerie answered, 'Self-inflicted. I've done all the wrong things, said all the wrong things, all at the wrong time, Kerry.' She looked down unhappily at the bunch of wild flowers she was holding. 'I picked these out of habit, and I've no one to give them to, to share them with.'

'Am I right in thinking Tinisha is behind this?'

'Partly.' Valerie nodded, tearfully. 'But I'm mostly to blame, Kerry, I took too much for granted. To go back to London with Guy would guarantee that we'd both be miserable. I thought I could start a new life down here.'

'With Tinisha?'

Kerry found that she was holding her breath after asking that question. If Valerie had made the move that Kerry was beginning to think she had made, then she must have suffered cruelly. If a lover showed even a hint of possession, Tinisha panicked, experiencing something similar to suffocation. She would have reacted badly, and Valerie was a sensitive person.

'Yes, I suppose I got what I asked for. But I really thought she felt something for me, Kerry.'

'I'm sure that she does, Valerie,' Kerry said consolingly, 'but Tinisha is such a loner that I doubt she was even born in bed with her mother.'

'You're saying that it isn't me that she rejected?' Valerie enquired hopefully.

With a shake of her head, Kerry answered. 'I can assure you that it isn't. Tinisha wants sex without commitment. To be fair to her, she does make that plain.'

'Because I know that, it makes me feel all the more silly,' Valerie said miserably.

'You're not on your own,' Kerry said, with a wan smile. 'I made the same mistake, but fortunately I kept it to myself.'

'What would you say you feel for Tinisha?' Valerie enquired, desperately interested.

'Love, I suppose.' Kerry gave a little shrug.

'Unrequited, the same as myself,' Valerie agreed with a solemn nod.

'Probably not,' Kerry argued. 'Tinisha is a very deep person, a deep thinker. She once told me that when you get caught in a relationship, then all the charming lures are withdrawn. She called it a dismal process that has to be avoided. She only let me stay at the bungalow overnight a couple of times. According to Tinisha, people are defenceless and at their most vulnerable when they are asleep.'

'I think I might understand what she meant by that, Kerry.'

Kerry gave a whimsical smile. 'I've tried to. I wish that I'd asked her to explain these things to me.'

'You can still do so, Kerry. I know that I'm being stupid, but I am envious of you remaining here with her when I'm gone.'

They were distracted for a moment by a movement close by. A squirrel clucked disapproval of their presence, then disappeared into a hollow tree. Like the Cheshire Cat's arsehole, the squirrel's bushy grey tail was last to go.

218

'I'm not staying here.' Kerry astonished Valerie with her announcement. 'I just have to get away. I'm leaving tomorrow.'

Seeing that Kerry was close to tears, Valerie reached out to her. In Valerie's arms, Kerry was comforted. But she was also aroused at the feeling of Valerie's warm body against her own. Kerry ran her hands over the sheer perfection of a tiny waist, narrow hips and strong thighs. Her mouth came against Valerie's, and she felt the press of her breasts. Although aware that she had wanted Valerie for some time, Kerry wasn't aware until now how terrifically strong was her desire. Their kissing became more daring. Valerie's breath was pure and sweet, her saliva sheer nectar on the tongue.

Encouraged when Valerie didn't resist the hand she put up her skirt, Kerry thrilled when the other woman parted her legs. The kissing was already having an effect. The narrow nylon crotch of Valerie's panties was sodden as Kerry moved it carefully to one side. She groaned, lovingly whispering Valerie's name as she felt a slim hand find its way up between her own legs. Kerry opened them, pushing her hips forwards to give Valerie all the help she needed. Kerry's cunt was being felt and fingered. Valerie's kisses became harder and deeper. Kerry answered with an urgency that inflamed her.

But then Valerie suddenly ended the passion and cooled the heat. Kerry first noticed a sudden coldness between her thighs as Valerie hastily removed her hand. Then they were standing a little way apart, clasping each other's forearms. Breathlessness made speaking difficult for Valerie.

'There hasn't been a right time for you and me yet, but I believe that there could be.'

'I don't understand,' Kerry said, afraid to welcome the feeling of hope rising in her.

'Kerry,' Valerie said softly, brushing Kerry's lips with hers in a brief kiss. 'Tell me, where do you intend to go when you leave here tomorrow?'

'I was planning on London.'

'That's a big step, Kerry. Might I suggest something?'

'Of course.'

Silent in thought for some time, Valerie then said, 'You make think this a crazy idea. I've been doing a lot of thinking, too.

About honesty, about standing on my own two feet, about the difference between what society says is OK and what is actually right for me – and I have to admit that it was really Tinisha who set me off on this particular train of thought. I have to go back home with Guy and the children to sort everything out. Our marriage is finished so, when the children are settled, I will be leaving Guy. I'd like to see you again, Kerry.'

Valerie had spoken her last sentence in a half-whisper. 'Are you saying we could be together then?' Kerry asked.

'Maybe.' But Valerie's smile was brilliant.

Kerry stared at Valerie for a moment, and then she, too, smiled. 'That would be wonderful.' Then a sobering thought hit her. 'But it would mean me staying down here until you sent for me.'

Hugging her again, Valerie shook her head. 'Not necessarily. I have a sister who lives not far from me. You could stay with her until I've sorted things out with Guy.'

Kerry grinned, and reached for Valerie's hand. The sun filtered through gold–edged leaves and danced shadows around them as they held each other and kissed.

Tinisha Weaver moved the easel. There was still quite a lot of the summer season to go. But she could tell by the way the sun behaved that autumn was just around a not too distant corner. Far below in the bay and the village the new arrivals were doing all the things that the people who had gone back home that morning had done. A pleasure cruiser carved an arc of white foam through a blue sea that was otherwise as smooth as plate glass. The boat was packed. They would be city folk, delighted by but more than a little frightened of the strangeness of distant horizons. The sounds from the beach seemed louder to Tinisha that afternoon. Maybe she was more finely tuned to the emotions of people because of what had happened. Kerry had gone off to London. Valerie had gone home with her family without calling to collect her portrait. Tinisha wasn't too upset by that. Right now, the painting was taking on a brilliance.

Geraldine Dumphy had become a close friend, and Marje Tredogan was still thriving, making regular repayments to the bank.

Marje had also made it abundantly clear that she would welcome more visits from Geraldine and Tinisha, preferably but not necessarily together.

For the moment, though, Tinisha let Geraldine and Marje remain in a lovers' limbo. Their personal odours remained tantalisingly around her; their perfume was in everything she touched; the taste of them was still on her lips. Holding that sort of thing in the memory was the mark of an expert lover. These traces would fade in time, faster from material things than they would from her memory. But by then there would be new scents to breathe, new mouths to savour. Tinisha adjusted the easel, tricked the light into falling exactly where she wanted it, and tried out the colour she had just mixed on the portrait in front of her. The eyes in the portrait sought hers. To lock glances with a creation of your own was a pathway to schizophrenia. Tinisha was too uncertain about reality to risk daydreams.

What had been Valerie on the canvas was now more what Tinisha would imagine Valerie's wraith would look like. Tinisha had done it again. She had unconsciously performed the same trick with Valerie as she had with her own portrait. She had painted the woman's alter ego. There was a resemblance still to the young Grace Kelly in looks, the delicate mask that Valerie presented to the world. But the raunchy, sexy, uninhibited Valerie that Tinisha had enjoyed on the bed wasn't showing through the way that Tinisha had expected. Her art had taken another turn in her subconscious, ever since the evening she'd viewed her own revealing portrait and decided that it wasn't so difficult to mix a bit of kindness in with her naturally rather ruthless libido. She had the satisfying feeling that if she were to attempt another self-portrait, she would quite like what she saw this time around. And even the portrait that should be Valerie – but wasn't – had a quality that astonished Tinisha. Though unable to describe herself as a religious person, she recognised something that seemed almost angelic about the portrait. It was so striking that she was in awe of it. Moved by the mystery of it, Tinisha contemplated the impact that her new-style portrait would have at her next exhibition in Kensington.

Tinisha brushed a small amount of paint on the jawline. Something was happening down at the holiday cottage. A green four-wheel-drive vehicle had pulled in to park where the Zennor hatchback had stood for the past two weeks. Two guys, young and athletic, full of whatever it is makes young guys behave like kids, leaped eagerly out of the car's front doors. With her brush poised and the paint in danger of drying too soon in the heat, Tinisha waited expectantly.

The back doors of the vehicle opened, one more slowly than the other. The first woman to alight was in a mildly agitated state. Dark-haired, she paced anxiously up and down on a dancer's legs as the two men searched for the door key. They upturned stones close to the door and searched through shrubbery without success. Tinisha knew that the cottage owners left the key above the lintel for incoming holidaymakers. But she was neither within distance, nor did she care enough, to convey that information.

Shortening her parading up and down, quickening her steps, the dark girl was becoming more and more agitated. She had a firm dancer's arse to go with the long dancer's legs. Tinisha found the undulating buttocks, the high hips and the wide shoulders enticing.

The second woman had got out of the car. Sophisticated, older than her companion, she was impeccably groomed and expensively coiffeured. She walked as effortlessly as someone who had made a study of it. Tinisha let her brush slide into a jar of turpentine. This pair interested her immensely. The younger one would be much easier to seduce than her companion, but Tinisha would bet the proceeds of this autumn's sale of her work that getting the majestic one into bed would be much more rewarding.

With the key still eluding the two men, the younger woman did a little half-run to the scant protection afforded by a couple of bushes. Terribly thrilled, Tinisha watched her struggle to pull up her tight black dress. Now she understood the dark-haired woman's agitation, as she watched her tug down a tiny pair of panties to squat, knees spread wide apart. It was too far away to see detail, but it was plain that she was urinating. Tinisha's breathing quickened.

The girl remained crouching. A small bird took a cooling bath in the shallow dish Tinisha had placed at the edge of the patio. As it fussed in the water, its mate kept watch from the limb of a tree. The bird stopped bathing and flew back up to the limb. There the two birds sat together, watching Tinisha. Unusually for her, she hadn't really noticed them. Her eyes, her mind, and her yearning were all focused on the dark-haired woman down below.

A shout, weakened and distorted by distance, announced a joyful finding of the key. The girl stood up. In full view of the two men and the woman, she was fully exposed until she pulled her briefs up and her skirt down. Tinisha envied the trio their close-up of the urine droplets that would be sparkling like jewels in the dark pubic hair. The mental imagery had her move her right hand up under her skirt to caress her wetly responsive cunt.

The young woman's legs and hips filled the black skirt without straining it. Tinisha's practised eye noticed how the sheen and tone of the black varied as the girl walked. They all went in through the door of the cottage.

Sexual arousal made it useless for Tinisha to attempt further work. She wondered if the women would reappear. If they did it would only to be to collect luggage from the car. She would see nothing more today that would match the thrill of watching that girl squat. Tomorrow, Tinisha thought, would see the start of a new painting and – who knows? – perhaps, even a friendship with the new female arrivals. But for some reason, her thoughts turned to someone else. Someone who had a bit of experience.

Quickly cleaning her brushes, putting the palette to soak in soapy water, she rushed into the bungalow to the telephone. Some mental quirk had her punch out the number with her middle finger. A woman answered.

It was odd how voices aged at the same pace as the body. Tinisha could tell it was a woman of at least middle age at the other end of the line.

'Is that Mrs Fuller?'

'It is.'

'Oh, hello, Mrs Fuller,' Tinisha said confidently. 'We've never met. I'm Tinisha Weaver.'

'Oh, it's nice to speak to you, Miss Weaver. Elke's told me all about you.'

Not *all* about me. Tinisha thought, and smirked inwardly. She said the expected, 'All good, I hope,' then got down to business.

'I'm sorry to disturb you at this time on a Saturday, Mrs Fuller, but is Elke there?'

'I'm afraid not.'

'Oh dear. It's a bit awkward. As you will know, Elke starts working for me on Monday, but I've an emergency right now I could use her help with.'

'There's no problem, Miss Wea–'

'Tinisha, please.'

'There's no problem . . . Tinisha.' The woman stumbled over the name. 'I know where Elke is, and my Stan's only in the next room watching telly. He'll go and fetch her.'

'As long as it's no trouble.'

'Don't you worry, Miss Weaver, I'll send her up to your place right away,' Mrs Fuller pledged.

Elated, Tinisha thanked the woman and hung up. She had time for a perfumed shower to prepare herself for the gorgeous Elke.

SAPPHIRE NEW BOOKS

NO ANGEL
Marian Malone

Leather. Fetishes. SM. The words conjure up a multitude of feelings for erotic fiction writer Sally Avery, for Sally has a secret. Despite her explicitly written prose, she is relatively inexperienced when it comes to forbidden pleasures. Frightened by the depth of her yearnings, she starts to explore her darker side with other women. Her journey of self-discovery begins in the sleazy, sexy fetish clubs of Brighton . . .

£6.99   ISBN 0 352 33462 2

HIGH ART
Tanya Dolan

Tinisha — a gorgeous, non-monogamous painter — is queen when it comes to the high art of seduction. If only the beautiful women of Cornwall would stop throwing themselves at her, she might be able to get some portraits done, as well.

£8.99   ISBN 0 352 33513 0

I MARRIED MADAM
Published in June 2000   #### Daphne Adams

Anna has a blast making the rounds of North London dyke pubs with her best friend Joan, but it's no cure for the rut she's fallen into with her girlfriend Vicky. Still, life gets more exciting when she meets enigmatic Marlene: a tall dark German who wears silk suits, smokes long expensive cigarettes and is, in short, a Dietrich-dream come true. A funny, bittersweet and very sexy tale about what *really* happens when opposites attract.

£8.99   ISBN 0 352 33514 2

PREVIOUSLY PUBLISHED

BIG DEAL
Helen Sandler

Lane and Carol have a deal that lets them play around with other partners. But things get out of hand when Lane takes to cruising gay men, while her femme girlfriend has secretly become the mistress of an ongoing all-girl student orgy. The fine print in the deal they've agreed on means things can only get hotter. It's time for a different set of rules – and forfeits.

£6.99   ISBN 0 352 33365 0

'The deal of a lifetime' – *The Guardian*

RIKA'S JEWEL
Astrid Fox

Norway, AD 1066. A group of female Viking warriors – Ingrid's Crew – have set sail to fight the Saxons in Britain, and Ingrid's young lover Rika is determined to follow them. But, urged on by dark-haired oarswoman Pia, Rika soon penetrates Ingrid's secret erotic cult back home in Norway. Will Rika overcome Ingrid's psychic hold, or will she succumb to the intoxicating rituals of the cult? Thrilling sword-and-sorcery in the style of Xena and Red Sonja!

£6.99   ISBN 0 352 33367 7

'Splendid stuff' – *Diva Magazine*
'★★★★!' – *SFX Magazine*

MILLENNIUM FEVER
Julia Wood

The millennium is approaching and so is Nikki's fortieth birthday. Married for twenty years, she is tired of playing the trophy wife in a small town where she can't adequately pursue her lofty career ambitions. In contrast, young writer Georgie has always been out and proud. But there's one thing they have in common – in the midst of millennial fever, they both want action and satisfaction. When they meet, the combination is explosive.

£6.99   ISBN 0 352 33368 5

'It's HOT!' – *About.com*

ALL THAT GLITTERS
Franca Nera

Marta Broderick: beautiful, successful art dealer; London lesbian. Marta inherits an art empire from the man who managed to spirit her out of East Berlin in the 1960s, Manny Schweitz. She's intent on completing Manny's unfinished business: recovering pieces of art stolen by the Nazis. Meanwhile, she's met the gorgeous but mysterious Judith Compton, and Marta's dark sexual addiction to Judith – along with her quest to return the treasures to the rightful owners – is taking her to dangerous places.

£6.99   ISBN 0 352 33426 6

'Never again will I be able to look again at an ice cube or a tube of Wintergreen without breaking into a sweat! As for champagne . . . it's too good to just drink!' – *Libertas!*

SWEET VIOLET
Ruby Vise

Violet is young, butch and new in town, looking for a way to get over her childhood sweetheart Katherine. And there are plenty of distractions in 1980s London, as the rarefied big-city dyke scene is both sexually and politically charged – full of everything from cosmic mother-earth worshippers to sexy girls in leather.

£6.99   ISBN 0 352 33458 4

'An easy, entertaining read, both funny and sad with believable erotic bits.' – *Libertas!*

GETAWAY
Suzanne Blaylock

Brilliantly talented Polly Sayers has had her first affair with a woman, stolen the code of an important new piece of software and done a runner all the way to a peaceful English coastal community. But things aren't as tranquil as they appear in this quiet haven, as Polly realises when she becomes immersed in an insular group of mysterious but very attractive women.

£6.99   ISBN 0 352 33443 6

'A smashing story – so sexy and sassy!' – *The Iron Woman*

- - - - - - - - - ✂ -

Please send me the books I have ticked above.

Name   ....

Address   ....

              ....

              ....

              .... Post Code ....

Send to: **Cash Sales, Sapphire Books, Thames Wharf Studios, Rainville Road, London W6 9HA.**

US customers: for prices and details of how to order books for delivery by mail, call 1-800-805-1083.

Please enclose a cheque or postal order, made payable to **Virgin Publishing Ltd**, to the value of the books you have ordered plus postage and packing costs as follows:

UK and BFPO – £1.00 for the first book, 50p for each subsequent book.

Overseas (including Republic of Ireland) – £2.00 for the first book, £1.00 for each subsequent book.

We accept all major credit cards, including VISA, ACCESS/MASTER-CARD, DINERS CLUB, AMEX and SWITCH.
Please write your card number and expiry date here:

....

Please allow up to 28 days for delivery.

Signature ....

- - - - - - - - ✂ -

WE NEED YOUR HELP . . .

to plan the future of Sapphire books –

Yours are the only opinions that matter. Sapphire is a new and exciting venture: the first British series of books devoted to lesbian erotic fiction written by and for women.

We're going to do our best to provide the sexiest books you can buy. And we'd like you to help in these early stages. Tell us what you want to read. There's a freepost address for your filled-in questionnaires, so you won't even need to buy a stamp.

THE SAPPHIRE QUESTIONNAIRE

SECTION ONE: ABOUT YOU

1.1 Sex (*we presume you are female, but just in case*)
Are you?
Female ☐
Male ☐

1.2 Age
under 21 ☐ 21–30 ☐
31–40 ☐ 41–50 ☐
51–60 ☐ over 60 ☐

1.3 At what age did you leave full-time education?
still in education ☐ 16 or younger ☐
17–19 ☐ 20 or older ☐

1.4 Occupation _____

1.5 Annual household income _____

1.6 We are perfectly happy for you to remain anonymous; but if you would like us to send you a free booklist of Sapphire books, please insert your name and address

_____

_____

_____

_____

SECTION TWO: ABOUT BUYING SAPPHIRE BOOKS

2.1 Where did you get this copy of *High Art*?
    Bought at chain book shop ☐
    Bought at independent book shop ☐
    Bought at supermarket ☐
    Bought at book exchange or used book shop ☐
    I borrowed it/found it ☐
    My partner bought it ☐

2.2 How did you find out about Sapphire books?
    I saw them in a shop ☐
    I saw them advertised in a magazine ☐
    A friend told me about them ☐
    I read about them in _____ ☐
    Other _____

2.3 Please tick the following statements you agree with:
    I would be less embarrassed about buying Sapphire
    books if the cover pictures were less explicit ☐
    I think that in general the pictures on Sapphire
    books are about right ☐
    I think Sapphire cover pictures should be as
    explicit as possible ☐

2.4 Would you read a Sapphire book in a public place – on a train for instance?
    Yes ☐   No ☐

SECTION THREE: ABOUT THIS SAPPHIRE BOOK

3.1 Do you think the sex content in this book is:
    Too much ☐   About right ☐
    Not enough ☐

3.2 Do you think the writing style in this book is:

     Too unreal/escapist ☐   About right ☐

     Too down to earth ☐

3.3 Do you think the story in this book is:

     Too complicated ☐   About right ☐

     Too boring/simple ☐

3.4 Do you think the cover of this book is:

     Too explicit ☐   About right ☐

     Not explicit enough ☐

Here's a space for any other comments:

SECTION FOUR: ABOUT OTHER SAPPHIRE BOOKS

4.1 How many Sapphire books have you read?

4.2 If more than one, which one did you prefer?

4.3 Why?

SECTION FIVE: ABOUT YOUR IDEAL EROTIC NOVEL

We want to publish the books you want to read – so this is your chance to tell us exactly what your ideal erotic novel would be like.

5.1 Using a scale of 1 to 5 (1 = no interest at all, 5 = your ideal), please rate the following possible settings for an erotic novel:

     Roman/Ancient World   ☐

     Medieval/barbarian/sword 'n' sorcery   ☐

     Renaissance/Elizabethan/Restoration   ☐

     Victorian/Edwardian   ☐

     1920s & 1930s   ☐

     Present day   ☐

     Future/Science Fiction   ☐

5.2 Using the same scale of 1 to 5, please rate the following themes you may find in an erotic novel:

Bondage/fetishism ☐
Romantic love ☐
SM/corporal punishment ☐
Bisexuality ☐
Gay male sex ☐
Group sex ☐
Watersports ☐
Rent/sex for money ☐

5.3 Using the same scale of 1 to 5, please rate the following styles in which an erotic novel could be written:

Gritty realism, down to earth ☐
Set in real life but ignoring its more unpleasant aspects ☐
Escapist fantasy, but just about believable ☐
Complete escapism, totally unrealistic ☐

5.4 In a book that features power differentials or sexual initiation, would you prefer the writing to be from the viewpoint of the dominant/experienced or submissive/inexperienced characters:

Dominant/Experienced ☐
Submissive/Inexperienced ☐
Both ☐

5.5 We'd like to include characters close to your ideal lover. What characteristics would your ideal lover have? Tick as many as you want:

Dominant	☐	Cruel	☐
Slim	☐	Young	☐
Big	☐	Naïve	☐
Voluptuous	☐	Caring	☐
Extroverted	☐	Rugged	☐
Bisexual	☐	Romantic	☐
Working Class	☐	Old	☐
Introverted	☐	Intellectual	☐
Butch	☐	Professional	☐
Femme	☐	Pervy	☐
Androgynous	☐	Ordinary	☐
Submissive	☐	Muscular	☐

Anything else? _____

5.6 Is there one particular setting or subject matter that your ideal erotic novel would contain:

_____

_____

SECTION SIX: LAST WORDS

6.1 What do you like best about Sapphire books?

_____

6.2 What do you most dislike about Sapphire books?

_____

6.3 In what way, if any, would you like to change Sapphire covers?

_____

6.4 Here's a space for any other comments:

_____

_____

_____

_____

Thanks for completing this questionnaire. Now either tear it out, or photocopy it, then put it in an envelope and send it to:

Sapphire/Virgin Publishing
FREEPOST LON3566
London
W6 9BR

You don't need a stamp if you're in the UK, but you'll need one if you're posting from overseas.